Back to the Banat

Victor Wendl

Dedicated to all descendants of ethnic Germans from Romania, Yugoslavia and Hungary.

Acknowledgments

In writing this book, I have received a great deal of help from many people:

I want to thank all of those Banat Germans who were gracious enough to share their experiences of survival during World War II – most notably Jakob Thalheimer whose first hand experiences in Yugoslavia were helpful in the creation of several chapters. Louis Meulstee's technical expertise in World War II radio communication devices added credibility to several characters in the novel in their operation of various types of clandestine equipment. A special thanks to Megan Norris Jones for copyediting the text. Her suggestions on making several major revisions strengthened the novel from its original writing. Thanks to Robert Altbauer for his illustration and cartography services in upgrading my map of the Banat. Original art work for the book cover was created by Scott Melby. Final book layout completed by Travis Wiggins.

My apologies to all survivors of the labor camps in Yugoslavia for my liberal use of many scenes in the creation of this fictional novel.

The Banat is bounded by the Danube River on the south, the Mures River on the north, the Tisza River on the west, and the Carpathian foothills on the east. The area is generally north of Belgrade in Yugoslavia and south of Arad in Romania. It is bounded on the west near Szeged, Hungary, all the way east towards Lugoj, Romania.

Nikolaus Engelmann

1 2 3 4 5 6 7 8 9 0   DOC/DOC   0 9 8 7 6 5 4 3 2 1

ISBN 978-0-9858375-0-1

THE BANAT

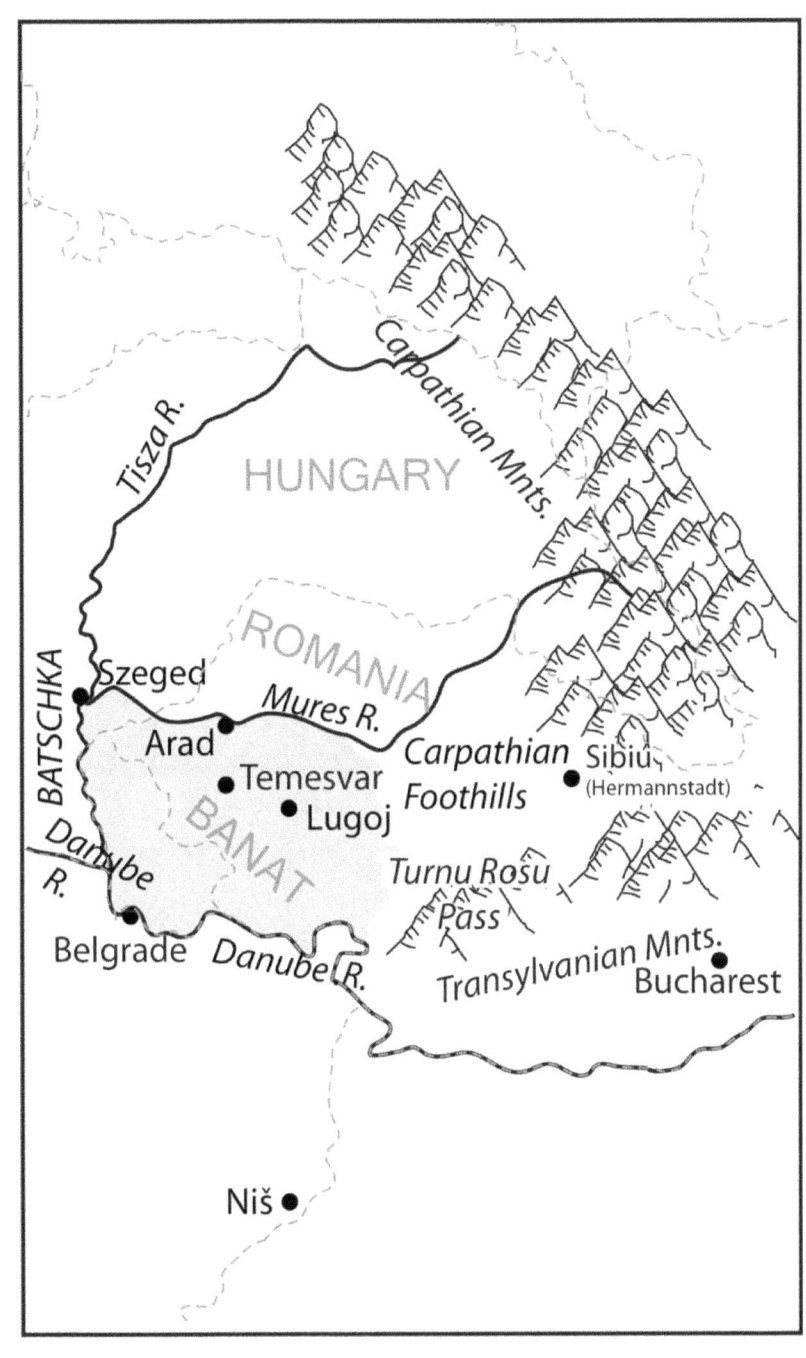

✝

Hungarian Banat
May 1919

"Not yet, Hansi," my father whispered. "We'll wait here."

He pulled back on my right ankle and slid my tiny body back to its original hiding place behind a lone mulberry tree.

"Do you think they saw me, Father?"

He didn't answer as I looked up at him. I could see the level of concentration in his face as he fixated on the Hungarian laborers loading the last of the livestock onto the railcar. My father was not the type of person who panicked in high-stress situations. It was a dark, overcast night outside our ethnic German village in Hungary. I could feel the blades of tall grass brush against my face as we waited in silence. Except for several bright lights near the livestock loading area in the distance, the grassy field around us was pitch black, hiding us from the Magyar workers in front of us.

"It's time, Hansi; let's go."

A Hungarian laborer slammed the railcar door shut and began following his fellow workers toward the long building stretching out in a parallel direction along the train tracks. My father and I left the safety of our hideout and began a slow crawl through the tall grass toward the loaded cargo train.

"Keep crawling like a snake," my father said.

"I'm doing it."

My father wanted to make a game out of the high stress situation, but I knew differently. I was only five years old, but I knew the trouble my father would get into if we were caught by one of those

Hungarian workers. I could barely see through the darkness as the two of us continued crawling toward the targeted railcar along the end of the train.

"I'm tired. Let's stop for just a minute."

"Keep moving. We're almost there."

He pushed me forward and increased the pace. I could feel the sharp edges of the stones below me work their way through my dark pants and dig under my skin. I'm sure if my mother were still alive she would have thrown a fit seeing me crawl through this dirt in my black vest and pants, which I only wore on Sundays for mass.

"Only a few more meters."

I could hear the panting in my father's voice from the hard work of slithering along the ground. As we approached the last railcar, the ground around us became soft. It was more trampled from all the activity during the day of loading livestock.

"Something stinks, Father."

"I know, Son. Try not to think about it."

The herd of sheep recently loaded onto the railcar had dropped plenty of manure on the ground. The waste particles from the filthy livestock now covered my clothes and hands like the marmalade my mother used to smear on the homemade bread that she baked on Saturdays.

"Keep quiet. Don't make any sound at all," my father said.

He elevated himself partially out of the trampled grass and examined the latch on the door to the wood-planked railcar. My father's plan was to smuggle us aboard the cargo train and make our way out of Hungary. As the horrible stench increased in intensity with a summer breeze, I watched my father fiddle with the latch in his thick, manure-stained fingers.

"My God!"

My father pushed several times with all his might against the rusty, metal latch, but it wouldn't release the rail door. After several attempts at opening the sliding door, his large body collapsed along the trampled grass next to me, in a state of exhausted frustration.

"Don't give up," I said.

I brushed some of the black, wet manure off my father's chin. The recent election of communist leaders into the Hungarian government disgusted my father. I knew he despised the thought of being an ethnic German minority under Hungarian communist rule, so he had decided to smuggle us out of the country.

"Look over there, Son."

My father pointed toward the long building where the Magyar laborers were taking a break after spending the day loading the railcars we were now trying to sneak into.

"Yes, Father, what about it?"

"If anyone comes out of that building, pull on my pants leg."

"Yes, Father."

"Don't get off the ground or scream out. Understand?"

"I know."

My father glanced up at the latch one more time and studied the mechanism that opened the sliding cargo door. I watched as he pulled out a small knife hidden in his right boot and repositioned the handle to hold it firmly with his fist. Moving quickly out of the dirt, he gave the latch a firm blow with the butt end of the dagger, but it wouldn't budge. In desperation, he struck the latch again with even greater force than before, forcing the rusty handle open. The sound echoed off the railcar until it faded into the distance beyond the loading area.

I could see in the distance the shadow of someone crack open the door to the long building that ran parallel to the rail tracks. Startled by the activity in the distance, I followed my father's command and yanked on his pants leg to get his attention.

"Jump in quickly," my father said.

I was swiftly lifted inside the cracked sliding door of the railcar as my father slithered in behind me. As I crawled between the sheep hooves packed inside, I was scared of being kicked or stepped on by one of the startled, filthy animals.

"Stay underneath me so you don't get hurt," my father said.

The two of us continued crawling on all fours toward the back of the stock car as the sheep grew even more confused from our forced entry into their area.

"Don't make any sound," my father said.

"I know already."

I could hear the workers chattering in Hungarian outside. Even though we lived in Hungary, my grasp of the language was extremely poor. Now that the Great War was over, the Austro-Hungarian Empire had dissolved, and I was technically Hungarian because of the location of our German village. I didn't feel like a Hungarian, probably because I only spoke German at home with my father and played with German-speaking children in our farming village.

"Sshh," my father whispered in my ear.

In the dark silence of the stock car, I could only pick up a few words of the Magyar workers' squawking. I think it had something to do with the latch on the cargo door being unlocked and how it could cost them their jobs if livestock fell out of the moving train.

"Oh no!" my father said.

I could feel my father's arms tighten around me as we tucked our curled up bodies under a bloated sheep that crushed against us in the darkness. Suddenly, the cargo door was flung open. I could barely see the Hungarian laborers through the intermittent sheep hooves as they gazed inside the cargo car, bursting at the seams with fattened sheep ready for butchering. The Magyar workers continued scanning the wood-planked walls of the railcar for any sign of peculiarity.

"Father—"

He quickly placed his hand over my small, open mouth before I could utter another word. The bloated sheep we lay under suddenly began to urinate. I could hear the sound of smelly urine hitting the rim of my father's black hat like rain pounding against an open umbrella. The rank odor from the animal manure coming off our clothes now mixed with the sheep's urine, making the task of lying perfectly still almost unbearable as the Hungarian workers continued gazing with suspicion into the open railcar.

The door finally shut with a slam, and total darkness returned to the livestock-filled railcar. I could feel my father's filthy hand move away from my mouth, and I knew the immediate danger had passed over us. As the Hungarian voices began to grow more distant, I risked uttering a slight noise as I repositioned my body in a more comfortable location away from the disgusting smell of the sheep I was crammed underneath. We waited for several moments until the workers' voices disappeared completely. With the passing of the immediate danger, my father pushed the surrounding sheep away, allowing us to sit upright against the planked wall of the livestock car.

"What's America like, Father?"

"It's a great place, Son. You're going to love it."

My father's plan was to eventually catch a ship to America and work overseas for a number of years. By then he figured the communists would be out of power in Hungary, and he could slip back into his village with the money he earned in America.

"I thought the Americans were our enemy?"

"No, Son, the war's over. Be quiet now, or they'll hear us."

The year was 1919, and according to letters we received from distant relatives who were farming in North Dakota, America was booming. Since the Great War, the discrimination against Germans living in America was running rampant, but it didn't concern my father. He felt that if he ever left the village he was born in, America would be the place to go, despite all the discrimination ethnic Germans faced overseas.

"I think we're moving, Father?"

"Yes, Son, I think you're right."

The wheels of the train began rolling. The only world I ever knew in my tiny, agrarian village in Hungary was now left behind for a life in America. I wondered about learning a new language and making new friends. My knowledge of America was limited to only what I read in books at my local school. I was excited but scared to leave everything behind.

"Who's going to grow our corn when we're gone, father?"

"No one. You met the farmer I sold our land to last week, remember."

"Oh, that's right."

"We'll buy it back when we return, even more land than we had before."

It was not uncommon for ethnic Germans like my father to go to America for a number of years and work. The strategy of working overseas allowed them to save enough money and vastly increase their land holdings when they returned to Hungary. I remember him lying to other people in his German village that he was changing his trade from farming to tailoring because it was less work. My father was the type of person who trusted no one. He feared someone would tell the Hungarian military about his plan of illegal emigration to America, ruining his chances of getting out of Hungary.

"When I get to America, I'm going to learn how to cook like mother did," I said.

"You can, Son, and much more."

My father looked down at me and pushed the strands of hair away from my face where they had pasted together from clumps of dried manure. I returned the favor and laughed as I peeled away several crusty pieces that filled the creases on my father's forehead. He was still a young man, but he seemed old to me. I would listen to him talk about the war with his friends, and I knew he had seen much death in his relatively young life. On more than one occasion I heard the story about life in the Kaiser's army and how the senseless killing and destruction seemed all a waste of time to him. My father was by no means a coward, but the war had taken a toll on him mentally.

"Good-bye, Mother"

"Good-bye," my father whispered.

As the train whisked by the outskirts of our village, I could barely make out the steeple of our Catholic church in between the cracks of the wooden boards that covered the walls of our railcar. I could still visualize the ceremony at the grave adjacent to the church where we buried my mother several months ago. Tuberculosis had ripped through our village and taken its toll on many families close to my father. I watched for months as my mother's cough worsened until she finally gave in to this modern day version of the black plague. Her death was the tipping point that caused my father to risk it all and head to America.

As the train clicked around a curve on the track, pushing my body against the wooden planks of the railcar, I could hear the sounds of gold coins jingle in a small pouch attached to my father's waist, keeping in time with the banging noise of animals' hooves repositioning themselves as they struggled to maintain their balance. My father's entire net worth was now attached to his belt, and if lost in this darkness, we would be destitute on the way to a foreign country. Ever since the time the Austrian empire took control of central Europe from the Turks, our family had owned farmland outside of our village. My father told me about family members who had emigrated to America before I was born. The positive letters we received from them must have motivated my father to sell his land and cut all ties to our community in Hungary. Who knows when I would be back again to the only home I ever knew?

"We're on our way to America, Hansi."

"We're on our way."

†

"Hans, it's time for dinner."

I could barely hear the voice bellow from the kitchen. My mind was still focused on the chatter coming out of the old radio that my father had purchased many years ago, shortly after his arrival in America.

"Come on, Hans! It's going to get cold!"

"Right. One more minute."

I usually responded to my father in English even though I could easily speak German in his Hungarian dialect. Ignoring the commands coming from the kitchen, I remained seated on my father's favorite chair in the living room, listening to the radio news reports of the conflict taking place in Europe. The broadcaster's voice crackled through the speaker as he spoke of the changes taking place in the puppet government of Yugoslavia now under German occupation.

"Hans, this is the last time already!" my father bellowed in his usual low-pitched voice.

The rule of thumb in my father's house was the third call for food was the one I listened to. It usually required him to get up and physically walk over to where I was located as opposed to a casual yell, but today I made an exception. As I made my way to the familiar wooden table in the kitchen, I thought about where I would be in this European conflict had my father decided to return to

Hungary instead of remaining in America for the last twenty-two years. As Hitler's invading army rolled over nations I now sympathized with, I wondered how differently I would view the war if I were one of those young German soldiers now engaged in battle overseas.

"Smells good, Lisa," I said.

I felt more comfortable calling my father's wife by her first name as opposed to "Mother." He met Lisa at one of the many German clubs that dotted the city of New York while I was away at law school and married her shortly afterward. Perhaps it was loneliness that caused him to take a second wife, but I didn't carry any anger at the thought of him remarrying.

"This *filtus kraut* is certainly better than what I ate in Wisconsin. A northern German trained to cook like a Hungarian. Pretty good, Father."

"Very funny. Eat your food before it gets cold," Lisa said.

I usually left a good portion of the stuffed cabbage uneaten on my plate, a habit I picked up when my less-than-gourmet father had cooked for me. The cooking at home had vastly improved now that Lisa was around. She was a first-generation American whose family had arrived from Germany around the turn of the century. She was of Prussian background, and her first husband, also German, had been killed in the Great War fighting in the American army. I'm sure her family was not exactly enthusiastic about my father being her second husband. The Prussians living in New York viewed themselves as higher class than ethnic Germans from Hungary, especially immigrants like my father who had stepped off the boat at Ellis Island over 20 years ago.

"It looks like the Germans are making some new friends in Yugoslavia."

It had been more than six months since the Germans rolled their Panzer Corps into Belgrade with only two hundred soldiers killed in the takeover. Another eastern European nation was now under occupation by the German military.

"I'm glad I'm not over there," my father said.

He continued alternating between cutting and chewing the ground meat surrounded in a thin layer of light green cabbage leaves. By the way my father spoke, I could tell he had only a casual interest in the events taking place in Europe.

"What do you think is going to happen to our people?" I asked.

"I don't know."

I always referred to ethnic Germans living in Hungary as our people. It was a habit I picked up from my father when he spoke about the Banat Germans, a term used to describe ethnic Germans living in Hungary, Yugoslavia, or Romania.

"I don't know how you can sit there and not have any opinion on what's going on. The Nazi party is against everything this country stands for: freedom, liberty. This is why you came here in the first place."

That was the budding young lawyer in me talking. Fresh out of the University of Wisconsin Law School, I was ready to show my stuff. It had not been easy on my father to pay for all that schooling, but he had been determined to see me move up the food chain among the social hierarchy of New York Germans. Having tailored clothing for wealthy people in the business community around New York, my father could see the economic power of an education in this country and was determined to get his son a piece of that action.

"Our people liked it better when Hungary was part of the Austrian Empire. If Hitler can recreate that environment, no Banat German is going to be complaining."

Before the Great War broke out, my father remembered life as a young man under the Austro-Hungarian flag as opposed to the Austrian Empire. His agrarian German village was under constant pressure from the Hungarian government to *Magyarize*, in an effort to turn a mixed bag of ethnicities into a single nation of Hungarians. Government infringement on their personal lives had become ever more of a problem. Schools no longer could teach in German. German last names were changed to Hungarian.

After the communist government took control of Hungary shortly before we left for America, discrimination against ethnic German minorities like my father worsened in our village. My father knew the Banat Germans living in Yugoslavia had the same discrimination problems as he had living under Hungarian rule. Now that Hitler was in control of Yugoslavia, my father thought it would give Germans living there more freedom to preserve their culture and way of life.

"People at school think we're going to get sucked into this one," I said.

"Let's change the subject to some more immediate concerns. You've been sitting around the house, and I want to know what you're doing about a job."

My father set his sharpened knife down on the wooden table and finished chewing the last of his stuffed cabbage as he waited for my response. His attention span wasn't long when the topics of world events or politics came up. It was October of 1941. The country was still on a slow crawl out of its greatest depression in history, and young attorneys like myself were having a difficult time finding work around New York.

"Any leads lined up?"

My father grabbed the wooden knife handle with his thick fingers and pointed it into the air.

"Actually, yes," I said.

"Now we're going somewhere."

My father was not one to spend a lot of time smelling the roses. Law school was now over for me, and the next logical step was to get a job. He knew the market was tough around New York. But several months doing day labor jobs for others in his primarily ethnic German neighborhood of Yorkville on the Upper East Side of Manhattan was long enough for the son of an immigrant to be lounging around on his version of a vacation.

"One of my instructors back in Madison sent me a letter and lined me up something," I said. "He wrote to me about some job working in a new government agency here in New York."

I was not super enthusiastic about becoming a government bureaucrat, but since I didn't have any other leads, I had agreed to the interview. My goal by the end of the summer was to land at least one secure position. With the summer days now over, I was staring at only one interview, which kind of depressed me.

"What kind of job are you applying for?"

"I don't know. I'll find out at the interview," I said.

My father glared in confusion at me. I returned to my half empty plate in fear of making eye contact with him.

"You know, I don't think you're taking this seriously," he said. "How do you expect to make an impression on the interviewer if you don't even know what the job is about?"

"Let him go. He'll find out tomorrow," Lisa said.

She always acted as a mediator when things started to heat up between my father and me.

"No, wait a minute here. When I became a tailor in this country, I looked for a job as a tailor. I never went to a job interview where I didn't know beforehand that the job involved using scissors and thread."

I glanced up from my plate and began the painful process of enduring another "back in my day" speech. My father continued lecturing me while simultaneously waving the sharpened blade around the kitchen like a baton in the hands of some sadistic conductor. The skin on his face began turning a deeper shade of red as he continued to lecture me.

"Look, I'm going to the stupid interview!"

I interrupted his speech, causing his fleshy cheeks to turn even darker in color.

"The job isn't going to matter anyway! We're going to war soon, and if we do, I'm joining up like many of my American friends!"

My father was never one to follow the crowd, no matter how unrelenting the pressure. His ability to endure the isolation of not giving up some portion of his individuality by joining the madness of crowd behavior was impressive. If the mass of humanity moved in one direction over a cliff, I knew he would never capitulate and join them. I could tell it made the old man furious to think of me mindlessly joining the military because my American pals were signing up.

"What kind of an idea is that?" he asked. "You don't know what it's like to be in war. I do, and it's not worth it, no matter what the cause."

His eyes were practically popping out of his head he was so angry. My father didn't discuss politics much, but he was not stupid. He knew the isolationist position that most German-Americans preferred regarding the war in Europe could lose the political upper hand, and because of my young age, I would have to serve in some way.

"I never had the opportunities you did. You have an education. If war breaks out, why not put your education to use in the war effort. Take some job in some back office somewhere and ride it out. I know I would."

"I really don't want to talk about this anymore. I'm out of here," I said.

I pushed my arms against the heavy, wooden table and skid my chair across the kitchen floor. I knew my father and I would never see eye to eye on this issue. It was pointless discussing it any further, so I pushed my shoulder against the thick front door to our building and walked out to the sidewalk to cool down.

I felt differently than he did about America. Maybe it was the result of my education, or the fact I grew up here. I didn't know for sure. After all, I was an attorney on paper, trained to uphold the Constitution of the United States. The democratic mentality was indoctrinated in me because of my law training, forcing me to despise Hitler's oppressive regime.

My father carried no legacy of achievement from others that helped him know when to zig or zag in the jungle of America. Everything he achieved in this country, he felt it was through his own hard work and intelligence. My father's small real estate investments shrewdly purchased at the bottom of the depression with the gold coins he brought from Hungary had enabled me to get a college education. As I continued walking along the city street, I knew my father felt the education I received would all be a waste if I were shot and killed. America in his mind had only one purpose: it was a place where he could make money and move his family ahead.

As I playfully kicked a soccer ball back at one of the ethnic German children living in our neighborhood, I tried to see where my father's perspective came from. His antimilitary sentiments came out of his years of service in the Kaiser's army during the Great War. One of my father's friends from Hungary, now living in New York not far from us, told me about how my father considered hanging himself rather then endure more bloodshed fighting under the Austro-Hungarian flag. Taking a bullet for a fellow German or some random American in some future war was all the same to him, a waste of time.

The next morning, I responded on time to my lone interview in a bleak job market. My brief conversation on the phone with one of the secretaries was sketchy at best. I was supposed to show up at the Rockefeller Center in room 3603, but I was lucky to find the office at all, since there wasn't even a number posted on the door.

"Have a seat in the corner on some of those boxes. Sorry about the mess," she said.

"Sure."

As her squeaky voice continued firing back answers to questions rapidly coming in from the multiple phone lines running across her desk, I brushed aside the dust on one of the boxes with my white handkerchief and planted myself. As the row of black phones continued ringing, I envisioned myself sitting in the room for hours virtually unnoticed amidst the sea of bureaucratic confusion and noise. I grew increasingly frustrated as specks of dust on the edge of the wooden crate worked their way on my pants leg. I'm sure my father would have rumbled a few words at me if he were here. The idea of not making a good first impression because of dirt on one of his tailored suits designed specifically for job interviews would have caught me some flack.

"What's your name again?" the secretary asked.

"It's John, John Miller," I said.

"Right."

She quickly abandoned the chaotic environment and slipped through an interior door leading to another office. People continued moving in and out, dropping off additional desks and file cabinets, and the noise from the ringing phones became almost intolerable. I could tell that meeting with the unemployed son of a German immigrant like myself was the last thing on this woman's agenda for today. As I grew ever more restless on my makeshift chair, I began walking around the lobby-in-progress, gazing at the view in between letters etched on the glass of the interior office door. The secretary continued talking with the gentleman parked behind a disorganized, giant desk in the middle of the room. I could barely make him out through the dull glass covering the door, but I assumed the intellectual-looking fellow would be my interviewer. I saw the woman turn her body toward the interior door I was peeking through. Concerned about looking too nosy on an initial interview, I rushed back to my filthy crate and waited for her entrance.

"You can go in now," she said.

"Thanks."

My body suddenly tightened up as I slipped through the door leading to the interviewer's office. The curtain opened as I walked inside. I was now on stage.

"Go ahead and take a seat."

"John Miller."

"Allen Dulles. Sit down."

I quickly shook his hand and sat in the chair he pointed to. He shoved the black phone receiver against his ear and continued talking for several moments while I waited in agony before the official interview started.

"Sorry about the mess. We moved in several weeks ago, and we're still trying to get all the bugs worked out," he said.

I knew a few pieces of information about the fellow from a letter I received from the instructor at the University of Wisconsin who had set up the interview. The balding interviewer was a former diplomat who had served in various capacities around Europe before practicing law in New York. Sizing me up through his beady glasses, he struck me as someone who had never worked a manual labor job in his entire life. The clenched jaw hidden under his pale features gave an initial impression of someone under tremendous pressure to convert the disorganized mess surrounding us into a smoothly run government agency.

"You have a résumé with you or did my secretary take it when you came in?"

"Here you go."

I reached across his green metallic desk and handed him a freshly typed piece of white paper outlining my academic credentials. He read it over for several minutes and looked up at me and grinned. I smiled uncomfortably back at him, hoping his cheeks would begin moving to break the uncomfortable silence. My résumé gave no indication that I was any different from any other red-blooded American kid with some good college grades, but underneath my newly tailored suit, I was the son of an immigrant, slightly insecure about my humble beginnings. I knew the two of us would find it difficult to find some common ground if I spent the afternoon chatting with him, so I hoped his questioning would focus on the potential job opportunity at this startup government agency.

"We're with COI, the newly formed Coordinator of Information office," he said.

"I see."

I tried to look as interested as possible as I listened to him describe the apparently insignificant purpose of this agency, a place where I was hoping to crawl into a job and get my father off my back.

"We're setting up an oral intelligence unit here in New York."

"What's the purpose of the intelligence gathering?"

I couldn't believe what I asked the former diplomat. I thought it might make me look more interested, but I now regretted even opening my mouth.

"We're gathering information on the events occurring in Europe from local newspapers written in German as well as conducting interviews from some of the immigrants fresh off the boat. We're hoping to gain some insights from them about the conflict overseas."

"How are you using attorneys like myself?"

He waited a moment before responding to my question. I had been under the impression that my newly minted barrister certification was the reason for my interview in the first place.

"How's your German?"

He responded to my question with another question as he continued staring at the bottom of my résumé indicating my fluency in German. My German accent was less noticeable than his New York dialect. I doubt the fellow would have picked up on it at all, if I hadn't written it on the paper he held in between his fingers.

"Pretty good," I said.

"How'd you learn German?"

"I was born in Hungary. My parents are ethnic Germans."

"What're the Germans doing in Hungary?"

I could tell by the confused look on his face that he knew very little about the history of my ethnic group. Government bureaucrats from America probably didn't spend a lot of time worrying about ethnic minorities from countries not on his short list of European world powers.

"My ethnic group is scattered across farming villages in Romania, Yugoslavia, and Hungary. These Germans have been there since the early 1700s when the Turks were driven out."

"Why did you come to America?"

"My father wanted to make some money over here. I think he was sick of the discrimination against Germans under Hungarian rule, so he packed up and left. I was a little kid, so I naturally went with him."

I omitted on purpose the small detail about how my father hated the communist regime in power at the time we left Hungary. I thought it might look bad since I was going for a federal agency job, and I didn't want to give off an impression that I came from a family who is anti-government.

He continued to bombard me with questions about my background and feelings toward the conflict in Europe. My time spent in this country and my law background seemed to be of little interest to him. As I continued answering his questions, I gazed at the large maps surrounding the walls of his cluttered, green office. I could tell from the placement of the tiny, black pins jabbed into the European maps, they matched the stories coming out of my father's old radio on locations under German military control.

"How do you feel about the current German government?"

I knew this question was coming, and I wanted to paint myself as American as I possibly could. I felt somehow that my German background might hurt my ability to get a job with the war escalating overseas.

"I came here as a kid. Freedom and democracy are part of my core values. Any government that doesn't buy into those values, I'm against, regardless of what nationality."

A partial cracked smile pushed the right side of his cheek into the air, as if something devious had popped in the veteran's mind.

"Wait outside for a minute," he said.

"OK."

I returned to my cluttered corner in the lobby and thought about my first dramatic role as a desperate, young lawyer looking for work. As I continued waiting, I hoped I had left a good enough impression that he might make me an offer today. I wasn't rich, so money was important to me, but getting my father off my back with a job that even remotely matched my skill set was a real bonus.

"Come on back, John."

"Sure."

I jumped toward the door of the bureaucrat's office and waited as his frame crushed into the seat behind his green, metal desk.

"This New York office is expanding quickly, John," he said. "I need people like you: bilingual who can read some of these local German papers and prepare intelligence reports so we can get a better feel on how the Germans think about all this stuff."

"Are you offering me a job?"

I stared at him in eager anticipation at finally receiving a job offer.

"I'm afraid I can't hire you."

My face went flush. It was my only lead for a job, and the interviewer had rejected me.

"We can get people twice your age to do that for us," he said. "Younger people like yourself with your unique background can serve this country in better ways. I just got off the phone with my superior in Washington. Would you be interested in taking an interview for another position?"

I was still psychologically devastated by the words of rejection and barely caught his offer for a second shot at a job.

"Yes, definitely."

I didn't have any other leads lined up, and since he wasn't going to hire me, it seemed stupid not to take the interview.

"I want you there by tomorrow morning to meet with someone in charge of COI," he said forcefully. "I know it's short notice, but they definitely want to talk to you."

"You mean Washington D.C.?"

"Yes, my secretary will arrange for hotel and transportation. From now on, any conversations about what you're interviewing for are strictly confidential."

Those commands weren't hard to follow considering I knew nothing about the job. That afternoon, after receiving the information on the location of the interview, I rushed home and began packing my bags for Washington. I told Lisa about the second interview and headed immediately to the train station. I didn't even wait for my father to return home from work, missing the opportunity to ease some of his concerns about my leisurely pursuit of gainful employment.

As the train pulled out of New York toward the nation's capitol, I thought about how little I knew about the job I was trying to land. Why wasn't I allowed to share details with anyone about the approaching interview? What did my government want me to get involved with? After a trip stressful from too much worry about my approaching interview, the train pulled into the capitol around midnight, and I took a cab to the hotel. It was my first time in Washington D.C., but I was too nervous and exhausted to fully appreciate the unique opportunity.

After an uncomfortable several hours napping in the hotel, I awoke at 6:00 a.m. to the familiar, annoying ring from my old alarm clock that I packed with me in fear of missing my scheduled interview. I dressed quickly in my tailored suit, which now gave off a slight odor from the perspiration that had soaked in from yesterday's interview back in New York. The front desk clerk pointed me in the direction of E Street where my interview was supposed to take place. It was within walking distance from the hotel, giving me an opportunity to catch a glimpse of the city on the way over.

As I walked along the crowded morning streets, I could see the tense faces of the men passing by in dress military uniform. Service in the military never interested me while in college, but now with the war going on in Europe and the difficulty of finding work, military service as a job outlet had moved up the food chain. Yesterday's interview back in New York had increased my sensitivity to the fact that the war in Europe was reaching a critical stage.

"Hold it here, kid," the guard said. "Where you headed?"

A guard standing ruler straight along the empty hallway of the Apex building I had entered, stuck his expanded chest in front of my face and blocked me from any further movement. His direct way of talking and military uniform seemed authoritative to a civilian like myself, and I didn't want to anger the guy.

"I'm here for an interview," I said.

He scanned my exterior jacket with his beady eyes in search of some sort of identification, coming up empty.

"Who you interviewing with?" he asked.

"COI," I said.

I used the acronym COI instead of Coordinator of Information in the hopes that it would make me look somehow more informed to this pesky, tall obstacle standing in my way. I continued staring up at him. It was a cheap attempt to signal that I wasn't somebody to fool around with, if he wanted to keep this cushy job watching people enter this government building.

"Keep this on you at all times, and don't forget to give it back to me before you leave."

"OK," I said.

He quickly stuck a visitor badge in the palm of my hand, and I was on my way again. As I walked through the barren hallway in search of the section devoted to COI, I noticed other folks wandering the building, seemingly as lost as I was. Refusing to ask anyone for help, I finally stumbled on a makeshift directory taped on a wall and quickly headed toward the set of rooms that contained the Office of Coordinator of Information.

Now armed with a visitor pass, I breezed through the military guards posted at the entrance of the corridor and passed into the section of the building for my scheduled interview

"Excuse me," I said.

I decided to talk to the attractive brunette about ten years older than I sitting behind the desk along the hallway in this locked-down section of the building.

"I'm here for my scheduled interview. I was sent by Allen Dulles from New York."

I figured by mentioning the name of the man in charge who had interviewed me back in New York could somehow avoid some red tape and lead me to the man that would offer me that great job. The young lawyer with a language background in German had arrived from afar, and it was time for everyone to take notice.

"Go ahead and take a seat in room 12 down the hall," she said.

As I entered the giant room, I noticed all four walls were covered with dark drapes hanging from the ceiling to the floor. Military people would periodically enter the room and push aside one of the drapes, revealing huge maps from around the world.

"Who are you scheduled to see?" the attractive dark-haired woman came back and asked.

"Allen Dulles, the man I saw in New York, didn't say. He gave me the address of the COI office, and that's it."

She turned back with a sarcastic smirk on her face, as if I was crazy for coming all the way to Washington D.C. without even knowing whom I was supposed to meet.

I waited for what seemed like hours, slowly drifting to sleep in my chair, still tired from the late train ride and a restless sleep worrying about this interview. Suddenly, my body shook like a bomb had struck the Apex building.

"WAKE UP!"

I stared into the eyes of the brunette.

"Yes," I said. "Sorry. Must have fallen asleep."

"Bill Donovan will see you now."

"Great."

After forcing myself awake, I entered the room adjacent to the planning area and approached a group of men in military uniform sitting around a desk having a discussion about some organizational chart in front of them. I waited patiently in the corner until the briefing was complete and several of the military bureaucrats left the office.

"I'm Bill Donovan," the energetic man over twice my age said.

He shook my hand firmly, taking a seat behind his desk. "I received the call from Allen yesterday. Now your background is what again? From Hungary, but you're German?"

Like most Americans this was slightly confusing to this newly minted head of COI.

"I was born in a small German farming community in Hungary. I came to this country as a child with my father."

He approached a panel to the right of his desk and slid open the drapes, exposing a large map of Eastern Europe.

"Are these Germans recent immigrants to Hungary?" he asked.

"Nope. Probably been there for over 200 years."

"And they're still German. Not like me. I'm Irish, but in name only."

"That's right. They're definitely German, not totally integrated."

He stopped for a moment and scribbled a few notes in his book on the desk in front of him.

"Now let me throw something out at you," Donovan said. "Could you easily communicate with, let's say, one of these Germans in one of these villages?"

Donovan's pen pointed at the map.

"Yes, most definitely. There might be a slight difference in dialect depending on what part of Eastern Europe you're from, but that's about it."

I remembered talking with one my father's friends, an ethnic German born in Yugoslavia. His German dialect was very similar to my father's, even though the two of them emigrated from different countries before arriving in New York. My father's friend from Yugoslavia was easier to understand than several students I knew at the University of Wisconsin, who were originally from Berlin.

"Let me explain what's happening and why we called some son of an immigrant with a law degree all the way to Washington," Donovan said. "The war's coming, son, and we're going to be in this thing. My feeling is that we need to get some people undercover in certain strategic locations around Europe so we can get some first-hand information from people we can trust about what's going on. We need people like you with your unique background to help us out."

"What about military training? I'm an attorney," I said.

I was startled at the suggestion that I would be a good candidate for undercover work.

"Maybe I have a soft spot for lawyers working in intelligence gathering since I have a law degree from Columbia myself."

Rows of lines appeared around his eyes as he cracked a smile. I could tell the man was under a lot of pressure to gather some useful information about events unfolding in Europe. He went on about how intelligence gathering was currently being conducted piecemeal from multiple government agencies, and the COI was tasked with consolidating this ad hoc network under one government agency

"We'll provide the training. Besides, you have a natural cover for this type of job. You're one of these Germans. You'll blend in easily with them, and that's where we'll stick you."

I felt a sudden knot in my stomach. I was expecting an offer for a desk job in Washington, but instead I was being propositioned for undercover work in Europe.

"I have to think this one over," I said in a quiet voice. "This is certainly not what I expected,"

"There isn't much time, John. I need a response soon," Donovan said. "If you don't take this job, you're probably going to be drafted, and your law pursuits will be put on hold anyway. We're going to be in this thing sooner or later."

"Let me think it over."

He picked up the ringing phone and quickly shook my hand as I moved toward the exit.

"You'd be doing the country a great service! This country gave you an education, opportunity. That's what we're fighting for over there!" Donovan shouted.

It was his last sales pitch as I headed out the door.

On the train ride back to New York, I thought about the job opportunity presented to me. Fresh out of law school, it was a far stretch from the first job I thought I'd be offered. It was quite an eye-opening experience witnessing the planning taking place behind the scenes in anticipation of America being dragged into the European conflict.

Donovan was right about one thing. If I decided not to join his intelligence-gathering operation at COI, I'd probably be drafted anyway. Not joining COI didn't necessarily translate into getting out of military service. Besides, like many of my American friends from school, I was already planning to join if we declared war on

Germany. Up to this point, the war had been strictly a radio program for me, but that was all about to change if I took the job offer.

As the train pushed along the tracks, I closed my eyes and leaned my head against the cold glass of the window. The cool chill felt good against my cheeks, relieving me temporarily from the humid conditions aboard the stuffy compartment. I dozed off and on with visions of greatness returning from Europe as the war hero, saving countless lives through daring feats of espionage behind enemy lines. Those romanticized visions were quickly dashed as thoughts of my father's experience in war took hold of me. After the war was over, law firms throughout New York would be climbing over one another to hire a war hero like myself in some partnership track position. My father could even appreciate the logic in joining the military for that reason. Who was I kidding? I'm sure he'd be furious at the thought of me overseas in some intelligence-gathering role. Donovan needed an answer soon, but I was too exhausted at the moment to even think about what my response might be.

✝

"Come on, defend yourself!"

"I'm trying!"

The muscular instructor grabbed my wrist and twisted my lanky arm around my back, quickly snatching the P-38 semiautomatic weapon out of my fist.

"You're dead," the instructor said.

With my arm still locked behind me, I could feel the barrel of the weapon pressing against my scalp as the trainer mockingly blew my brains out.

"Could you take another man's life if you were put in this situation?"

"What?"

His muscles bulged from his uniform like swollen air balloons under a layer of tight skin. I was in tremendous pain from the arm lock, making it virtually impossible to concentrate on his question.

"You heard me. Could you take another man's life to defend yourself?"

"I think I could."

The instructor sensed the conflict within me as I tried to provide a convincing answer to his question. His background was in psychology and defensive tactics, a combination that enabled him to pick up easily on my inability to harness my killer instinct. He twisted me around and knocked me to the ground, disgusted at my response.

"Yes, I could. If put in that situation," I said.

My answer lacked a degree of confidence that the nameless instructor was looking for. Once I had killed a couple of rabbits with a .22 caliber rifle while working on a distant relative's farm in North Dakota, but that was the extent of my experience in killing anything.

"I'm not going to waste my time signing you up for additional training in SA/G school. It's clear you'd be useless as an assassin. We don't have the time or the resources to drive this conflict from your being."

The instructor slipped the German P-38 semiautomatic back into his side holster and pulled out a small knife from his pocket.

"This is more your style, legal boy. I'm going to schedule some training time with an instructor on how to defend yourself with a knife in case you're discovered."

"Yes, sir."

I took the knife from his hand and lightly etched a cross into the hard ground with the sharp edge of the blade, pretending in my mind that I wasn't a part of all this espionage training. The simple act brought back memories of my father when we lived back in Hungary. I could still see him carving the sign of the cross over the top of a fresh loaf of bread before slicing it into smaller pieces for us to eat.

"Let me make it clear to you," the instructor said. "You're not an assassin. The knife is only used for defense. If your cover's blown, the objective will be to abandon your mission and stay alive. Understand?"

"Yes, sir."

I never asked any questions when I was under instruction from this muscle-bound officer. He always seemed angry with me, never cracking even the slightest smile. For security reasons, neither I nor any of the other seven students knew the real names of any of our instructors. For a joke, we decided to give the bulky fellow the nickname "Hot Bath." I envisioned him being forced as a baby to endure boiling hot water when his mother bathed him, resulting in deep-rooted personality problems now as an adult.

"By the way, they approved your security clearance."

"Excellent," I said.

I was a little concerned about getting through the rigorous background check given my ethnic German background and time spent in Hungary. If the clearance didn't go through, I probably would end up serving in the upcoming war against Germany some other way. Now with the security clearance behind me, I hoped the endless questions into my past would begin to slow down. Although my nameless instructors never mentioned it outright, I knew the constant probing was designed to gauge the risk of me turning into a double agent while in isolation overseas on a mission. I found it ludicrous that my superiors even entertained the idea, considering I had lived most of my life in America.

"How's your cipher coming along?"

"It's memorized, sir."

My unique cipher, designed to disguise my correspondence when I communicated by radio, had become second nature to me after several weeks of training. The Germans listening to my radio communications would have a difficult time interpreting the information based on the secret code I had now committed to memory.

"You have a meeting scheduled with the commander tomorrow morning at 0800."

"Yes, sir."

"That'll be all."

Without saying another word, I left the instructor and headed toward my barracks, which had been my home for the last six weeks. The other seven students and I were the first class at the new SA/B training school hidden about twenty miles outside of Washington. The place was jokingly referred to by my espionage classmates as "The Farm," given its barren surroundings sprawling over one hundred acres of open terrain. America was creeping closer to involvement in the conflict in Europe. Deciding to make the jump and take up Donovan's offer by enlisting in SA/B, the intelligence gathering division of COI, seemed the right choice.

As I walked across the deserted compound toward the barracks, I thought about my decision to join Bill Donovan's Coordinator of Information office. The organization was tasked with gathering foreign intelligence, and I would be involved in that effort. No one knew about the espionage role I was being groomed to play for my government, not even my father, who thought I was serving in some administrative capacity testing new equipment for the military. I felt uneasy about lying to him about enrolling in espionage training, considering all the sacrifices he had made in raising me without a mother, but there was nothing I could do about it. Absolute secrecy was mandated for all candidates like myself signing on to the training program on The Farm.

I entered the front door of my half-empty barracks with its neat rows of beds, still mostly vacant as the training program's ramp-up continued. Subsequent classes would be bigger than mine, and they had already brought in the beds for them. I dropped my head onto the stiff, off-white pillow and began wondering about the assignment I would be given now that the training part of the program was near completion.

I could tell by the intensity of the sessions that my instructors were under pressure to get people over to Europe to get some first-hand information on what was happening. As I wondered about where I might be sent overseas, I began flipping in between my fingers a Hungarian gold coin that my father had given me for luck, hoping the repetitive act would eventually lull me to sleep. Like most ethnic Germans in Hungary, my father had a streak of superstition in him that he never talked about. Giving me the last of his lucky gold coins that he had brought from Hungary probably gave him a feeling of control in an environment that, at times, seemed completely out of his control.

The next morning, I woke up early for my meeting across campus with the military commander in charge of operations at The Farm. I only met the nameless commander one other time in a group setting with some of the other early candidates in the program. As I ran across the open terrain to his private office, I was eager to hear what the man had to say about my performance in the program.

"I'm here to see the commander," I said as I stepped through the door.

"He's expecting you," the secretary said.

The Farm had only been operational for about six weeks, but it seemed longer thanks to this commander in charge who was about to pass judgment on my performance in the program. Given how smoothly everything seemed to be running at the newly opened training facility, his level of organization seemed impressive. As I stepped into his impeccably laid out office, I knew practically nothing about the man other than his educational background, which was in psychology.

"Come in and take a seat," he said in a monotone voice.

I took a seat on the wooden chair exactly centered in front of his neat, metallic desk. He walked over to the clean row of vertical file cabinets lined up razor straight against the wall and pulled my file, scanning the pages as he returned to his desk. Triggered by some text scribbled on the page in front of him, the commander looked up at me, as if trying to gauge in my face some overlooked flaw that made me unattractive as a candidate for overseas undercover work.

"Your instructors told me you've mastered your cipher."

"I'm comfortable using it and with operating the suitcase radio."

Operating the SSTR-1 radio transmitter along with my memorized cipher is all anybody seemed to care about in the program. I suppose it made sense considering my intelligence gathering would all be pointless if I couldn't send the coded information back on my radio transmitter. I sensed a general mistrust among the hierarchy in using immigrants such as myself for espionage work. I could tell by their mannerisms and way of talking they came from wealthy families, the elite of East coast society not used to mixing with people of my sort. After reviewing the entire file, he looked up, staring at me with his unblinking eyes for what seemed like an uncomfortable length of time.

"I suppose you heard that your security clearance went through."

"Yes. Yes, I did."

He stared, almost looking for a subtle sign of too much enthusiasm at my security clearance being approved, as if I had pulled something over on our government. He looked down at the beige cover of my file one last time and walked over to a map of Europe on the wall behind his desk. It was a smaller version of the exact map I had seen in Donovan's office back at COI in Washington D.C., but with fewer black pins jabbed inside the paper.

"A project from the Central European desk has been reclassified as 'approved and in preparation.' It would fit with a person of your background."

I nodded.

"There are resistance movements right now underway against the Germans in Yugoslavia. We're receiving conflicting reports about what's going on down there."

He moved his hand across the map of Yugoslavia and indicated where the sketchy reports of rebel attacks against Germans were coming from.

"We have to increase the quality of information we're getting about these resistance movements so we can find out who to provide with military support. It'll be your job to untangle this mess of information and get some information back on what's going on down there."

The concept of intelligence gathering suddenly took on a cold reality as my endless lectures and exercises on espionage would be now put to use in Yugoslavia.

"Any additional information in terms of troop movement, morale, etc. that you happen to stumble upon should also be sent back."

I continued gazing upon the map of Central Europe pinned on the wall behind his orderly desk. I moved out of my chair and slowly walked toward his location.

"Where am I going to be located?"

The commander scanned his notes before responding.

"We're going to plant you in Theresiafeld. It's this small agrarian German community not far from Belgrade."

His index finger moved across the map and stopped on a small dot, north of Belgrade in Yugoslavia.

"It's a good strategic location to pick up some chit chat on resistance info against the Germans. Besides, it's a natural cover for you, given your ethnic German background."

It suddenly hit me how real this was all becoming. My government had formally asked me to go behind enemy lines as a spy. I would now be wearing the mask of a man that I would have become, if my father hadn't left Hungary many years ago.

"Will I have a contact person once I get over there?"

"I'm afraid we can't help you much in that department. Once you arrive in Theresiafeld, you're going to have to carve out a life for yourself and sort of blend in with the village. We'll be monitoring your radio transmissions, but you won't know who's listening on the other end."

My throat hurt a bit as I swallowed. If I didn't know the identity of the person receiving my radio transmissions, I couldn't provide the enemy any usable information on him if captured and subjected to torture.

"The person listening will relay the info to England where it'll be analyzed and prepared into memos for analysis."

"I understand."

"Remember, if your cover is ever blown, immediately abandon your mission and head for home. We're not telling anyone, not even the Russians, about the intelligence network we're establishing in Yugoslavia, and we intend to keep it that way."

"Yes sir."

"You'll be completely alone, but that'll be your safety net."

As I continued staring at the tiny black dot on the map that marked my target location of Theresiafeld, I found it odd that the skills and knowledge I acquired in this country would have to be temporarily abandoned while on my mission in Yugoslavia. I would have to rely on information picked up as a child in Hungary in order to maintain my cover.

"How long you think I'll be down there?" I asked.

"We'll get word to you when your mission is completed."

His response was not reassuring. I knew in the back of my mind it could be years before I would see my father and return to this country again. Who knows how long the conflict in Europe would last and my role as a spy in Yugoslavia would continue.

"I'm going back to the Banat," I said in a quiet voice as I continued staring at the tiny black dot marking Theresiafeld on the map.

"What did you say?"

I looked at the commander and realized I was talking to myself.

"The Banat is a term used by people of my ethnic background to describe the geographical area I'm being assigned to."

The trained psychologist now controlling every aspect of The Farm placed his arm over my shoulder as a token of comfort.

"That's right, son, we're sending you back into the Banat."

Vienna, Austria,
December 1941

A young priest walked along the side aisle of his church. His path was guided by the dim, natural light from the early winter morning, creeping through the jagged pieces of colored glass. The long row of windows he passed stretched toward the arches rising to the roof of the building. Avoiding eye contact with several women praying in silence in the wooden pews he passed, the priest slid through the ornately carved door of the confessional and disappeared from view of the outside world. In his mind, the darkness of the confessional was not a place where parishioners came for absolution, but rather was a personal sanctuary from his very existence. His vision impaired in the black emptiness, he ran his fingers along the side of his cassock in search of a slit hiding his flask from view. After a quick swig of hard liquor, he leaned his head against the back of the chair and closed his eyes. It was not unusual for him to linger in his favorite confessional for hours. It was an oasis from his vow of obedience in the service of the Roman Catholic Church, and he was only rudely interrupted from his slumber by the occasional parishioner seeking absolution from sin.

With the war escalating in Europe, his daily ritual after mass of passing out acts of contrition for insignificant venial sins seemed more of a nuisance than ever. His grand scheme planned years ago on his father's farm in Austria was at the threshold of completion. It would not be much longer before his role as a priest could be cast aside, and he would be free to pursue his true passion as part of the educated elite of Vienna, absolved of any outstanding student debt.

He cracked the confessional door open, providing light for his old wristwatch. Irritated by the view on the tiny clock face, he dragged himself out of his makeshift cave and headed to his meeting.

Once there, the young priest continued sitting in a dazed state as his pastor thumbed through the endless records he meticulously maintained for the Bishop. He didn't hear his name the first time it was called, so the pastor repeated it more loudly the second time.

"Father Peter!"

"Oh excuse me," he said. "I was up working late last night, and I'm a little tired."

The priest never worked late, but it always seemed like a good excuse. Boasting of his diligence to his superior always seemed convenient before the start of another endless meeting that his pastor forced him to attend.

"Yesterday, I received a call from admissions," the pastor said. "They received the balance of your tuition payment."

"Excellent."

It was the last of Father Peter's tuition expenses, left over from his long days in the seminary here in Vienna. He was now a young priest on paper only and free of the shackles of student loans that had cramped his less-than-virtuous lifestyle.

"My benefactor wanted to make a contribution to the church restoration. Did you receive the donation?" Father Peter asked.

"She sent it. An unbelievably generous woman," the pastor said.

Tante Anna, a half-senile, rich woman who lived near his father's tiny farm in Austria, lent him the money to get an education. It was the ambitious young man's meal ticket out of the village and in with the social elite of Vienna. The only stipulation the wealthy, old spinster made was the requirement of a priestly vocation for Peter; otherwise, his enormous student loan would have to be repaid in full. Father Peter's plan was to serve some time in his version of purgatory as an assistant to an administrator for the archdiocese in Vienna. The dark scheme was to quietly bide his time in the priesthood until the sickly, ancient woman croaked and then slither out of his service to the church completely debt free.

"When do you want to leave for Frau Mayer's New Year's Eve party?" Father Peter asked.

"I guess in about an hour," the pastor said.

He was given the task of development, raising money for several church restoration projects. Part of his job was soliciting wealthy Roman Catholics in Vienna like Frau Mayer to help fund the endless reconstruction of several dilapidated local churches. When the assistant's position came up, the ambitious Father Peter quickly jumped on it. His assignments enabled him to interact with some of the wealthiest people in Vienna. These duties relieved him of the burden of direct contact with the emerging poor as Europe's war-distracted economy dripped into the sewer.

"Well, if you don't need me for anything else, then, ah, I'm going to pray in my room for awhile before we head out."

"Fine. I have the latest numbers on the donations for the renovation. I think the bishop will be pleased."

"Great."

Father Peter never missed an opportunity to sell his own prayer and meditation to his superiors in the service of the archdiocese. His religious ambivalence was in sharp contrast to his workaholic pastor, a dedicated servant of the Catholic church who constantly entangled him with new altruistic projects. The man's other hobby was to seek out new ways to eliminate Father Peter's already limited free time, annoying him to no end. With the war in full swing, the pastor seemed to reach an almost dizzying pace, taking on a steady stream of new projects thrown at him from every frayed corner along the perimeter of Vienna. His nemesis, who devoted ceaseless work hours to the Roman Catholic empire, was a fool in the eyes of Father Peter. His meddling into the limited space that Father Peter managed to carve for himself outside of service to the church was unending.

As the door of his pastor's office shut behind him, Father Peter withdrew the small metal flask he had concealed under his work cassock, taking a quick mouthful of *Doppeltgebrannter* schnapps as he started walking to his bedroom. This shiny, metal container, a present from Tante Anna was the last remnant of any ties still remaining to his humble beginnings of growing up virtually destitute on his father's tiny farm.

As word of Tante Anna's health grew worse with every passing day, he began to see the hazy, dim light at the end of the tunnel when his final ties to the priesthood could be cut loose forever. His devious plan in using the Roman Catholic Church to upgrade his lowly beginnings would soon end in complete victory.

Although he looked forward to the day when he no longer defined himself as a priest, his annoying vocation was a tolerable existence, provided he could remain in Vienna among the elite who supported all of this mindless benevolent activity. In between spells of intoxication, Father Peter enjoyed the opera and intellectual debates at various dinner parties, venues of opportunity used in his mind to suck money out of rich Catholics. If it weren't for his interaction with people in Viennese high society, life in the priestly vocation would be virtually intolerable.

"Ready to go?" the pastor asked as he knocked on Father Peter's bedroom door, rousing him from a daydream.

"Yes."

He took another massive gulp of schnapps and tucked the metal flask in a desk drawer.

Father Peter concentrated as he walked, attempting to avoid the occasional bump on the shoulder of his pastor as they moved away from the Danube canal toward Frau Mayer's house. He thought about how shrewd his decision to become a priest looked in hindsight. Some of his childhood friends now served as draftees in the military while he soaked up Riesling wine, insulated from all the bloodshed.

"Looking forward to the party?" the pastor asked.

"I guess it should be all right."

Always the disciplined con man, Father Peter loved playing down his enthusiasm in attending high-end gatherings, even though he salivated over them with great anticipation. Now that the war was in full force, gatherings of the elite seemed shorter in supply in Vienna, but not eliminated. Father Peter always tagged along when the pastor received an invitation. He felt he was doing the benefactors of the church a favor by showing up in priestly garb; relieving the top wrung of Viennese society the feeling of guilt that comes with partying while others around them are dying on the battlefield. With a priest gorging on *Faschingkrapfen* jelly doughnuts on the eve of another year at war, Father Peter gave them all absolution for enjoying a round of casual gluttony.

As Frau Mayer's ancient butler placed their coats in the hall closet, the priests made their way through the maze of well-dressed guests in the direction of Strauss waltz music echoing in the distance. Father Peter negotiated a quick separation from the pastor as he entered the converted great room, which doubled as a dance hall during the *Fasching* party season that lasted till the start of Lent. He discreetly made his way through the twirling dance couples crowded on the floor, until he arrived at the long table covered with neat rows of fine crystal glasses filled to the brim with champagne. The young priest watched his pastor from across the room work a bit of subtle Viennese schmooze on his elderly hostess as he pounded back several glasses of champagne. No doubt before the evening ended, several thousand schilling could be wrung out of the pocket book of Frau Mayer on some new church initiative that would entangle Father Peter in the cold months to come.

The hours passed quickly as Father Peter washed back a river of alcohol. The sea of bubbly dulled his hearing, forcing him to stumble closer to the ten-piece orchestra entertaining the wealthy merchant class of Vienna. The full spectrum of temptations was everywhere as Father Peter strategically stopped his drunken frame next to a group of well-dressed women roughly his own age. Suddenly, the music stopped, and the electric lights dimmed. As the hands of the wall clock approached the start of another year, only the candlelight flickering sporadically around the makeshift ballroom could be seen, revealing the faces of guests waiting in total silence for the final seconds to pass.

The priest's glazed eyes returned to a woman standing near him as he followed the ends of her long, pleated dress to the floor.

"Happy New Year!"

The chimes of midnight rang out.

"Happy New Year!"

Father Peter tossed back another mouthful of champagne as his eyes stared at the high cheekbones of the woman pressed tightly against the face of a friend standing next to her under the candlelight. The sounds of *böller* popped outside, chasing away the evil spirits of the old year, a brief respite from the war that crept ever closer to the gates of Vienna. He set his empty champagne glass on a table behind him and moved his arm along the back of the young woman, touching her hand as she twirled around. As her body pressed up against him in the darkness, the priest could sense her start to pull away. He forced her closer, touching her lips with his own in a way that hinted of someone out of his natural element.

"Huh? Oh my God!" the startled woman said.

"It's all right. Don't." Father Peter said.

The electric lights snapped back on. He could see the shocked look on her face as she stared at the white collar revealing his Roman Catholic vocation. Without saying another word, she quickly moved away from him and returned to her group of friends. A bit shaken by the inappropriate behavior, Father Peter turned the other way and found the table guarding his half-empty champagne glass.

As the orchestra jump-started the party to its previous steady state, he gulped down the last mouthful of lukewarm champagne. The crystal glass angled away from Father Peter's lips, and he looked through a jumble of drunken heads bobbing around the crowded dance floor. Staring back at him from across the room was Bishop Gabriel. He quickly turned away and repositioned his guilty face behind a couple returning to the makeshift dance floor.

Did the bishop see the kiss? Was he looking when the lights flickered back on, revealing his moment of temptation? Father Peter doubted this man, perched several levels above him on the church hierarchy, even cared. Under the influence of the champagne, the minor waver from priestly conduct left his mind within minutes.

The following week, Father Peter showed up in his usual late style for another one of the endless, boring meetings his pastor set up to chart the progress on a church renovation program.

"Morning, Father," he said.

"Bishop Gabriel wants to see you."

The pastor cut right to the business of the bishop's request.

"What's it about?" he asked.

"I don't know, but please give him these."

The workaholic pastor handed Father Peter the paperwork containing the latest figures on donations for the renovation fund drive. Even as the war continued straining the financial resources of the elite of Vienna, the pastor's tireless efforts always seemed to keep the fundraising going.

"Is there anything else you want to review with me?" Father Peter asked.

"It can wait," he responded. "Head on over. He's expecting you."

Within minutes, Father Peter had slipped on his coat and walked down the street to the bishop's office. As he walked along through the rainy mess, his thoughts returned to last week's Fasching kickoff at Frau Mayer's house. Did the incident with the young woman at the New Year's Eve party catch his superior's eye? As he hurried along, the dulling effect of alcohol at the party no longer tempered the seriousness of his indiscretion. Never before had the bishop met with Father Peter without others attending the meeting. Why else would he be calling for him? The sound of his shoe soles pressing against the marble steps echoed throughout the majestic building as he headed to the bishop's office. Being in this grandiose building always frightened him; probably from some latent insecurity given his modest beginnings as the poor son of an Austrian dairy farmer.

Father Peter opened the ornately engraved wooden door to Bishop Gabriel's office. The bishop made no attempt to change his position. He continued facing away from him, looking out the window at the streets of Vienna covered in rainwater.

"Bishop Gabriel, it's Father Peter."

The continued silence made him feel even more uncomfortable. The young priest felt like pulling out the flask hidden under his jacket and taking a quick gulp of his hard liquor before the bishop turned around. Maybe he could leave the office and come back another time, but he knew it was too late.

"Bishop Gabriel?"

He slowly turned around and walked toward him. As he stretched out his long, bony arm, Father Peter gave a quick kiss on his ring and backed several steps away from him.

"How is the fundraising coming along, my son?"

"Here are the latest figures. I think you'll be pleased at our efforts."

Father Peter always overplayed his significance in the progress of the church renovation project whenever the pastor wasn't around. He set the monthly report on the bishop's desk, hoping that his role in the fundraising would more than offset the damage he did to his reputation last week at Frau Mayer's house.

"These are hard times for men of our vocation," the bishop said as he thumbed through the report. "The hardship and stress the war puts on the average man is a tragedy."

"Yes, I agree."

His insincere agreement with the bishop's words only seemed logical. Father Peter's mundane daily existence in his administrative role for the archdiocese in no way helped him to empathize with the families affected by the broader conflict surrounding him. As Germany regained control of territory lost after the Great War, Father Peter's life remained insulated from all the killing. He was surrounded by a protective layer of Viennese culture and sophistication.

"I have a request to ask of you, Father Peter."

"Yes, Bishop, anything at all."

Father Peter slid into an old leather chair in front of Bishop Gabriel's desk. He called them requests, but in reality they were orders that no priest shackled to the vow of obedience under his tyranny ever refused.

"I received word that a small German village in Yugoslavia has been without a priest for some time now," the bishop said. "I'm recommending you take over the position as pastor of that parish."

Father Peter's mouth practically sank to the marble floor at these words. The transfer of priests from Vienna to ethnic German villages in Yugoslavia was a lingering practice from the days when that part of Europe was still under the control of the Austrian Empire.

Father Peter knew he had to put up a fight if he wanted to remain in Vienna. "Why me?" he asked. "Why not someone from that region?"

"It's always difficult to find priests to service parishes in some of these agrarian villages. Besides, I think it'll be a good idea for you to spend some time away from Vienna."

He was in a world of trouble. The only thing that made life tolerable as a priest was Vienna, and now it was slipping away from him. He spent his entire life scheming to get out of a tiny Austrian farming village, only to be forced to one even more remote somewhere in Yugoslavia. While he waited for his benefactor to pass away and relieve him once and for all of his tuition debt, his remaining years in the priesthood would be like a prison, locked up from everything in the secular world that Vienna offered.

"But my service in the development for several of our renovation projects is not yet completed."

It was his last, desperate attempt to remain in Vienna, so he clung to a restoration project that only moments ago he had found routine and uninteresting.

"Several of our seminarians will be ordained a priest in the next several months. One of them can take over your duties."

The Bishop squinted his eyes, watching the young priest's desperate attempt to find a way out of obedience to the church.

"Is there possibly another assignment within the limits of Vienna that I could be transferred to instead of Yugoslavia?" Father Peter asked.

"No."

It was the final kiss of death from his intimidating superior. No was the answer, and there was nothing he could do about it.

"When do I leave for Yugoslavia?"

"Someone from my office will be in touch with you and fill you in on the details. Sometime early this summer should be enough time for your replacement to feel comfortable performing your current assigned duties."

"But—"

"That's all, Peter. Thank you."

Without saying another word, he raised himself out of his chair and stretched out his hand for Father Peter's lips to press against his ring, signaling the end of their conversation. As he walked down the marble steps, Father Peter thought about the stupidity of his actions on New Year's Eve. The bishop never mentioned the incident with the girl, but he knew it was the catalyst that had caused his transfer. A little less champagne, and the entire episode probably wouldn't have occurred.

When he returned to his pastor's office, he was still shocked by the wretched turn of events. "You're not going to believe what happened," he said.

"What?" The pastor set his ornately decorated fountain pen on the scribbled pad of paper and shrugged his shoulders in confusion.

"I'm being transferred!"

"Why?"

"How do I know?" he said. "Well, I think I do know."

Father Peter decided to temporarily drop the religious front he usually put on in front of the pastor and confess his venial sin to the man. He wanted to get the incident off his chest, and the pastor happened to be the closest person around.

"You know what kind of a person he is?" the pastor said. "Remember that incident with that young man in your seminary class. What's his name again?"

"Thomas."

"Right."

The pastor was referring to one of Father Peter's classmates in his last year of training in the seminary. Bishop Gabriel dismissed the young seminarian from school after he found out about an alleged affair during his time in the seminary. The young man was at a crossroads and had finally given up the woman, making a final commitment to a religious vocation. Upon finding out about the incident, the bishop dismissed him from the seminary, and the church lost a good priest. Father Peter's fear of Bishop Gabriel had grown after that incident. He never felt completely candid in a confessional booth with another priest on the bishop's staff again.

"Yugoslavia of all places. How dangerous do you think it is?" the pastor asked.

"I haven't even thought about that." Father Peter said.

The news of leaving Vienna had overwhelmed his thoughts, blocking out any concerns regarding the war and his own personal safety.

"Probably not too bad. The Germans have been in control of the country for some time now," the pastor said.

"I can't believe it." Father Peter said and put his face into his sweaty palms and shook his head in disgust. "Maybe I should leave the priesthood."

If he went down this path, it would result in a complete reversal of Tante Anna's decision to repay his student loan debt. Even in her current frail condition, he was confident that leaving the priesthood would anger her enough to execute that decision. Even under the stress of his current plight, no one knew about his deep secret to eventually drop out of the priesthood, and he wanted to keep it that way.

"Are you serious about dropping out?" the pastor asked. "You may only be down there for a couple of years!"

Father Peter waited for a moment before answering the pastor's question. He had become a patient man over the years, determined to complete his devious plan, even if it meant serving some time in Yugoslavia waiting for the eventual demise of his benefactor. Not even the all-powerful Bishop Gabriel could stop him from the objective formed many years ago during his humble beginning milking cows on his father's farm.

"No, I'm not dropping out," he said. "It looks like I'm headed to Yugoslavia."

Sadness turned to anger at the thought of life in some insignificant agrarian community deep in Yugoslavia. It was like receiving word from a commanding officer in the German military that a transfer to the Russian front was imminent. A death sentence.

Maybe the transfer was God punishing him for years playing the role of a priest, using the church as a scholarship fund for his own self-serving interests. Words could not begin to describe his raging anger. He wanted revenge against Bishop Gabriel, the Roman Catholic Church, even God himself. He envisioned God looking down upon him, laughing at his circumstances. Father Peter would never give up. He was determined to have the last laugh in the end. But for now, his life in Vienna, the city he loved more then anything, was coming to an end. He was on his way to Yugoslavia.

✝

Vienna, Austria

June 1942

I repositioned my suitcase under the restaurant table in between my legs. My portable receiver, transmitter, and six-volt power source were secure inside. My fear of losing the small case was almost as intense as opening my mouth and talking to strangers here in Vienna. The idea of losing my lone communication device and severing the umbilical connection to an unknown listener on the other end petrified me.

"What do you want?" the waitress asked.

I stared at the rude, middle-aged waitress as her thick forearms slid along the pad of paper scratching out the start of another breakfast order in the crowded café.

"Please hurry," the waitress said.

Understanding her Viennese dialect required concentration for an ethnic German born in Hungary like myself. My father back in New York didn't have many friends born in Vienna, so I wasn't used to the German chatter growing up as a kid.

"Ah, nothing. Thank you"

I grabbed my suitcase and quickly lifted myself out of the booth, walking out the front door in a state of panic. My body still froze every time I interacted with any of the local Viennese merchants for fear of being discovered as an American spy. When anyone looked at my flushed, panic-ridden face for too long, I envisioned an advertisement stamped across my forehead saying, "I AM YOUR ENEMY, TURN ME IN TO THE AUTHORITIES."

I decided to endure my hunger pains a little while longer, as I rushed past an oncoming red *S-Bahn*, floating over a thin track in the middle of the busy street. Avoiding eye contact with any one of the local Austrians crowding the Vienna West Station, I headed for an isolated bench and waited for my scheduled departure deep into Yugoslavia.

A well-mannered young boy near my cold, metal bench playfully handed me a newspaper fallen on the cement floor of the station. At least I could talk with children without panicking. All I needed was a little more confidence to begin interacting with some of these Austrians.

I unraveled the crumpled, wet newspaper the young boy gave me and read some of the Nazi propaganda that filled the press of Vienna. Austria was now under the complete control of the German propaganda machine. The slanted words coming off the soaked pages were the counterpoint version of the news announcer's rhetoric bellowing from my father's old RCA radio back home.

A cool breeze pushed through the open door of the Viennese train station, rattling my damp paper. Germany had been at war with America for almost a year, making me an official war criminal if my cover as a blue-collar worker bound for Yugoslavia was ever blown. I continued reading the newspaper in fear. I felt if I dropped the soaking rag on the floor, one of these high-brow Viennese travelers might strike up a conversation with me, sending me into another panic attack.

The announcer's voice rang out across the platform. "Train bound for Budapest is now arriving on track three."

I jumped off my bench and tucked the ragged, old suitcase tightly under my right arm, terrified it would pop open and reveal my hidden radio transmitter in the false bottom. As I walked to the punctual train whistling into the station, I wondered what the folks racing past me thought about the war. On the surface, they appeared unaffected by the Nazi occupation, which struck me as odd. I had heard about sporadic resistance against German forces, but the overall momentum still seemed with the Axis powers, resulting in relative stability for Austria.

"All aboard, Budapest!" The conductor shouted the train's destination as he dropped the metal steps connected by a hinge, allowing travelers to climb into the railcar with greater ease. I walked through the center aisle of the empty train, moving quickly through several second-class railcars before grabbing one of the empty seats.

As I reluctantly slid my weathered suitcase above me on the luggage rack, I wondered if it would be searched upon crossing the border into Hungary or Yugoslavia. I wanted to keep it on my lap, but I feared it would attract too much attention. It was pointless worrying about it any longer. The radio communication device was carefully hidden along the false bottom, and the possibility of border patrol workers searching every piece of luggage on the train seemed unlikely.

I settled back in my second-class seat for the long journey and wondered about the existence of any enemies listening to my cipher, transmitting valuable information back to our allies. The radio signal could easily be tracked down if someone looked for it. My concern eased a bit as I thought about how insignificant the tiny, agrarian village of Theresiafeld was from a military standpoint. No one in German intelligence would think an American spy was planted there.

Within several minutes the punctual train crawled out of the Viennese station. A sense of relief came over me that the seat next to me remained unoccupied. The stress of forced communication with a stranger sitting next to me while in transit to Yugoslavia seemed unthinkable.

Suddenly the sound of luggage banging up against the arm rests of passenger chairs caused me to glance down the center aisle of my railcar. I could see a blond man roughly my age move toward my row with little regard to striking anyone with his bulky, leather luggage.

"Is this seat occupied?" he asked.

I shook my head no. The stranger methodically wiped off the smallest of dust particles from his hand-crafted leather suitcase and stacked it neatly above him before sitting next to me. As he opened his newspaper, I glanced at his impeccably clean shoes and pants.

His outward appearance contrasted with my blue-collar work clothes, the natural cover of a laborer taking a job in Theresiafeld, Yugoslavia.

Trying to avoid eye contact with him, I looked out my window as the last traces of the Stefansdom steeple of Vienna faded in the distance. I now moved eastward into territory that Adolf Hitler and his war machine had slowly taken during the last several years. It would be a long stretch before getting off the train in the city of Belgrade. The thought of sitting next to this stranger with the expensive luggage made my stomach lurch.

"Excuse me," I said, pushing the stranger's open newspaper aside as I crawled over him to make a fast break to the restroom. Quickly latching the door of the restroom behind me, I dropped to my knees and shoved my face in the toilet and began vomiting. The combination of the train's motion and my stress caused me to lose what little food remained in my stomach. I was a nervous wreck, clearly unfit for espionage. As I knelt there with my head in the toilet, the vomiting and motion sickness brought back memories of my original trip as a young boy aboard the ocean liner that had taken my father and me to a new life in America.

Someone knocked on the door behind me and began wrestling with the latch, attempting to hasten my exit from the tiny restroom.

"One minute please!" I said.

I had to regain my composure before returning to my seat. I reached into my right pocket and touched the lucky gold coin my father gave me before leaving New York. As I rubbed the coin in between my fingers, I took a deep breath and wiped my mouth clean with an old, embroidered, handkerchief belonging to my mother before she died.

"Sorry."

I moved past the restless passenger waiting to use the restroom and hustled back to my seat.

The train continued eastward to the Hungarian border. I relaxed a bit, hoping to muster up enough courage to strike up a few words with the young stranger sitting next to me buried in his paper.

"Hmm."

The stranger said something. Was it a word? Did he want to talk to me? I glanced over at him and took a good look at his cynical face glaring at the newspaper article. I could see the look of disgust as he read through the tainted words in print generated by the tightly controlled Austrian media.

My limited read on him was of someone ambivalent to the war. His reaction to the article gave me a renewed sense of calm. Maybe he was a free-spirited Austrian? If my new cover in Europe were blown, would the stranger next to me even care that I was an American?

I decided to try a little conversation. "Another several hours, and we'll be in Budapest," I said.

My stomach settled a bit. It was my first attempt at voluntary communication with someone. It felt good to finally break the ice. His head remained motionless after hearing my voice. Slowly, the stranger's eyes moved out of his newspaper and took a quick scan of the not-so-well-dressed laborer sitting next to him. Unimpressed by what he saw, the stranger glanced at his watch to confirm my thesis and returned to his paper without uttering another word. In the stranger's mind, I guess a peasant such as myself had little to offer in the form of interesting conversation to pass the time. Nonetheless pleased with my bold attempt at communication, I concentrated on the Austrian countryside buzzing across my window.

After the train stopped at the border, I decided once again to coax the young man seated next to me into a conversation.

"Looks like we're at the Austrian border."

The stranger didn't respond.

He moved out of his seat and pulled down from the overhead rack one of his giant, leather suitcases. As the young man unbuttoned his coat and slid it into his suitcase, I was surprised to see the white collar strapped tightly around his neck, revealing his priestly vocation. He gave a quick look back at me to see my reaction at discovering he was a priest. My annoying attempts at conversation with the priest probably gave an impression of unworldliness, a general geographical stupidity for belaboring the obvious by recognizing the train would stop at the Austrian border.

"How long do you think we'll be at the border?" I asked.

"Haven't a clue."

It was clear that my stupid question annoyed the priest. "Pass, please!"

The young priest and I handed our passports to the border patrolman entering from the rear of the train. My passport had checked out upon my initial arrival in Europe without a hitch, and I was confident that it would hold up against the scrutiny of an overworked border patrol guard.

"Where's your final destination, Father?" the patrol guard asked.

"Theresiafeld, Yugoslavia," the priest said.

As the words came out of the young priest's mouth, I could hardly believe what I was hearing.

"And how about yours, Hans Mueller?"

"Theresiafeld also," I said.

I had never heard anyone say my undercover name before, and I felt uncomfortable responding to it. Everyone called me John at home except for my father. When I was given the outline of my mission back on The Farm, they decided to Germanize my real name, which was easy to remember. My last name was originally spelled "Mueller" before I immigrated to America with my father. When we passed through Ellis Island, the immigration inspector misspelled our last name to "Miller," which my father didn't bother trying to correct. My last name remained "Miller" until I started undercover work, when the American government ironically switched it back again to its original spelling, "Mueller."

The border patrolman tossed the passports into our laps and proceeded to the next passenger. Within minutes, the inspection of the train was complete, and we crossed the border into Hungary.

"So you're headed to Theresiafeld?" I said.

"Yes, that's correct," the priest said.

"I'm also headed there."

"Yes, I know."

The young priest was obviously not as excited as I was at the news of being headed to the same final destination. I felt somehow relieved that I would not be the only newcomer to the tiny village.

"Is this your first trip to Yugoslavia?" I asked.

"Yes," the priest answered.

"Where are you from originally?"

"Austria."

"I'm originally from a small farming village in Hungary myself."

"That's excellent," the priest responded sarcastically.

As I grew more confident, I continued boring the man with my fictional background as the man I might have become had my father decided to return to his ethnic German village in Hungary. It was clear the young priest was not impressed with my fictional cover so thoroughly rehearsed back in spy school on The Farm.

"Think you'll miss Vienna?" I asked.

He lowered his eyes and pulled out a small, metal flask hidden under his black suit jacket.

"Yes, I'm sure I will."

As I watched him take a large gulp from the shiny, metal container, I wondered how he ever came to choose the priesthood as his calling. The stranger did not give off an initial impression as a religious man. Doing God's work seemed more like a day job to him, not a spiritual vocation.

As we pulled out of the Budapest train station, I looked out my window and watched tiny bits of moonlight reflect off the ridges of the dark blue water of the Danube River. It was my last glimpse of the Danube as the tracks slowly drifted southeast through Hungary, lulling me into a light sleep. In my dream, an image appeared of my earliest descendants making the long journey by barge down the Danube River. Unlike my lofty ambitions of becoming a lawyer, these early German colonists desired only an escape from oppressive taxation in their original homeland and an opportunity to acquire some inexpensive land to farm. I was now on a mission that could potentially destroy this agrarian way of life carved out more than 200 years ago by these early German pioneers.

The silence between the jagged bumps on the track increased in length as the train decelerated, and I returned to the reality of my mission in the crowded interior of the railcar. I glanced at my traveling companion, sleeping in a crunched position. An empty metal flask dangled from his fingers to the rocking of the train. As the train slowed, the priest's body slowly came to life. I could see the moonlight coming through the window, reflecting off his glazed-over eyes, revealing the effects of hard liquor consumption. His excessive drinking seemed to fill empty holes where his religious faith failed to ease some hidden pain. In some strange way, I felt sorry for him.

We pulled into the station, and I practically jumped out of my seat as I looked out my window.

"Are those Wehrmacht soldiers?" I asked.

"Yes."

My heart started pounding faster, looking at the German soldiers in their polished uniforms waiting for a transport along the pavement parallel to our train. Since my initial arrival in Europe, this was my first glimpse at such a large number of German troops in one location, and the sight of them frightened me.

"Where do you think they're going?" I asked.

"Probably on leave and headed back to Germany," the priest said.

It was my first attempt at intelligence gathering, and it was from a priest of all people. I wanted to use my radio transmitter immediately, but I knew the information would be worthless to the European desk. As the train pulled out of the station, I continued staring through my cloudy window as the sight of Wehrmacht soldiers faded in the distance.

We continued for hours through the barren plains of Yugoslavia. My partially intoxicated traveling companion fell quickly back to sleep, making the long train ride even more unbearable without anyone to practice my cover with.

"Father, we're here."

I shook the priest several times, but he didn't respond.

"We're in Belgrade. Wake up."

"All right, already."

I didn't mean to make him angry, but I didn't want my only contact in Theresiafeld to miss his stop. I watched as he pulled his large leather suitcases off the rack and stumbled to the exit.

I knew the farming village was roughly twenty kilometers north of Belgrade, but I was clueless on how to get there. Hoping my priestly traveling companion might have the problem already figured out, I decided to follow him from a safe distance. He stumbled through the Belgrade train station, dragging his expensive luggage as he hobbled along. I watched as a well-groomed man in neat work clothes approached the priest, pulling several of the leather suitcases from his hand while they chatted. Their conversation continued for a while, and I decided to approach the newly acquainted group.

"Father, excuse me. Do you have any ideas on how to get to Theresiafeld?"

I knew he didn't know, but I hoped the individual he spoke to would jump in and rescue me from my dilemma. Clearly annoyed by my presence, the priest didn't say a word as he looked back at his contact person, hoping to be relieved of any further interaction with me.

"You can come with us. I'll take you back to Theresiafeld," the other man said in German.

The stranger's dialect was more like my father's, and it felt good not to struggle to understand him. I gave the stranger a nod as he grabbed the rest of the priest's leather suitcases and headed out of the station into the cold night air. As he continued talking with the priest, I was surprised how similar his German dialect was to my own, giving me another slight edge in the slow process of trying to drift into Theresiafeld without attracting too much attention to myself. My small suitcase, the lone piece of luggage containing the hidden radio transmitter, started to get heavy as we made our final approach to the local man's horse and wagon.

"Hop in," he said.

I slid my suitcase across the back of his wagon, covered in pieces of dried hay probably left over from last season's wheat harvest, and jumped aboard.

"Be careful with that!" the priest screamed at the driver who was tossing his bulky, leather luggage on the rear of the wagon next to me. Without asking, the inconsiderate priest took a seat in the front, and I hitched a ride in the back.

"Thanks for giving me a ride into Theresiafeld," I said.

"No problem," the driver replied.

As we rolled along in the hay-covered wagon for the final leg of the journey, I wondered where I would stay and how I'd carve out a life for myself in between bouts of information gathering.

"Everybody all right back there?" the driver asked.

"Yes, no problem," I responded.

The priest didn't glance back at me, totally unconcerned about my well being as our bodies continued bobbing along the uneven dirt road.

"Do you have any family in Theresiafeld Father Peter?" the wagon driver asked.

"None"

I never asked the young priest's name the entire train ride from Vienna. Even though he had no interest in me, it felt good knowing at least one person in this community of Germans. The wagon rolled past the last of the open field now stripped of crops from the harvest and broke into an alternate landscape. The neat rows of whitewashed houses that bordered both sides of the wagon were like Janissary guards at attention, protecting us from the wind when the Ottoman Turkish empire controlled the plains of the Banat.

My mission was to acquire information that would help in the war effort through interaction with these Banat Germans from Theresiafeld, and it would begin today.

†

Yugoslavian Banat
June 1942

"One more minute!" I called.

The knock on the door had startled me, and I scrambled to shove my radio transmitter back in the false bottom of my worn suitcase.

"I have some information for you, Herr Mueller."

My fidgety landlord for the last several weeks continued knocking on my bedroom door.

"I'm almost ready!"

I slammed the lid to my suitcase and slid it between the dark-stained wooden bedposts that rose to the ceiling. I let the innkeeper into my rental room, doubling over the last several weeks as a makeshift headquarters for information gathering in Theresiafeld.

"Good news, Herr Mueller."

My temporary German landlord, the proud owner of this local *gasthaus* in Theresiafeld, seemed always eager to please me, probably because I always paid my rent on time.

"What is it?" I asked.

"I managed to get you in the game tonight."

"Excellent. What time?"

"Come down to the bar around 10 o'clock."

I had managed to bribe the gasthaus proprietor into squeezing me into a well-known card game that took place most Saturday nights at his establishment. A small group of relatively well-dressed men gathered in the smoke-filled back room, taking part in a Theresiafelder version of high-stakes poker. The merchant class who took part in the infamous game were influential people around the village. After several rounds of hard schnapps at the card game tonight, I hoped they might leak some information that might be valuable to the allies in the war effort.

"Don't tell anyone I'm encouraging some of my guests to get involved in this game."

"Oh, I won't."

The always-nervous gasthaus owner seemed like a religious man with a practical twist. I think he wanted to be perceived by the gossipy villagers of Theresiafeld as an honest proprietor and not one who promotes high-stakes gambling in his establishment. I don't think anybody knew he received a percentage for organizing the game and supplying the liquor, but I gathered his cut was enough to allow his morals to be somewhat compromised.

Since my arrival in Theresiafeld, I had stumbled upon no information of substance that might help the Allies. In the early weeks, I stayed secluded in the gasthaus, only occasionally creeping down to the adjoining tavern for a quick bite to eat. As I grew more comfortable with my undercover role, I began talking to the mixed bag of Serbs, Germans, and Croats who made their stay at the gasthaus while traveling through Theresiafeld. Unlike the more diverse group passing through the gasthaus, the local population in Theresiafeld was almost entirely ethnic German, which made communication easier for me, considering I couldn't speak a word of Serbo-Croatian.

"I'll see you later tonight," I said.

"Yes, Herr Mueller. Till tonight, then."

I slipped several dinars into the innkeeper's hand and walked him to the wooden door of my room, quickly locking it behind him as he left. Once again, I had forgotten to ask him what his nickname was, and I wanted to call him back, but I had to return to my radio transmission. I had forgotten about the annoying practice in Banat German villages of everyone being tagged with a nickname, making it more difficult for an outsider to remember anyone's name.

After a short nap, I slipped into my black slippers that a local shoemaker had crafted for me and headed downstairs to the adjoining tavern. The shoes and clothing I had recently purchased gave me a less suspicious exterior look when snooping around town, allowing me to blend in more easily with the local population of Banat Germans.

"Are they here?" I asked.

"Go on back!"

The innkeeper shouted over the noise of the Saturday night crowd, as beer continued flowing through the chilled pipes moving up from the basement. I moved past one of the locals playfully letting his child take a drag out of his pipe and headed toward the back of the gasthaus. Having scoped out some of the card players from conversations with other Theresiafelders, I was confident that if I could slip into the game, I could land some high-quality information for the European desk back home.

I greeted several of the drunken regulars in attendance. Even under the influence of alcohol, a glossy-eyed Theresiafelder could pick up my slight Hungarian German dialect, revealing to the local that I wasn't born in this village. At first I was concerned about blowing my cover every time I opened my mouth, but most of the local population didn't seem to care, provided I was of German background.

I watched as several more card players made their way to the semiprivate back room of the gasthaus. Within a few minutes, I had brushed off the drunken acquaintances befriended in the tavern over the past several weeks and headed on back.

Pushing aside the dark gray curtain that separated the noisy tavern from the back room, I entered without saying a word. There was only a single electric light hanging from a long cord illuminating the well crafted wooden table in the middle of the room, so I moved in closer to let the other card players take a good look at my face.

"Good evening. I'm here for the game," I said.

"Are you the one who's going to be my partner tonight?" asked a gentleman who limped out of the dark, smoky corner of the tiny room to the wooden table where I was standing.

"I guess I am," I said.

"Johann Reichinger."

The partially disabled man wrapped his thick fingers around my hand for a quick greeting and took a seat across from me at the table. The game of choice for the card players was *fuchser*, a typical game played in the Banat that my father had taught me as a child. I was used to playing with an American deck of 52 cards with my buddies from law school, but I didn't figure it would be a problem switching back to the old shorter Hungarian deck again. The game worked in sets of pairs, and my nervous landlord had managed to sell Johann Reichinger, one of the wealthiest landowners in Theresiafeld, on the idea of my being his partner for tonight's game. I didn't know much about the landowner who bent over to one side as he walked toward the card table. I was told he was one of the larger landowners in Theresiafeld, and land in an agrarian community was how wealth was defined. From what I could gather, the landowner I was teamed up with farmed at least twenty times the total ground my father did before we left Hungary.

"This is my friend for the last 100 years, Fetter Matz," Reichinger said.

"Matz."

"And this is—"

"My name is Valmer."

The man dropped his cigarette butt on the wooden floor and moved in uncomfortably close to my face, as if trying to read my facial tells to gather clues before the card game began.

I lit up a filterless cigarette, a habit I had decided to pick up, given so many men in the village seemed to be chain smokers. I thought about the improvements in the quality of life for Banat Germans relative to when I was growing up in my father's village back in Hungary. Despite the brutal hardships of disease, discrimination, and war, this German farming community seemed on the surface to be stronger than the one I had left. Electric power had pushed aside old kerosene lanterns. Mechanical tractors, which now stood dormant until the fall harvest, replaced the metal plow and horse on most of the farms surrounding this agrarian community.

There was no doubt in my mind that the quality of life for the average farmer in Theresiafeld, my microscope on the greater war surrounding Europe, had improved since the days of my childhood.

"Valmer, pass out the cards already," Reichinger said.

As he manipulated the Hungarian cards with the few fingers remaining on his hand, Valmer stared at me from across the table with the classic dead eyes of a shrewd gambler. I had heard rumors that several years back the astute card player had placed a big land bet against one of the locals in cards and managed to win the farmer's entire land holdings.

"You know how to play fuchser, don't you Magyar?" Valmer slid the Hungarian cards face down to the three other players seated around the wooden table.

"Yes, I do."

I could see the faces around the room begin to focus on the ornate figures hidden from view as they peeled the cards off the table.

"You're not going to get steaming mad like a typical Magyar if I take your money tonight?" Valmer said.

I smirked back at him, studying several cards in my hand.

The designated card dealer with the missing fingers had picked up on my Hungarian-German dialect immediately and jokingly labeled me as a hot-blooded Hungarian. The ethnic Germans in this part of Europe always had a slight elitist streak in them when they compared themselves to other ethnic groups on the plains of the Banat. With Germany now in control of Yugoslavia, the friendly rivalry between the ethnic groups now teetered dangerously close to rage. A slow crescendo of derogatory labels mutating into nationalistic overtones had crept its way through the ranks in every dark corner of this tidy little gasthaus.

As the last of the Hungarian cards slid my way across the wooden table, I laughed to myself at the irony of the situation. The name of the card game I was playing was also my code name when sending messages via my radio transmitter. "The Fox," the name I signed off with when sending radio transmissions out of Theresiafeld, now played fuchser, German for "fox."

"How's your son doing, Matz?" Reichinger asked as he stared at his hand.

"He's doing all right. He should be home in a couple of weeks now that the camp commandant saw a postcard I wrote him in German."

"What happened?" I asked.

"My son was serving in the Yugoslavian cavalry when the German military invaded. He was taken back to Germany as a prisoner."

"Matz's family was never known for good timing," Reichinger said as he tossed a card marked with acorns into the middle of the pile. My initial impression of Reichinger, my partner in this card game, was not a man sensitive about other people's problems, even one as serious as a friend's son serving a prison term in Germany.

"How does Germany ever expect to control Europe if they're stupid enough to take our own people as prisoners?" Matz asked.

A small stack of discarded acorn and shell cards began building up in the middle of the table, and the conversation grew more interesting as we slipped into talk about the war. This was the exact situation my superiors back home envisioned when they recruited me for espionage training.

"What if the war takes a turn for the worse and the Germans start losing?" Fetter Matz asked. "A friend of mine who's in the German military claimed that his unit was hit by some Croatian rebel named Tito."

I listened intently as I continued staring at Valmer's three-fingered hand, glued against the backside of his cards. I was hoping he would jump in the conversation. I had heard from a contact in the gasthaus that his wine trading business enabled him to interact with many people around the Banat, giving him access to information about the war that many people in Theresiafeld might not know.

"No one knows for sure if this Tito even exists," Reichinger said. "I heard he might have been killed already. Those Serbian terrorist groups are probably keeping his name alive to rally support behind their cause."

"What about this Serbian national, Mihajlović, I thought his group of Chetniks were the real terrorist enemy of the German military?" Valmer asked.

"Some Serbs I do business with hear rumors that Mihajlović may be cutting a deal with the Germans," Reichinger said.

"How do they know that?" Valmer asked.

"When was the last time you heard on the radio Chetniks fighting the German military," Reichinger said.

I ducked my eyes back down at my weak hand of Hungarian playing cards as Valmer stared at me.

"These Chetniks and Partisans are completely disorganized. I hear they're even fighting among themselves," Reichinger said. "Mihajlović, Tito—it doesn't matter. None of those rebels are going to organize a real military resistance to our own German troops."

"Our military expert has spoken," Fetter Matz said. "Reichinger didn't serve in World War I because of his bad back, and now he lectures us."

"When the military front moved through Theresiafeld in the last war, we abandoned the village for a short while," Valmer said. "After the war ended, we all returned home. It'll probably be the same way this time if things go the wrong way for Germany."

As the conversation grew in intensity, the cards continued popping out of the wealthy hands of the players surrounding the table. The card pile grew under the dim light, peeking out of the cigarette smoke rising above.

"You're wrong, Valmer!" Reichinger shouted. "It's not going to be like last time! The Germans aren't going to lose control of Yugoslavia!"

I took a quick shot of my spritzer, a popular mixed drink of local wine and soda water, calming my nerves as I continued soaking in the heated debate. As the overconfident lecturing of Reichinger mixed with the smoky haze filling the back room of the Gasthaus, the game of fuchser dragged on through the night. I struggled to keep my bloodshot eyes open as I soaked in the information.

"I'm tired of all this negative talk!" Reichinger said as he pounded his fist against the wooden table.

The jolt woke me from a partial slumber, sending Valmer's neat pile of dinar winnings floating to the hard wooden floor below us.

"I don't care if the Americans are in the war! You hear the victories reported on the radio."

"I'll drink to that," I said. Raising my glass pretending to be in a mild drunken state.

The *doppeldeutsch* cards were shuffled a dozen more times as the card game continued for another several hours. Now that I accomplished my goal of getting some information for the war effort, I began betting recklessly, hoping to be driven out of the game.

"Our new man on the card table tonight hasn't said too much. Who do you think is going to win this war, Magyar?"

As Valmer voiced the intimidating question, I sat there frozen, staring at the massive quantity of Yugoslavian dinars in the center of the wooden table.

"Don't know," I said.

"Well take a guess. It's like fuchser. You have to have an opinion about your opponent before you decide to destroy them or make big bets against them."

I found his question loaded in some way, and it made me feel uneasy. I wanted to walk off the table and return to my room, but Valmer needed a response. I waited several moments longer, hoping the shrewd gambler would ask someone else a question and I could get off without a confrontation. The waiting continued. From my endless lectures back on The Farm in Washington, I didn't want my response to attract much attention to myself or appear mindlessly patriotic.

"Whoever wins, everyone still needs bread across Europe, and the Germans scattered across the Banat will be there to provide it."

I controlled my fear with every ounce of energy remaining, taking a big gulp from my half-empty spritzer glass.

"Good answer, Magyar."

Valmer grinned at me as he laid his William Tell face card on top of my stack of dinars in the center of the wooden table. It was the final kiss of death for my partner, Reichinger, and me in this game of fuchser.

"That's it, my friends. I've lost enough money this evening."

I had to get out of there. I felt my legs shaking under the wooden table from the fear of blowing my cover.

"Come down anytime, Magyar. Your money is always good here."

"Right."

Valmer peeled up the left corner of each paper dinar, working slowly through his stack with his three digits as he counted his winnings in a whisper.

"What do you do here in Theresiafeld?" Valmer asked.

"The job I thought I was going to take didn't come through. I'm looking for work, especially after tonight's performance."

I worried for a moment he was going to probe further at the mythical job I was after. Under the influence of the alcohol spritzers, I wasn't in the correct mental condition to continue playing my cover any longer.

"My wife's having a party next Sunday after mass," Reichinger said. "Kind of a welcome party for our new priest in Theresiafeld. Why don't you show up? Maybe we can figure out a way you can win back some of that money you lost me tonight."

"Thanks."

Concerned about receiving some more intimidating questions from Valmer, I quickly left the smoke-filled room, bobbing past the remaining guests, and headed upstairs for the night. I pressed my body against the mattress, still trembling from the fear of being discovered as a spy.

My head sank deep into the large goose feather pillow on my bed. I thought about my impressions of the locals in Theresiafeld over the last several weeks. I found the attitude of most Germans in this agrarian village to the war to be different than I had originally expected. There were some like Reichinger, my partner in the card game tonight, who were hardcore believers in Germany and religiously believed the radio broadcasts of great victories on the battlefield. But most of the Theresiafelders I encountered had simpler ambitions: a good price for their crop, family and friends safe from the conflict, and a preservation of their ethnic identity, which was constantly under attack by the Serbian majority.

The next day, after spending the morning sobering up, I snuck out to the location where I had buried my suitcase radio and sent off an encrypted message.

THE FOX RECOMMENDS SWITCHING RESISTANCE SUPPORT FROM THE CHETNIKS UNDER MIHAJLOVIĆ TO JOSIP BROZ TITO AND HIS COMMUNIST PARTISANS.

It was the first piece of quality intelligence I managed to acquire since my arrival in Theresiafeld. It felt good knowing that I was helping the war effort in some small way.

✝

Yugoslavian Banat
July 1942

"Excuse me!" I called out to the woman hidden under a large, black scarf as she walked out of the Baroque-style Catholic Church located near Theresiafeld's town square. The elderly woman with a slight hunch didn't hear me as she concentrated on the uneven, gravel road crunching against her worn shoes. Sunday mass had ended more than an hour ago, but many of the women like herself were slow to exit the church because they stayed to pray for family members drafted into the German military.

"Ah, excuse me."

"How can I help you?" her old voice crackled under the black shawl loosely wrapped around her wrinkly face.

"I'm looking for Reichinger's farm?" I asked.

She stretched out her hand, cut full of deep grooves from years of hard work bundling wheat into bushels. I followed her crooked finger as it pointed in the direction of the open pasture, which surrounded the neat rows of whitewashed houses that made up Theresiafeld.

My boots slid along the ruler-straight gravel road out to the open field where local farmers would parade their livestock almost daily during the summer time. Peeking through the trampled countryside, an occasional blade of green grass shuffled across my dark pants leg, signaling the start of an early spring planting season this year in Yugoslavia.

I walked for about an hour until a glimpse of the Reichinger estate was visible in front of several sandy, shallow hills that barely stuck out from the flat terrain surrounding the village. I could see in the distance the dusty smoke of a wagon wheel as several guests of Reichinger rolled past the surrounding whitewashed fence and disappeared into the courtyard. I followed the wagon behind a large, iron gate, separating Reichinger's monumental land holdings from the neat interior of his compound.

"Come in. Come in."

A middle-aged woman opened the creaking door of the main house, guiding me in to an impeccably clean day room jammed full with a chattering German hoard of Theresiafelders. The dark complexion of my female greeter at the door contrasted with the face of every light-skinned guest at Reichinger's house party.

"Can I ask your name?"

"Hans Mueller. I was invited by Johann Reichinger."

The black-eyed woman walked in the direction of the familiar baritone voice of Reichinger lecturing from down the hall. The servant was of Gypsy origin, and I hadn't seen one since I had left my Hungarian village as a child. Although I knew nothing about this servant, my first impression of her was entirely negative. This was probably learned from my father, who despised the entire ethnic group from his dealings with them back in Hungary. I remembered my father hiring a Gypsy one harvest season to help with the brutal manual labor of gathering wheat into bushels, but he was forced to fire the black-eyed thief when he caught him pilfering some of our dishes.

"Hans!"

I could see the free hand of Reichinger waving in the air above the guests, motioning me to join him in the kitchen.

"Hans, come on back here!"

I drifted toward the back of the kitchen where the bellowing Reichinger stood before a long table of sliced liverwurst and bread, holding court for several Banat men in attendance at his wife's party.

"Herr Reichinger, thanks again for the invitation."

"Watch for my wife; we're not supposed to eat yet."

He looked nervously in both directions, making sure his spouse wasn't lurking somewhere as he snatched a bite-sized sandwich, shoving it deep into his oversized mouth.

"Is this all your land surrounding us?" I asked.

He shook his head in agreement.

He didn't seem impressed by the size of his land holdings as his mouth continued chewing down the last of his ground up pig-liver and bread.

"What's your background, Hans?"

I didn't pay any attention to his question because I was looking at the somber faces of his relatives in framed pictures on the wall.

"What do you mean?" I asked.

"You know, what's your training, work background?"

"I worked during the harvest season for several large farmers in Hungary."

The deformed farmer who I played cards with only a week ago looked at me disappointed. It wasn't uncommon for poor Banat Germans who didn't own any land like myself to work for other farmers during the harvest season. Since my cover was a blue-collar worker from Hungary, it seemed like a good line to tell Reichinger, whose upper body angled to one side from his waistline. I think he would have liked me to be of higher status, but it was too late. My cover was established in Washington, and there was nothing I could do about it.

"Is that your family?"

Reichinger turned his twisted body and glared with his blue-eyes at the picture I was staring at.

"That's me as a child with my father and mother."

Reichinger's tiny frame stood next to a black and white photo of a stern man hidden behind a thick moustache.

"Are your parents at the party?" I asked.

"They're all dead now," Reichinger said. "My father died from tuberculosis when I was eighteen."

"I'm sorry to hear that. My mother also died from that," I said.

"Who knows? Maybe it's better that he's dead. We never got along anyway."

It was hard to imagine Reichinger and myself having similar backgrounds in the form of a dead parent. The death of Reichinger's father had made him a wealthy man at a relatively young age through the simple trick of inheritance, but I detected no sense of gratitude from receiving his father's substantial estate. I envisioned the wealthy farmer throwing these lavish parties out of a desperate need for acceptance, which probably came from a lack of love by his father during childhood.

"I want to show you something," Reichinger said.

"What is it?" I asked.

"We'll only be gone for about an hour. By the time we get back, my wife will let you eat something."

He pushed me through the day room crowded with German guests and several Gypsy servants. I could see the priest I traveled with from Vienna sitting in the corner of the room. Valmer, the three-fingered card shark, placed his Hohner accordion on the floor and began pouring the guest of honor another glass of wine.

"Do you like living this far from the others in Theresiafeld?" I asked as we headed out the door.

"Never thought about it before. My father built the home after a couple of good seasons. Maybe he didn't want to be around other Theresiafelders."

As he hobbled alongside me across the dusty fields, I could sense a deep scar still left behind from his dead father. Moving ever farther away from his fenced-in compound, I found the image of Reichinger's land very similar to my distant cousin's place back in North Dakota. Like my cousin's farm, where I had worked one summer before starting law school, Reichinger's main house was located on his farmland. This arrangement was unlike the rest of the villagers in Theresiafeld, who practiced a more European model of farming. Most in Theresiafeld lived alongside one another in town and took a wagon out to their land to work the field.

"Up this hill, Hans. This is what I want you to look at."

The limping Reichinger forced me ahead of him as we moved up the incline. I noticed he didn't like walking in front of me, probably out of fear at being laughed at from the funny way he limped along the sandy soil.

"This is it!"

From our hilltop position, I looked down the other side of the incline and gazed at the giant swamp, which covered the ground as far as the eye could see.

"The Reichinger family has been farming in Theresiafeld practically since the Turks were driven out in the early 1700's," Reichinger said.

He dropped his hands over his knees, allowing himself to catch his breath from the long climb up the hill. We stared at a marshy, green wasteland rotting below us on the other side.

"My family started small with only fifteen hectares of land, but slowly we acquired more. My great-grandfather bought the land we're standing on from a Serb and picked up the unusable swamp as part of the package."

"This is a huge swamp, Herr Reichinger."

From our perch on the hill, I could see the surrounding elevation trapping the swamp water from running off and freeing the land for usable farming. Excluding the disgusting sight of the green blob, the view from the hilltop was beautiful. We overlooked Theresiafeld in the distance, with its lone steeple peeking over the ruler-straight rows of whitewashed Banat German homes in the village. The intermittent acacia trees contrasted with the flat, sandy soil used for growing wheat, the lifeblood of the Banat Germans that allowed agrarian life to continue in Theresiafeld.

"My father wanted to drain this swamp and convert the land for agricultural use, but he never could get enough money to pull it off."

As I stared out at the massive sea of green, filthy water, I tried to figure out how much it would cost to complete such a massive drainage project.

"I'm going to accomplish what my father couldn't do in his lifetime. I'm going to rid my farm of this swamp and convert it to usable land."

"Doesn't that seem risky? Taking on a project of this size with the war going on?"

"This damn war is going to come to an end one day, and when it does, my life will go on pretty much as it always has, just like it will for everybody else living in Theresiafeld."

As Reichinger stared out at his green nemesis, I could see the determined warrior trapped under his partially disabled body. By draining the swamp, he would vastly increase the size of his usable farmland and in his own mind, become a better man than his father.

"How are you going to drain it?" I asked.

"I intend to dig a trench several kilometers in length all the way to an adjoining river. The drainage canal will keep the land dry and allow me to put the land to use."

"I can't even imagine the amount of work that's going to take!"

"That's why you're going to help me, Hans."

I looked away from the giant swamp of green slush and stared back at the wealthy farmer, struggling to balance his crooked body along the uneven soil.

"What?" I asked.

"You heard me. You said you needed a job."

"Well, yes, I need to find work."

I obviously couldn't tell Reichinger that I had a job already working in intelligence-gathering for the Office of Strategic Services (OSS), but I wasn't exactly excited about taking on the backbreaking labor of digging a ditch for some rich farmer trying to outdo a dead father.

"It's settled then," Reichinger said. "You're coming to work for me."

As we made our way down the incline of the hill overlooking the swamp, I thought about Reichinger's job offer. I was starting to grow bored at the gasthaus in Theresiafeld, and, eventually, it would start to look suspicious for a laborer like me to constantly spend dinars losing at cards without some form of income to support myself. Besides, the ditch-digging job was consistent with my cover and would let me increase my interaction with Reichinger, who seemed all too eager to open his mouth and toss war stories at me.

A week later, I packed up my suitcase radio and what minimal belongings I had acquired over the last several weeks and relocated to a building adjacent to Reichinger's main house. I was now a young lawyer from New York in the menial business of digging ditches. The building I relocated to contained clean rows of finely crafted, wooden bunk beds, used in housing seasonal workers who drifted into Reichinger's compound around planting time. These roaming workers on the plains of the Banat stayed until the last grain of wheat was separated from the dry chaff when jammed through Reichinger's oversized threshing machine.

After I moved the last of my things over to Reichinger's well maintained building, I tossed my broken down suitcase under my bunk near a window overlooking the barren, sandy fields and fell asleep for an afternoon nap.

From somewhere in my sleep I heard it. Click. Click. As I jerked awake I saw one of the Gypsies, brought on to help with the upcoming crop harvest, opening a rusty latch on my suitcase, almost revealing my hidden radio communication device.

"Hey get away from there!" I shouted.

"Sorry," the black-eyed thief said in a broken German.

He scuttled out of the building, frightened by my nervous reaction. Without saying another word, I relocked the hinges to my suitcase and exited the Reichinger compound in search of a better place to store my radio transmitter. The thieving hands now making their way onto Reichinger's compound could destroy what small inroads I had made in integrating into this community.

I'm sure Reichinger would have preferred to hire none of the filthy rats, but their presence in Theresiafeld was a necessary evil. The Banat German farmers needed the Gypsies who, if the price were right, didn't mind taking seasonal work that others passed over.

Darkness drifted over the farm, and I quietly slipped out of the compound. With my suitcase radio tucked in an old pillow cover, I stumbled over the fertile ground in search of a strategic hiding place for my equipment. As I approached the outskirts of Theresiafeld, I noticed a group of tightly bunched acacia trees not far from view of the Roman Catholic Church in the middle of the village. I ran past the tree line and dropped to the ground, checking the surrounding open fields for any sign of nosy Theresiafelders wondering what I was up to.

"That's the spot!" I thought as I carefully stepped around a patch of *brennessel* weeds in the clearing, surrounding the cluster of acacia trees. The weeds from the plant create intense itching for the victim who touches it. I remembered playing in a big patch of the itchy stuff in my father's village in Hungary. The result was endless painful hours of intense scratching from the plant's chemicals that had rubbed onto my skin. It was the perfect place to hide the radio components that enabled me to communicate with my mystery contact person on the other end. I carefully moved around the patch of brennessel and began digging with my bare hands through the dry, crusty top layer of dirt. Within a short walk from my new residence on the Reichinger farm and protected from all sides by acacia trees, the location was ideal for transmitting future messages to my contact person listening somewhere on the open plains of the Banat.

The tips of my fingernails turned dark as I continued scooping large handfuls of soil to the surface. As I dug ever deeper, the soil grew black, nurtured from years of dormancy under a bed of water that covered the Pannonian basin thousands of years before the Germans ever arrived on its fertile plains. I pulled the radio transmitter out for a quick inspection and wrapped it back in the pillowcase stolen from my room back at the gasthaus. I quickly covered the radio with loose soil and slithered away from my new transmission location as fast as I could. Relying on stealth tactics picked up at spy school back on The Farm, I walked back to my new employer's estate from a different direction than I had originally left to hide my tracks.

Brushing off the black soil clinging to my pants, I thought as I walked about how far I had come in only a few weeks in

Theresiafeld. I was now a partially integrated member of this ethnic German village, and my blue-collar cover was more natural than ever. The vision my government had of planting me in the Yugoslavian Banat and becoming a deep probe to aid in the war effort was completed.

✝

Yugoslavian Banat
April 1943

"Keep pushing!" I shouted.

"I'm trying, but it won't budge!"

The Gypsy continued to angle the end of his shovel against the tree stump as I tugged on the reins of the horse in front of him.

"Push!"

Slowly the tree began to uproot, and the two of us rested for a moment from the backbreaking labor. More deep-rooted trees and rocks would have to be pulled, as the canal digging crept farther away from our starting point at the river to its eventual destination along the edge of the marshy swamp on Reichinger's property.

"Give me some of that."

I wiped the sweat off my forehead with my oversized white handkerchief and collapsed next to several of my workers who were gulping wine out of a green glass bottle.

"One more time around with the bottle, Hans. One more time."

I took a quick gulp out of the bottle and passed it along to my only German coworker, an extremely unintelligent fellow whose gambling habits had cost him his land and who was now reduced to bone-crushing labor working for wealthy farmers like Reichinger. Banat Germans living in Theresiafeld who didn't own any land or have a trade were forced to take on jobs like this one. This landless, unskilled class hitched a spot on the lowest rung of the agrarian caste system in the Banat. Their spot on the food chain was marked by exhausting work fulfilling a wealthy farmer's dream of building a canal and draining a swamp to increase the size of his usable farmland.

I had made my home on Reichinger's farm for nine months, and my body had slowly grown accustomed to shoveling soil and carving out a drainage canal on the open plains. Through the simple trick of being born German, Johann Reichinger elevated me to the position of foreman among the ethnically diverse band of drifters making up my work crew. As the canal digging slowly progressed toward our marshy swamp several kilometers in the distance, I found myself growing in satisfaction at the quality work I performed. One day the war would be over, but the canal would remain as a memorial to my time spent in the Banat. Even though my canal digging performance was irrelevant to my espionage mission in Theresiafeld, I wanted to be respected by my crew and employer. For what reason, I didn't have a clue.

"Let's do it," I said. "Back to work."

I could see Reichinger in the distance. The dry soil exploded above the hooves of his favorite black stallion as he rode closer to our location. His ability to arrive at the job site at the exact time I called for a break was uncanny, almost telepathic. I grabbed my iron shovel, which leaned against the covered wagon, signaling my crew that it was time to return to digging.

"I calculated how far your crew moved over the last several weeks, and I don't think we're going to make it in time," Reichinger said.

In my overstressed employer's mind, we were behind schedule. The German military had confiscated Reichinger's tractor to help with the war effort. His wheat fields would now have to be cut by hand, and the men in my crew would be diverted from the canal project to help with the harvest in the fall. It was the same story in other villages across the Yugoslavian Banat. By diverting hauling equipment to the German military machine, farmers were pushed to the breaking point.

"We need more horses to move the large stones and trees in our path," I said.

"Spoken like someone who doesn't have to pay for any of this," Reichinger said. "Are you veering to the right? I think we're not headed to the swamp."

He moved his horse around and scanned the area ahead of our partially completed canal. Reichinger never dismounted from his horse when barking out commands to his work crew. Sitting high atop his black, muscular steed, Reichinger created an illusion that he was not physically handicapped, an image he wanted to project to his workers.

"I don't think we're off. It looks pretty straight," I said.

"Well, I don't. Start veering more to the right," Reichinger said.

"Yes, sir."

Reichinger shouted out a last order as he trotted alongside the partially completed canal. As the digging continued, and the fall harvest season approached, the once-bubbly Reichinger transformed incrementally into a hostile creature as his obsession with completing the canal project increased. It was as if his original objective to increase the size of his usable ground for farming had transformed into a twisted, illogical goal of destroying the swamp as an end unto itself. Like an enemy of the German military, in Reichinger's mind, the green, murky blob standing in the distance had to be destroyed, and the canal was the only way to do it.

"What are you doing? Further to the right!"

As Reichinger galloped back to the location of my crew, he pointed his finger into the air, directing several of my black-eyed Gypsies to start digging in a different location. His thick-headed mind was made up as to the optimal route to the marshy swamp. With every new command raging from Reichinger's mouth, morale among my work crew deteriorated as their hatred for their obsessive employer grew.

Reichinger turned the bridle with his right hand and forcefully moved his muscular horse back to where I was standing.

"Go into town on Saturday and buy another horse," Reichinger said. "We've got to move faster if we want to reach the swamp in time."

"Where do I—"

"Do it!"

Without another word, Reichinger galloped off into the distance. During the last several months, my relationship with Reichinger had changed. I was now one of his indentured servants on the ditch-digging team. Like everyone else who worked for this stressed tyrant, I was treated with a general disrespect. Even though I had started to hate the deformed little man, I was pleased when he asked me to handle the acquisition of a workhorse. It showed that he trusted me and renewed my faith that my cover in intelligence gathering was secure.

The crew and I continued shoveling dirt and relocating giant boulders embedded in the soil until close to sunset. As our wagon moved slowly across the sandy dirt back to the Reichinger compound, I stared at the sweat-drenched faces of my crew under the backdrop of the cloth shell that covered the roof of our wagon. The team assembled was like a microcosm of ethnic groups across the Banat: Serbs, Croats, Gypsies, and Germans working alongside one another to accomplish the goal of completing the massive drainage canal. I found it odd how well this diverse band of ethnic groups worked together. Bound together in a life of poverty, my canal-digging crew operated as a cohesive unit, yet outside the confines of Theresiafeld these same groups raged with nationalistic hatred toward one another as the war dragged on.

"Anybody know where I can purchase some horses?"

As we bumped along, I asked a general question to my exhausted crew. They rested on wooden benches strapped to the edges of the covered wagon as we headed for Reichinger's compound.

"Any ideas?"

I stared at the lone Banat German in my work crew, hoping for a response. He had a bad habit of gulping too much wine during our afternoon break. Our shared ethnic identity gave me a false sense of security in terms of his valued opinion.

"I don't know," he said.

His responses usually met all my expectations as completely useless in terms of providing quality guidance. Maybe it was envy at not receiving the foreman position that lead to his indifference to helping me.

As the wagon rolled toward the iron black gate of the fenced-in compound, one of my ditch-digging Gypsies responded in broken German, "I know where you can find some horses."

"Where?" I asked.

I didn't trust the Gypsy, but since I didn't have any other leads, I listened to what he had to say.

"There'll be a group of people at the market tomorrow selling knives. They might be able to help you."

"Are they, ah, some of your people?"

The worker didn't answer as his dark face nodded in agreement with me. I didn't like to use the word "Gypsy" around these black-eyed vagabonds who strolled from farm to farm around Theresiafeld looking for odd jobs. It seemed that every time someone in town spoke in German about a Gypsy, it came out in some sort of negative way. By even saying the word, I thought it might offend my fellow laborer.

"Why don't you come along with me tomorrow?"

Dragging my Gypsy coworker along to buy some workhorses seemed like a good idea. I hoped he knew these nomadic tradesmen well enough to increase my chances of getting a good deal.

"No," the Gypsy said.

"Why not?"

"You wouldn't understand. I'm not of their group."

As the bumpy wagon ride came to a halt, I disregarded the black-eyed Gypsy's confusing response about not being in their group, whatever that meant. I climbed off the covered wagon and followed my men through the food line for our daily ritual of receiving a free meal. Seasonal workers were the muscle on Reichinger's estate. Feeding them for their toil was customary in Theresiafeld.

As the weekly wages were passed out, I dunked one last bite of the homemade bread in the meaty layer of goulash sauce still lingering on my plate. I watched several of my laborers slip behind the whitewashed fence of the Reichinger compound, escaping into the darkness of the open plains. It was a ritual some of these drifters performed every weekend, never remaining for too long on the estate. Ever since I caught one of them going through my suitcase, I had a general mistrust toward these wanderers working on Reichinger's farm. Occasionally one of these Gypsy migrants would miss a day or even a week of work, resulting in endless delays on the canal project. I was surprised Reichinger didn't fire any of these laborers. His overwhelming desire to complete the long drainage canal before the start of the harvest in the fall outweighed their dereliction of responsibility. I mistrusted these migrant Gypsy workers who I toiled in the field with daily, and I found their carefree approach to life foreign to my more regimented upbringing. Nevertheless, I wanted to learn more about these mysterious nomads who wandered through the various German villages that dotted the map of Yugoslavia.

The next morning, I took one of the horses from Reichinger's private stable and navigated toward the church steeple. It stood like a beacon across the sandy plains to Theresiafeld. I made my way through the gravel street near the Baroque church now doubling as a market for eggs, produce, and other miscellaneous goods sold among the area residents. I walked through the market buzzing with merchants perched behind their makeshift stands and searched for the Gypsy merchants selling horses.

"Hans! Hans, come here!" a voice called from the crowd.

A woman behind a wooden sales stand waved a homemade pillow in my face, but I ignored her and scanned the crowd to locate the source of the voice. "Hans!"

I waved back at a droopy-faced card player I had met when I lived at the gasthaus in town. I made my way through the frenzy of humanity crowded into the tiny square. Amid the sea of bargain hunters in the Saturday morning market, I could see Reichinger's old friend Fetter Matz chatting with our new priest.

"I'm leaving. Maybe he can help you," I heard Father Peter say as I walked up to them.

Without even saying hello, Father Peter abandoned our location, clutching the homemade blood sausages that Fetter Matz peddled from his stand. I was disappointed that the priest didn't want to stick around and talk with me. Despite his discouragement, I was still hoping to form some kind of friendship with my fellow newcomer.

"Hans, I have a favor to ask you," Fetter Matz said.

"What is it?" I asked.

"Do you know anybody in the military in Germany?"

Startled by his question, the panicky feeling that overwhelmed me during my early days in Theresiafeld returned once again. I stood there frozen, watching him retwist the end of a pig's large intestine that he used as a natural casing for one of his homemade sausages.

"Why do you think I know someone in Germany?"

"Father Peter told me you arrived with him on the train from Austria."

"No, I'm sorry I don't."

I began scanning the area in search of the Gypsy merchants, hoping to dodge any further awkward questions Fetter Matz would throw at a deep cover spy like myself.

"Out of curiosity, why do you need a military contact in Germany?"

"Remember how I told you my son was in prison, captured during the German military invasion in Yugoslavia."

"Yeah?"

"Now that he's released, the German army set up a new division from the *Volkdeutschers*, and he's probably going to be drafted."

Ethnic Germans not born in Germany were always referred to as Volkdeutschers.

"I'm hoping to get him into the Wehrmacht and sneak him out of service in this newly created Prinz Eugen SS."

Fetter Matz's son was extremely unlucky. He was an ethnic German serving in the Yugoslavian military and was taken prisoner by the German army after the invasion. Here was a young man now being drafted by a military force that earlier in the war, tried to have him killed. Volkdeutschers fresh off the farm were now being forced to zigzag from one side of the battlefield to the other by service as draftees in the once-voluntary Prinz Eugen SS.

"Why do you want him out of the SS?" I asked.

"I think he stands a better chance of making it through the war alive that way," Fetter Matz said. "Behind a desk in Germany decoding radio messages is better than the Russian front any day."

The pig farmer selling sausages continued chatting, providing some useful intelligence regarding the mounting German losses over the last winter on the Russian front. The German army needed fresh cannon fodder to replace the dead Volkdeutschers who had volunteered for military service. Drafting ethnic Germans across the Banat and placing them in the Prinz Eugen division showed a weakness in the German military machine. The fighting apparatus that rolled into Yugoslavia without much resistance now struggled to find fresh replacements.

I looked at Fetter Matz's son standing nearby, haggling with a woman wanting to barter some of her fresh eggs for a couple of his father's sausage links. Since his son wasn't born in Germany, it was difficult for ethnic Germans to get into service in the Wehrmacht, which encompassed mainly soldiers that were born in Germany.

"How are you going to get him out of Yugoslavia?"

"Bribery. What else?"

Fetter Matz's drooping cheeks flapped in the wind as he spoke. The well-to-do pig farmer recited his elaborate scheme for smuggling his son out of Yugoslavia and into the perceived safety of the Wehrmacht. Unlike the idealistic view of German military dominance spouting out of the radio, many of the Banat Germans in Theresiafeld had less lofty ambitions. They were more concerned with keeping their family out of harm's way while they rode out the war. Many of that generation knew first-hand of the bloodshed during World War I and didn't want their children to endure the same agony.

"I have to go, Matz. We'll see you at another card game soon. I'm now working for Reichinger, so I've got fresh money to lose."

I moved through the market square and managed to catch the dark face of a Gypsy merchant running a knife along a flat stone used for sharpening. His jet-black hair and face were easy to spot over the light complexions of Theresiafelders crowding the general market area.

"I was told you have horses for sale," I said.

He stopped sharpening the dull edge of the knife and tossed it on a pile of ornately decorated dishes on his table. When they weren't in the business of stealing, the Gypsies wandering into Theresiafeld were known for their skill in making knives and tools for the always-practical Banat German craftsman.

"We don't have any horses," the Gypsy said.

"Look, I've got money." I said, pulling a wad of dinars from my pocket. "I want you to tell me where I can buy a horse."

The shriveled Gypsy moved in closer and quietly looked me over from head to toe. Gaping dark holes remained in his mouth where teeth had been plucked clean. His clothing smelled worse than one of the local farm pigs, but I tried not to gag for fear of losing the toothless man's help.

"Who sent you?"

"One of your people who works on Reichinger's farm."

The Gypsies looked at one another as if the name meant something to them. In my mind, it was irrelevant what they thought of my employer. No doubt his reputation as an abusive boss was well known among the community of Gypsies that wandered through Theresiafeld looking for day jobs.

"Meet me in front of the church at nine this evening. I'll take you to someone who can sell you some horses."

As the broken German sputtered from his mouth, tiny particles of phlegm shot from the gaps of his missing teeth and landed in my face.

"I'll be there."

Later that afternoon, I rode back from the market place. My limited training as a spy led me to believe there was an ulterior motive for this toothless vagabond wanting to help me. With the confiscation of my employer's tractor by the German military, I desperately needed to buy a horse to help with the canal project. Without the additional horse, we might not complete the drainage canal in time, and my fragile relationship with Reichinger would be on shaky ground. Reichinger's contacts with influential people around Theresiafeld gave me access to information that aided the Allies in the war effort. I didn't want to jeopardize my relationship with him by failing to close a deal on a workhorse.

The meeting with the Gypsy was risky, but after wrestling with the idea all afternoon, my mind was made up. I would rendezvous with the toothless vagabond, attempt to secure a horse, and—I hoped—keep my relationship with Reichinger on good terms.

I galloped through the dimness, barely catching a glimpse of my animal's front hooves as it lifted its muscular legs out of the sandy soil surrounding me.

Upon reaching Theresiafeld, I directed the stallion along the main gravel road, cutting through the middle of the village. As I headed toward the Catholic Church for my rendezvous with the Gypsy, I caught a glimpse of an old woman through the window of one of the houses that lined the road. I could see the rosary clenched in her fist, and she sat motionless likely praying for an end to all the killing that engulfed the European continent like a fire sweeping through a dried-up field of wheat.

"You're late!" the Gypsy said as I stopped my horse near the steps of the Roman Catholic Church and stared at the Gypsy waiting for me on horseback.

"I'm here now," I said. "Let's go."

I motioned with my outstretched hand for him to lead the way. The two of us moved along, passing the cemetery near the outskirts of town. Under the moonlight, I followed the Gypsy's lead in total silence for nearly an hour. Suddenly, the faint glimmer of firelight grew ever larger as our horses galloped toward its source, a semicircle of covered wagons in the distance.

"Wait here," he said.

I waited nervously as he maneuvered his horse up the slight incline to the camp. I watched the group of dark faces reposition themselves around the campfire while the horse approached. I could hear the sound of a lone violin coming from a young Gypsy boy sitting near the burning flames. It could be heard over the warm wind that rustled the colorful pans clinging to the tarps stretched over their covered wagons.

I tied my horse onto a broken tree as the Gypsy disappeared into one of the covered wagons that doubled as a mobile gasthaus for these roaming creatures of the Banat. What kind of people were these drifters? Why did they wander? I had heard stories about these people when I was growing up in Hungary. According to legend, they were the descendants of the Biblical Cain, forced to wander with no permanent home of their own as penance for killing Abel in the Garden of Eden.

I waited while the meeting continued behind the wooden door of a wagon trimmed in bright colors. I grew nervous, hoping for someone to open the whimsical door, which was covered in a sporadic layer of strange symbols. It didn't surprise me that Germans from Theresiafeld were in a constant state of tension with these people. The lifestyle differences of the two groups were incompatible. I didn't meet a single person in our village who had a kind word to say about any of them.

I could see my Gypsy guide waving his dark hand in the air, signaling me to enter the camp. As I walked up the incline, I could feel their black eyes, bugging out of their faces as they stared at me from around the campfire. I was afraid. Their brown facial features were similar to the Gypsies I knew in Theresiafeld, but their black, rimless hats and tattered dark clothing gave them a more rugged appearance. Untamed, wild, like the Banat before the arrival of agrarian colonists from Germany in the early eighteenth century.

I pretended to brush some dry grass off my lower pants leg, making sure my knife was safely tucked under my boot, in case I was attacked by one of the dark-haired thieves surrounding me. As I approached my Gypsy guide, I saw a set of leather boots bouncing down the ornamental steps that edged off the back of a covered wagon.

"I assume you're the one who wants to purchase the horses?" asked a Gypsy woman in surprisingly good German. I nodded in agreement. "Over this way," she said.

Her smooth, flowing language skills gave me a false sense of security as she sized me up with her exotic, blue eyes. I enjoyed looking at the muscular legs that peeked out of a tear in her long, tattered dress as we made our way to the horses tied to a thick rope strung between two covered wagons.

"Pick the one you want and give me a price," the woman said.

I found her direct request rude, but I began studying the quality of the horses.

"Where are they from?" I asked.

I approached the first horse and began stroking its right front leg with my hand.

"A stud farm in Paratz, Romania."

I nodded to the woman, acting like I recognized the stables from the Romanian Banat as a mark of quality. Horse breeding among Banat Germans had died out as the animal faded in military value. However, when farm equipment was taken by the German military, the horse had made a nostalgic comeback as a substitute for confiscated tractors. The Gypsies were quick to see a new opportunity with the war underway. The nomadic group jumped aggressively back into the horse trade, taking advantage of desperate farmers like Reichinger.

"Bring those closer to the firelight," I directed after I had picked through the lot and selected several horses I was interested in. The Gypsy sales woman shouted to a young, dark-haired boy in the mysterious language only these people understood. The boy, whose dark, ragged hair practically ran to the sandy soil, moved the animals closer to the campfire.

I pressed my hand against the chest of the muscular animal and felt the steady, slow breathing of a healthy, young horse. Within a finger's distance from the horse's nostrils, I caught a familiar odor that I couldn't quite place. I closed my eyes and concentrated on the sharp smell coming from the horse's snout. It was the identical smell that filled my father's basement in New York after making a batch of his homemade soap. Although we could easily afford it, my thrifty father never felt the need to purchase soap in a store when the oversized, homemade bars served perfectly well.

"Which one do you want?" she demanded impatiently.

"Give me a minute!" I responded.

At first I thought the strong, soap smell was from washing the animal, but after careful inspection, I caught a glimpse of the soap sticks jammed up the flared nostrils of the horse I inspected. The simple trick forced the horse to breathe in a steady manner, creating the illusion to an unwary buyer like myself that you were purchasing a younger, healthier animal.

"Which one?" the Gypsy woman asked again.

She was growing impatient, but I laughed to myself at the cleverness of her little scam. I could hear the faint sound of a bell clinging in the distance, causing the horses to come alive, disturbing my inspection.

"I guess I'll take this one," I said.

I picked out the horse whose damp nostrils seemed to reek the least from homemade soap. After several moments haggling over the price, I negotiated a final settlement and ended the annoying process with the impatient woman.

"What's the animal's name?" I asked.

"It's your horse."

I hoped my friendly question might calm the anxious woman now that the business transaction was behind us.

"I think I'll call him Mercy," I said.

Once I knew I was headed to Theresiafeld for my intelligence gathering assignment, I had decided to brush up on some history of the Banat. Count Claudius Mercy was governor of the region during the time of the Austrian Empire. He implemented a number of canal-digging projects that increased the amount of usable farmland for German colonists settling in the new frontier. Since the horse was bought to help on Reichinger's ditch-digging project, I thought the name Mercy suited the stallion

"Walk over to my horse, I'll pay you there."

I kept Reichinger's money for the horse deal hidden under my leather saddle. I was afraid if I brought it into the camp, one of these black-eyed opportunists might lift it from me.

"Is the horse for yourself, *gadjo*, or the farmer you work for?"

The bridle twisted in my hand as I led the forceful animal down the incline away from the camp. The Gypsy woman called me gadjo. I had grown accustomed to hearing the word from other Gypsies who worked with me on Reichinger's farm. I think it was the generic term given to all people who weren't of her nomadic group.

"The farmer I work for," I responded.

"Reichinger must be doing well if he can afford to buy another horse," she continued.

"We're digging a canal, and some of our equipment has been seized by the German military. That's why he needs the animal," I explained.

As I pulled the Yugoslavian dinars out from under my horse's saddle, I wondered how she knew the Reichinger name. Maybe I had mentioned it to the toothless Gypsy who led me to the camp? Now more seasoned in my role in the Banat as an undercover American spy, I had started to pick up on little things like a name being dropped, revealing the woman's desire to pull some information out of me. As I handed her the wad of paper money, I grew more curious about her interest in Reichinger. I didn't want to probe too deeply, for fear of upsetting the woman with her band of travelers sitting around the fire close by.

"How is Renate doing?"

She knew the name of Reichinger's only child. It was clear she had some former contact with this wealthy German family, and I wanted to find out more. "I only began working for the family recently. I don't know Renate that well."

I stared into her exotic eyes as we stood together a short distance from the circle of Gypsy wagons. I could still hear the pieces of dishware and cooking equipment dangling on the edge of their wagon covers, clanking in the wind. I didn't mind her asking me questions as my curiosity grew.

"How do you know the Reichinger family?" I asked.

She looked at me for a long time before responding. Her hair and skin color seemed lighter in complexion than the other Gypsies starting to sing around the firelight.

"You are not from Theresiafeld," she said.

"I was born in Hungary," I said. "Reichinger offered me a job working on his farm, and I took it."

"Reichinger is not the type of man he pretends to be."

"I've noticed. His personality changed as soon as I started working for him. Not all of us can be born as wealthy landowners."

I wanted her to feel comfortable talking to me. I thought by creating the illusion that Reichinger and I were distant from each other it would cause her to open up and possibly toss me some juicy piece of gossip about my employer.

"My mother worked for Reichinger many years ago," she said.

She looked down at the sandy soil as she spoke.

"You lived on his farm," I said.

"Reichinger kicked her off his land."

"What for?"

I could feel her grow more relaxed as we continued talking.

"I don't know for sure. When Reichinger remarried—"

"This is Reichinger's second wife?"

I stopped her in mid-sentence, somewhat surprised that Reichinger never mentioned this was his second wife.

"Yeah. After he remarried, the two of them said they didn't need my mother's help on the farm anymore and told us to pack our bags and leave."

I could tell she was angry at the thought of being forced off the Reichinger estate.

"I'm sorry your mother lost her job."

The exotic Gypsy woman grabbed the reins on my horse as it grew unsettled.

"What happened to his first wife?"

"She died from some kind of fever, probably coming off that swamp near his house."

Reichinger's obsessive behavior toward the canal-digging project became clearer to me. The illness that had killed Reichinger's first wife drew its strength from the marshy swamp near his fenced-in compound. It was a lingering killer that had brought many of the original German colonists to an early grave. By completing the canal, he would drain the marshy swamp and destroy the ruthless enemy that killed his first wife.

"Why did you leave Theresiafeld?"

"We were poor and had no place to go. Food was scarce, and my mother got sick. She died shortly afterward, and there was no family in Theresiafeld that would hire me, so I left."

"My mother died also when I was little. I know how it feels," I said.

I hoped by disclosing the fact that I grew up without a mother would make the Gypsy woman take more of an interest in me. She turned her blue eyes toward the sounds of music by the campfire in the distance. There was a hidden anger in her face as she recalled her difficult childhood.

"Did you lose your entire family, gadjo? Everything, everyone close to you?" The Gypsy woman's words grew in anger as she spoke. I empathized with her situation given the fact I immigrated to America shortly after my mother died, leaving the only home I knew in Hungary behind. I felt a sudden slight desire to share with her my secret occupation as a spy for the American government.

"I lost everything thanks to Reichinger. They kicked us off their farm like stray dogs. I wish he were dead. You hear me? Dead!"

I waited a moment until she calmed herself. Her angry outburst had attracted attention from some of the other Gypsies around the campfire in the distance. I could see in the distance along the hillside a tiny, shriveled up woman take a closer interest in my conversation with the gypsy woman. She yelled out a few words in their secret language, but the young woman waved her arm to calm her concerns.

"I only work for Reichinger," I told her. "I'm sorry that he abandoned you."

I reached into my leather saddlebag and pulled out a bottle of the local Theresiafelder wine given to me as a gift from Valmer. When he wasn't taking dinars off me at the card table, Valmer was a *kupetz*, trained in the skill of knowing quality wine that he sold to various innkeepers around the Banat. I wanted to keep the bottle for myself, but I felt by giving it to this Gypsy woman it might enable me to cultivate a friendship with her for future intelligence gathering. She cracked a slight smile as I forced the green- colored bottle into her hand.

"Gypsies don't drink wine. We drink beer."

I jokingly tried to grab it back out of her hand, but she resisted. My act of generosity looked too flirtatious to some of her black-eyed friends, and some of them stopped their singing and joined the shriveled up woman moving in my direction. The elderly woman of this nomadic tribe clearly didn't take kindly to Banat Germans lingering around the camp and talking with one of their own.

"When are you coming through Theresiafeld again?" I asked.

My interest in her was complicated. Her future movements in this part of the Banat might not be entirely related to my espionage mission, but I was attracted to this exotic-looking Gypsy and wanted to stay and talk more, but I feared for my safety.

"My *vitsa* usually wanders back into Theresiafeld after the grape harvest in October." she responded with a puzzled look. I grabbed the reins of my newly purchased horse and maneuvered it away from the band of angry vagabonds making their way down the incline.

"You must go. The woman coming down the hill is concerned about *prikaza*."

I glanced down at the woman from my horse as she spouted out a few last words in her Gypsy language to calm the approaching mob.

"What does that mean?" I asked.

"It's Romany, the language of our people. It's bad luck if I talk to you any longer."

The tone in her voice didn't sound as if she believed in that superstition. Clutching the reins of my newly purchased workhorse, I kicked the animal I was riding and headed toward Theresiafeld. The sound of pots rustling over a violin faded as I rode away. I thought about my encounter with these strange people. I didn't know why I cared, but I feared with the changing military front, the trade route she followed with her band of nomads might be forced to alter. My hope of her returning to my tiny village along the southern edge of the Banat might prove futile.

I slowed the tired horses when I reached the outskirts of Theresiafeld and felt an increased desire to tell this woman who I really was and what I was doing in Yugoslavia. It was the first time since my arrival in Theresiafeld that I was relaxed enough to let myself feel this way.

Both of our life paths started from a similar humble position—a farming village in the Banat—but as we grew up, our lives drifted in completely opposite directions. The Gypsy woman and I both had to adapt to our foreign surroundings as best we knew how: I as an American learning a foreign language with formal educational training and hers as a nomadic salesman, peddling goods and adopting the culture of a nomadic way of life. Our lives now crashed together because of the war in Europe. This woman and I were more alike than she could ever imagine. We were both enemies of this community of Banat Germans living in Theresiafeld, one by duty to a country that fought against the German military and the other from personal hatred on behalf of her destroyed family.

The thought of never seeing this woman again saddened me as I rode onward in the dark emptiness of a fledgling wheat field toward Reichinger's estate.

✝

Yugoslavian Banat
July 1943

"Is that the last one?" I asked.

"Yeah."

My Gypsy coworker burrowed the last hole into the rocky hill and jammed the dynamite stick inside. As I laid the fuse at my feet, the Gypsy and I backtracked from the shallow hill to the location of the rest of my crew, shielding themselves behind our covered wagon in anticipation of the explosion.

"Who wants the honors?"

I looked into the sweaty faces of my coworkers, huddling behind the wagon as I waved the matchstick in the air, coaxing someone to step forward and light the fuse.

"Maybe Reichinger should," the Gypsy said.

"Look at him back there," another worker said. "He's too scared to come any closer."

Johann Reichinger would now spend long periods of time watching my team from a distance on his horse as his obsessive goal of draining the land came ever closer with each push of our shovels. If we could take out the hill in front of us, the path would be clear for a short dig to the final edge of the swamp.

"Go ahead. Light it."

The Gypsy flicked the match against the dust-covered heel of his old boot and lit the end of the fuse. Our filthy bodies braced against the wagon as the flame crawled along the sandy soil toward the planted dynamite.

Pow! The explosion rocked the ground below us. As the ground continued rumbling, a faint ring could be heard from the church bell hanging from the high steeple in Theresiafeld.

"Stay down! Don't get up yet!"

A shower of dirt continued falling over our huddled bodies from the massive explosion. I glanced at the broken-down workhorse, Mercy, which I had purchased from the Gypsy woman last year. As the soil continued falling over his hairy, dark back, I made a quick visual inspection of the worthless animal, making sure he wasn't injured from the blast. The horse's spirited demeanor as well as his usefulness to the canal-digging project had faded with each passing month. The Gypsies had scammed me into thinking I had purchased a spirited, young stallion, but the animal was now reduced to nothing more than pulling the wagon that carried my work crew to and from the job site.

"Can you see anything?" my coworker asked.

"I'm not sure."

I raised my head from the sandy soil and tried to see through the dust and smoke that obscured my view of the hill, hoping the dynamite explosion had solved our problem.

"Look!" my coworker yelled out, as a massive crater appeared through the dust where the hill had once stood. I walked slowly toward the bombarded location. There was no doubt about it. A view of the marshy, green pool of water could now be seen where the hill had once blocked our digging path.

"What's it look like?"

Reichinger screamed out as he galloped toward my location.

"I think we did it!" I yelled.

Perched on his stallion, Reichinger continued staring at the gaping hole carved out of the hill, revealing the sight of his green nemesis in the distance.

"Let's get back to work," Reichinger shouted. "We have a few hours left before nightfall."

Reichinger's haunted face and the deep bags floating under his eyes revealed the financial and emotional stress the canal project had taken on him. Riddled with cost overruns, the canal project had to be finished by early August. My crew needed to be shifted to the intense manual labor of harvesting the wheat crop.

"We should be able to reach the swamp sometime next week," I said.

Without saying another word, the beaten down Reichinger rode off from the demolished hill site and headed toward his fields bursting with wheat. The grain would help feed a ravaged European continent for the next winter.

We continued shoveling away debris from what was left of the hill. I found it interesting that Reichinger hadn't abandoned an excavation project of this monumental size. Despite young men leaving our village for war and farmers strapped for cash and equipment, we continued digging. This obsessed land baron remained confident that his farming way of life would go on pretty much as always after the war ended. An unbroken confidence in Germany remained with him despite a communist resurgence creeping farther into Eastern Europe.

Mosquitoes from the green marsh flew through the gaping hole carved out of the hill, stinging our faces as we continued the backbreaking labor before calling it a day. Over the last several months, I had grown weary of the canal digging, and I was looking forward to it coming to an end. As the quality of intelligence I was gathering from Reichinger dwindled, I had considered quitting the project, but I changed my mind. I didn't understand why, but I wanted to see the canal completed.

As the knotted tips of the wheat grew out of the sandy soil, a subtle feeling of guilt at betraying people in this community grew. The whiff of treason would be undetectable from my encrypted intelligence reports, but I feared the slight loss of positive control within me. Every month that passed, I integrated further into this community. The upper hand of defection from my primary purpose here required more discipline to push back. Maybe after the war ended, I could say I built something that had served the interests of the community in Theresiafeld, offsetting some of the damage I caused sending my coded radio transmissions.

Mercy lumbered past the iron gate with my wagon load of exhausted laborers, and I caught a glimpse of the daughter of Johann Reichinger. She was leaning against the stone well not far from the whitewashed barrier surrounding the compound. I jumped off the moving wagon as it rolled past the entrance gate and walked towards the old well in the distance.

"Renate, how are you?"

I casually cranked up the wooden bucket filled with cool well water, washing it over my sweaty face and hands. In the evening, I would watch from my bunk window while Reichinger's spoiled daughter leaned over the edge of the stone, circular wall that surrounded the well. She would stare for long stretches at a time into the dark abyss of the water below.

"Talk to me. Say something, girl."

My casual interest in Renate had grown, sparked a bit by the Gypsy woman's questions during our horse transaction. She continued gazing down the deep well. Looking for an answer to a problem bottled up inside her below the dark, watery abyss buried under the surface of the fertile soil.

"What do you want to know?" she said.

"You look like you have a problem. Maybe I can help."

I leaned forward and let the wooden bucket drop cold water over my head and back, cleansing me from the dust buildup layered over my skin.

"Oh, I don't know," she stalled.

"Go ahead, you can tell me."

Echoing off the stone wall surrounding the well, you could hear a teardrop hitting the water deep below the ground. Renate kept her head lowered over the wall.

"I guess it's my father," Renate said.

"He can be kind of demanding at times," I said.

"I hate him."

"Your father can't be all that bad. *Kirchweih* is approaching soon, and he'll make it up to you then. Maybe he'll get you a new dress."

The largest festival in Theresiafeld, Kirchweih, would be held shortly after the grape harvest, as was the tradition in most Banat German villages. When I was a small child in Hungary, I had watched the single men and women marching in the Kirchweih procession down our main street. It was always a time of great joy for my family. Renate's sadness confused me for someone so insulated from the war surrounding her.

She was used to the good things in life as the daughter of the largest landholder in Theresiafeld. Other women in the village envied her riding clothes and modern dresses. She lacked for nothing, even with the conflict strangling the resources of every villager across the Banat.

"You don't understand," Renate said. "This is going to be my last procession in the Kirchweih."

Renate was no longer the youngest woman that took part in the procession of couples. Her response to my question was a roundabout way of telling me she would be married soon. She was only seventeen years old, but as the daughter of a wealthy landowner, she would marry young.

"Who's your Kirchweih partner?"

By asking her the name of the boy she would be paired up with in the Kirchweih procession, I would know the young man she was destined to marry. As tears continued dripping into the well, it was obvious Renate didn't want to get married.

"My father's pressuring me to be with Fetter Matz's son."

"I thought he's in Germany. Didn't his father get him into the Wehrmacht?"

"His father never managed to get him in. He'll be on leave over Kirchweih," Renate said.

"Where is he right now?" I asked.

"He's somewhere in Russia. I think south of Moscow near Kursk."

"We need him here, protecting our village in the *Heimatschutz*."

A new Heimatschutz was formed to protect the village from the Partisan communist attacks being reported by other ethnic German villages in Yugoslavia. Despite the best efforts of his wealthy father, Fetter Matz's son was pulled from the Heimatshutz into active military duty in the Prinz Eugen SS.

My body cooled down from the well water. Gathering information about the war had become routine with Renate. Her contact with other young woman in Theresiafeld always managed to provide a morsel of news from letters they received from young Theresiafelders drafted into the SS. I found information gained from her sources to now be more useful than her father. As Reichinger withdrew from the world and obsessed over his canal project, Renate picked up the information slack.

"Fetter Matz's son is a good man. I think you'll be good together."

"Haven't you listened to what I've been saying? I don't want to be his partner in the Kirchweih."

I watched as she picked off the shriveled flowers that surrounded the rim of a black hat from last year's Kirchweih. She casually tossed the dried buds over the stone wall, watching them float to the bottom of the well. It was her job to redecorate the hat with fresh flowers, which would be given to her partner in the procession to wear on the day of the Kirchweih festival.

"Try to think of other peoples' problems. Many of the young men in our village are risking their lives at war," I said.

I watched as her flabby, pale arms, not forced to harden by labor in the fields, shook as she picked clean the last of the dead flowers surrounding the black hat.

Her problems seemed petty to me. She was the spoiled little girl of a stubborn landowner forced to follow tradition by marrying Fetter Matz's son, another of the wealthy upper crust of Theresiafeld. I reluctantly steered the conversation back to the information she picked up from men serving on patrols in our local Heimatschutz. It appeared the routine patrols around our village had revealed no terrorist attacks from Tito's Partisan soldiers.

My enthusiasm at helping the Allied war effort had dissipated over time. It irritated me to use Germans such as Renate as a source for information. She was disconnected from the war. Every day became more of a struggle to continue playing the role of an undercover agent in this tiny village.

"You may feel differently when he returns from the front."

"Why's that?"

"War has a way of changing people. He may also change."

I could see that Renate found faults in her assigned Kirchweih partner that were reflections of her own inadequacies. She didn't like Fetter Matz's son because he was a spoiled rich kid like herself. Maybe the war would change all that, and life with him as her husband might not be all that bad.

While the last drops of well water dried on my back, I pulled a few more pieces of information out of the spoiled daughter of Reichinger and left her sulking at the edge of the stone well. As I headed back toward my bunk for the evening, I could see the guards checking their rifles as they gathered near the entrance of the compound. Used by large farmers like Reichinger to ward off outsiders from stealing their precious crops, the guards scattered across the vast land holdings of the Reichinger family. The sea of brown wheat was only weeks away from harvest, and Reichinger, strapped for cash, needed all of it.

From a window near my bunk, I watched Renate in the moonlight. I fiddled with my father's lucky gold coin, hoping for the day when my role as a spy would come to an end.

Several weeks passed, and my physically exhausted work crew managed to finish our final approach to the marshy layer of green algae, days away from the ideal harvest of Reichinger's wheat crop. Yesterday, we held back at the edge of the swamp, giving Reichinger an opportunity to plan a grand spectacle among his wealthy peers, as the last several meters of the canal would be dug away. Many farmers in the village worried about their future with the war dragging on, but Reichinger's steadfast confidence remained that the Germans would prevail. By gathering a small group from the top wrung of the Theresiafeld caste system, he would show the superstitious group that the future was bright, and there was nothing to fear.

"Today's the day my friends!" Reichinger screamed. "Today's it!"

Reichinger climbed aboard his favorite black horse, excited at finally completing the canal-digging project. I tossed back a last cup of strong coffee and jumped aboard the wagon, following Johann Reichinger to the site of his green enemy. I watched from the wagon as he smoked a cigarette nervously from the back of his horse. The canal project had taken a massive toll on him both financially and physically, but his obsessive goal was on the verge of becoming a reality.

Through the morning hours, my crew shoveled out the last several meters of the canal, which snaked over the sandy plains to a small river several kilometers away. With large, white handkerchiefs protecting their noses and mouths from the stench of the swamp, Theresiafelders arrived from all directions to watch us chip away the final layers of crusty, dry soil.

"I'll take it from here, Hans."

In an uncharacteristic display of raw, physical labor, Reichinger grabbed the shovel out of my hand and began moving out large scoops of dirt as green, murky water stood at the threshold of busting into our man-made canal. Over the last several months, many of the Banat farmers in the village had made fun of my employer. Taking on a project of this magnitude drained his resources, but today Reichinger would get the last laugh as he clumsily dug away the last of the dirt.

"It looks like the canal is finally coming to an end."

I looked behind me and saw the face of the card shark, Valmer. The local Kupetz's wine trading business had slowed over the last month while he waited for the upcoming grape harvest. His activities closer to home enabled him to visit with Reichinger more often, and he always made a special effort to swing by the workers' quarters to chat with me.

"Now that the canal project is over, what are your plans, Magyar?"

He always gave me these open-ended questions and moved uncomfortably close to my face, attempting to somehow read my inner thoughts.

"Don't know yet."

"Do you like it here in Theresiafeld?"

"Sure."

"You've been here now for what, over a year?"

"Yep."

"It's a shame your luck at cards isn't as good as your luck at not being drafted. You'd own this land."

I cracked a smile and turned away from Valmer's uncomfortable comment. I was in the age bracket to be drafted in the German military, yet no one asked why I wasn't. It could have put a dent in my cover if the question took on momentum among the gossipy people in the village, but it did not.

"There it is! It's coming!"

I watched as the murky water crept across Reichinger's polished, French boot while he bent over his shovel, balancing his crooked body. Reichinger stepped out of the canal as the flowing green slush oozed into the narrow mouth of the newly completed, man-made canal. Valmer opened a bottle of his wine and began passing it around as cheers and applause sounded on the open field, signaling the start of the drainage process.

"Follow it down!" Reichinger said.

He hobbled alongside the finished canal as water filled the cracks of the dry, empty trench. Periodically, my work crew would jump in the canal and dig away some dirt that blocked the water flow, but otherwise the stream of green ooze flowed without interruption.

"We did it!"

With cheers of joy, the onlookers followed the flow of water as it made its way down the canal toward the mouth of a small tributary where the green slush drifted away for good. Our canal project was like a throwback to an earlier time in the Banat, when German colonists dug many canals like this one to drain the land for farming, enabling communities like Theresiafeld to grow and prosper.

"It's draining off! It's working!"

I slapped the back of my Gypsy coworker as the swamp water poured out of our man-made canal and into the small river.

"Congratulations!"

I stretched my hand out for my employer to shake. He and I were by no means friends, but we shared the feeling of accomplishment as the water flowed off of his estate.

The landless class of workers in my crew did the heavy lifting, but I saluted Reichinger for having the courage to take on the monumental task of digging the canal. Although I didn't know the exact figures, I knew it had taken a tremendous toll on Reichinger's financial resources.

The stress in my employer's face drained with the green water as it poured into a tributary, eventually leading to the Danube River along the southern edge of the Banat. He had destroyed his enemy once and for all. This deformed, little man now stood in victory as he took his revenge on the disease and pestilence that bred on this swamp and that had killed his first wife. By completing the canal, Reichinger savored the victory of outdoing the accomplishments of his dead father who couldn't pull off the monumental project in his lifetime. In one magnificent performance of man conquering nature, the twisted-spined Reichinger washed away the anger bottled up inside him as the flowing waters cleansed his soul.

From one hand to the next, Theresiafelders passed the bottle of wine, savoring the victory of man conquering nature through this simple act of digging a canal. In another season or two, the drained land could be used for farming, helping to feed a hungry European population trapped in war. I watched as the celebration continued. The tight-knit group of Banat Germans in this village could forget, for a brief moment, about the war raging around them and what the consequences would be to their way of life in Theresiafeld.

✝

Yugoslavian Banat
September 1943

My shoes echoed across the baroque interior of the old Catholic church as I moved slowly up the middle aisle, sliding into one of the empty wooden pews near the center.

A loud sound like a chair crashing to the floor came from the adjoining room near the altar as I pretended to pray in silence. A server boy opened the wooden door to the sacristy and gave the German parishioners a look of confusion. I abandoned my painful, wooden kneeler. Stepping on a woman's dark, pleated dress, traditional for the Kirchweih celebration, I stumbled out of the pew and headed toward the sacristy to investigate the loud noise.

"Father Peter!"

I ran toward the priest's lifeless body sprawled out on the hard, cement floor, grabbing his shoulder as I attempted to get the man to his feet.

"Father Peter, wake up!"

I forced the priest back on a wooden, foldout chair as a server boy peeked in from the adjoining dressing room, slipping his cassock over his black vests and pants, pretending to pay no attention to the spectacle.

"Who are you?" the priest asked.

He rubbed his face and looked at me with a blank stare. His rosy cheeks and nose told of an early start to the schnapps before the start of Kirchweih mass. I held his cold hand and tried to get him to his feet. It was eight o'clock in the morning, and his breath reeked from locally distilled *raki* made from plums.

The people of Theresiafeld didn't comment publicly on the young priest's excessive drinking, but the gossip had spread in private circles. Many of the Banat Germans remembered a time when they didn't have a permanent priest in residence within Theresiafeld, and I guessed they feared losing this one if they contacted authorities higher up in the church. The always-practical Theresiafelders overlooked slight wavers in Father Peter's priestly conduct for the greater good of having a leader for various religious functions.

"You've got to pull yourself together. Mass is starting soon."

It had been a brutal several months for the Banat Germans of Theresiafeld, and they had earned the right to a decent Kirchweih mass by this priest sent from Vienna. Many of the farmers like Reichinger were exhausted from labor shortages and equipment confiscation, increasing the manual workload needed to bring in their crop this year. As I integrated further into the daily rhythm of Theresiafeld, my affection for the people grew. A drunken priest incapable of leading the mass would be disruptive, and I wanted to prevent that from happening to this community.

"You've got to move," I said. "The Kirchweih mass is starting soon."

"I don't care," the priest said.

The slurred words coming from his mouth were surprising coming from someone who chose the priesthood as his vocation. I turned my head to a server boy struggling to keep his hand still to light a candle. He gazed in confusion at us, eavesdropping on the cynical comment coming from the priest's lips. My already low image of this drunken creature moved another notch down as he struggled to balance himself to a standing position.

"You've got to sober up."

I clenched my fist around his upper arm, dragging him toward his tiny residence that connected to the church.

"Ayyy!"

I caught a glimpse of a bloated German woman running out the back door with a handkerchief shoved across her weeping face. This live-in maid who helped Father Peter maintain the church had to have known of the priest's alcohol problem for some time. I guess the sight of him drunk before the start of one of the most important masses of the year was too much to handle.

I dropped the priest's drunken body on a wooden chair at the kitchen table and went for the pot of coffee. I scrambled around the kitchen, opening drawers and cabinets in a desperate attempt to find a match, hoping to light the stovetop and warm up some coffee.

"Oh my god!" I cried.

When I had pushed aside a clean stack of plates in the cabinet, I found myself staring in disbelief at a larger version of my own radio transmitter and receiver. What was this priest doing with a short wave radio? For obvious reasons of security, the OSS would have left me in the dark if other agents were operating in the Banat, but not one in Theresiafeld. During one of my previous radio sessions, this glaring omission seemed unlikely. I stood there motionless. I looked back at the priest, hoping he hadn't caught me staring at his radio transmitter. He looked older, more worn out in comparison to our initial contact back at the train station in Vienna. His head rested against the kitchen table, still suffering from a late night drinking binge.

I struggled to steady my shaking hand as I struck the match and lit the stove to reheat the coffee. I needed to calm down. Maybe he didn't know another spy existed in Theresiafeld. After all, I was living on Reichinger's compound a distance away from the church. The man was drunk all the time. How could he be smart enough to figure out I worked for the Americans? Maybe the drinking was all an act, and he grew closer every day to unlocking the mystery person sending coded radio messages out of Theresiafeld.

"Drink this, Father."

I looked at him suspiciously as he began sipping the reheated coffee. We sat in silence together for an uncomfortable length of time.

"You know, Hans, I spent my entire life scratching my way out of a small farming village back in Austria, only to be forced back to another one in Theresiafeld."

After stumbling upon his transmitter, I didn't believe a word he said. As his sobriety slowly returned, I thought about his clever act as a priest forced to endure service in this tiny, agrarian village. It was truly a beauty to watch his performance as he acted out his cover. I could see his well-crafted, leather suitcases opened against the wall still containing clothing that he refused to unpack, adding credibility to his ruse as a man desperately trying to escape from Theresiafeld.

"You shouldn't talk that way; it's not a death sentence. Maybe one day you'll be able to return to Vienna."

I didn't want to create an impression that something was wrong or that I was on to his act. Underneath my calm exterior, I was panicking inside, knowing that a German intelligence officer was creeping around Theresiafeld in search of me.

"I wanted to become part of the elite of Vienna, and now I'm here, lost in this sea of wheat and corn."

"You have to get ready for mass," I said. "I'll see you out front."

Given the discovery of this German radio transmitter, I suddenly grew insecure in my cover as a poor laborer from Hungary. Had I made any mistakes over the last year that might lead the priest into thinking I was a spy working for the Americans?

Fear returned to me as intense as it had been my first weeks after arriving in the village. The man I arrived with from Vienna was in the intelligence-gathering business like myself.

As I left the sacristy, I could hear him wheezing as he struggled to slip his priestly vestments over his head. I sidled down the aisle past a row of melted votive candles under the statue of some random saint. The candles were burnt to the base from the sea of parishioners praying for loved ones forced into service on the battlefield. I squeezed into a rear pew full of men dressed in traditional black vests and pants as the procession of young Kirchweih couples filed down the center aisle. Fetter Matz's son and his reluctant partner, Renate, lead the way as the couples filled the reserved pews near the front of the church. My mind was now preoccupied with visions of torture if I were discovered by this spy from Vienna.

After the last couple in the Kirchweih procession slid into the pew, the priest began the celebration, slurring through a string of Latin words. As the mass dragged on, my mind returned to the thought of mistakes I might have made in my cover over the last several months. Maybe the "Fox," the name I used when I signed off on my radio transmitter, didn't hide deep enough in the wheat fields, and I had grown careless as my mission dragged on.

"Take a good look around you, Magyar. This might be the last time you see a Kirchweih in Theresiafeld."

Still nervous after discovering the priest's radio equipment, I cocked my neck halfway around and stared at the familiar three-fingered hand pressing against the back of my wooden pew. I cracked a nervous smile back at the face of Valmer sitting directly behind me.

My anxiety continued as mass moved along. My complacency in Theresiafeld had increased as I had grown more relaxed in the village. I tried recalling past conversations with other villagers when I had boldly commented on mythical letters I had received from distant cousins in North Dakota, attracting attention to myself and my knowledge of America. My guard was down with so many others in the village commenting on friends or relatives they had in America. It could have cost me my life if it meant this Viennese priest could expose me.

"Try to think positive," I whispered to myself followed by several deep breaths from my kneeling position in the wooden pew.

After discovering that another spy existed in Theresiafeld, I found it impossible to enjoy the biggest festival of the year in our village. My mind drifted back to the activities taking place in the local church. I looked up to the altar and watched Fetter Matz's son and Renate approach Father Peter for the blessing of the rosemary bush filled with colorful ribbons clenched tightly in the fists of the young couple.

I watched as the trio performed the ritual blessing. The priest, barely sober, splashed droplets of holy water that clung to the prickly edges of the rosemary bush crushed in the couples' hands. In my mind, the priest was more interested in figuring out which one of the individuals crowded in a wooden pew in front of him was an American spy. Renate, the spoiled daughter of a wealthy farmer, was only interested in getting out of the engagement to a man she didn't love. Rounding out the pathetic trio, Fetter Matz's son followed along while his facial muscles stayed in their clenched position. It was obvious his mind was still in Russia where he now served on the front lines as a draftee in the SS Prinz Eugen division. As the odd trio completed the Kirchweih ritual, they seemed to fit with the screwed-up wartime.

Once the Kirchweih mass ended, the procession of young couples moved out of the church through the center aisle and proceeded along the gravel street. I remained in my pew as a column of black vests and women's *trachts* paraded by me. A small group of brass musicians scuttled soon after, joining the marching entourage.

"Well, Magyar, this is where I say good-bye," Valmer said.

I slipped out of my wooden pew and joined the other Theresiafelders dressed in traditional costumes as they clogged the gravel road in front of the church.

"What do you mean?" I asked.

"I'm leaving for good, my friend."

I looked at the card shark, astonished at his words. The local kupetz traveled quite a bit trading his wine, but leaving permanently seemed out of character for someone in this village.

"Are you serious?"

"Yeah. Sold the last of my wine stock and land, everything. Wanted to see one last Kirchweih before taking off."

I followed Valmer towards a group gathering around a makeshift wooden booth selling wine made from this year's grape harvest.

"So you think Germany's going to lose Yugoslavia? I asked.

"If you asked me that question two years ago, I would've said no, but now—"

"Reichinger must think you've lost your mind."

"How bout you? Do you think I'm crazy?"

In his usual annoying style, Valmer closed in on me. The stubble on his chin was a flicker away from my face as he waited for a response to his question. His bet had been placed, and it was against the Germans. He struck me as a man not easily swayed by the mania of German nationalism that mindlessly struck so many farmers in this community. Valmer's ability to endure the isolation of being a free-thinker impressed me. In a time when so many Theresiafelders joined the collective consciousness of the German hard-line position, he stuck out of the crowd of men dressed identically in black vest and pants. The land Valmer had won many years ago in a card game and the last of his wine stock were now liquidated. He was leaving the Banat for good in anticipation of hard times ahead.

"I think the Germans are going to hold," I said.

Saying something against the German position seemed unthinkable, now that I was aware of Father Peter lurking about Theresiafeld looking for an American spy.

"You think that, Magyar. You go ahead and think that."

Valmer let out an opened-mouth laugh. Almost swallowing my face like it was a home-grown watermelon.

"Good luck to you." He slapped me on the shoulder with his deformed right hand as musicians from the local brass band started assembling. Without saying another word, he pushed his black-rimmed hat deep over his scalp. Valmer strolled past the group gathering near the makeshift festival grounds and headed for his wagon. It was still covered in a layer of straw left over from the wheat harvest several weeks ago. Up to this point, life in Theresiafeld had seemed insulated from the direct violence of the war, but in Valmer's mind the end was near. Climbing aboard his wagon, he took a last look around, concentrating as he struggled to file the image of Theresiafeld in celebration into his long-term memory. Valmer forced his horses forward and rolled out of his beloved home for the last time.

That afternoon, I kept mostly to myself, still rattled from the morning's encounter with Father Peter. As the sounds of a ten-piece brass band bellowed across the outdoor dance floor, I pounded down several spritzers of soda water mixed with locally brewed wine, gazing at the dancing couples. The repetitive motion of black vests and women's trachts moving up and down on the wooden dance floor kept harmony with the steady beat of the polka music. I never picked up the dance step during my time in Theresiafeld. Maybe it was because none of the women in town particularly interested me. It didn't matter any more. I was by nature a loner, and my solitude came with being a spy.

My strategic seating location on one of the tables surrounding the dance floor allowed me to pick up some chatter among several guards in the Heimatschutz of Theresiafeld. These guardians of the surrounding village were on extra alert as news arrived from other German villages regarding raids from Tito's band of rebels, pushing ever harder against German control in Yugoslavia. In my early days in Theresiafeld, I reported about Tito as a potential threat to the German military in Yugoslavia, and I wondered if my transmissions amounted to further backing of his ragged group of communist rebels. A major factor that caused my father to pack up and leave his German village in the Hungarian Banat many years ago had been communism. As I slammed down another spritzer, I began to hate myself for being back in the Banat and aiding them.

Disgusted with hearing chatter about Tito's attacks on other German villages, I moved away from the Heimatschutz soldiers in silent shame at my treachery. After several more hours lighting up on spritzers, I stumbled away from the Kirchweih festival grounds and headed out of Theresiafeld.

I considered skipping the transmission because of the volume of alcohol I had drunk, but at the last minute I changed my mind. I had grown sloppy over the last month in sending radio messages. Sending some coded information on Tito's increased resistance against the Germans might redeem some of the damage to my spotty service record as an undercover spy. After several failed attempts at finding the location of my buried radio behind the Acacia trees, I finally dragged it out of the sandy soil and pulled it from the pillowcase.

"Get up slowly!"

I felt the cool edge of a blade pressing against my neck. I was paralyzed in fear. My body couldn't move. My first instinct was to run. I slowly reached along the side of my leg toward the knife hidden in my boot.

Several hard blows came crashing down on my face, disorientating me as I attempted to go for my knife. I fell to the ground, partially unconscious as my defensive weapon was pulled from its hidden location by my mystery attacker. Within moments, my hands were ripped behind my back and bound together with rope.

"Tell me who you are and what you're doing!"

My body was propped against the Acacia tree as I eyed my female opponent. I tried to free my hands, but the knot was too tight. She had the knife against my throat, and there was nothing I could do. I recognized her immediately as the blue-eyed Gypsy who sold me the broken-down stallion over a year ago.

"I'm an agent for the German military, recruited for intelligence gathering" I said.

My mission was now over. I hoped by telling her I worked for the German military, the Gypsy would fear repercussions from those who viewed her as inferior. The German military was still in control of Theresiafeld. Maybe she would be intimidated and run off? I had been discovered, and according to the training I received back on The Farm, my primary objective was to get out of these ropes and escape.

"We think some people inside Theresiafeld are supplying information to Tito. That's why I'm here."

She pushed the blade harder against my neck, and her face turned a shade of red, covering her light brown complexion.

"You're a fool to lie to me, gadjo," she said. "I could turn you into the German military for a nice profit, and we'll see if your story holds up against their interrogation."

It was clear she didn't believe me. Maybe she knew more information than I realized about Tito's operation. I heard many of the Gypsies worked for the communists, so maybe she was one of them.

"Wait a minute."

I didn't think she would kill me on the spot. As a Gypsy, she most likely would choose the route most lucrative to her and turn me in to the German authorities. I suddenly envisioned forms of torture inflicted upon me by their military interrogators, painfully squeezing from my mind every tiny sliver of information sent back to the allies over the last year.

"I'm an American gathering intelligence for the Allies. You've got to believe me."

Maybe it was desperation or the residual influence of the alcohol that changed my story. If she turned me in to the German military, they would get the information eventually from me. My only chance was to convince a woman who already held a grudge against the Germans who had abandoned her to let me off.

"Americano?" she said.

As my mouth and tongue struggled to pronounce the English words not spoken in over a year, I could feel the pressure of the blade move away from my neck. It was pointless to lie. Maybe by telling the truth, I would have a way out with the communists.

Her familiar blue eyes continued staring at me. I coughed up information, describing my true identity and background. It felt good in some way to divulge my true self to her. She stared at me for several more minutes, digging the pointy edge of my confiscated knife into the sandy soil as she digested the news. I hoped she would empathize with my situation. I knew she possessed a hatred for the Banat Germans, especially Reichinger, for kicking her off his farm. The fact that I was working against him had to mean something to her.

"Give me one good reason why I shouldn't turn you in, gadjo."

She moved closer to the acacia tree I leaned against, waiting for a response.

"You can have my money. Or, better yet, if you turn me into the American authorities, I can promise you even more."

I hoped to appeal to a practical Gypsy woman always interested in making some easy profits.

"Does Renate or anyone else know what you're doing here?"

"No. Besides, she has other problems right now."

"What do you mean?"

I couldn't believe her interest in Reichinger's daughter at a time like this. She had discovered me in the act of sending a radio transmission, and her mind now switched to the spoiled daughter of my employer.

"Her father is making her marry a man she doesn't love."

She turned her head toward the soil and clenched her teeth for a moment. I could tell the thought of Johann Reichinger ruining another woman's life disgusted her deeply.

The gypsy woman slid her dark hand into my vest pocket and pulled out the dinars that I had brought to Kirchweih. She slipped the money through a rip in her long skirt. In one swift motion, she reached behind me with my knife and cut the painfully tight ropes binding my wrists. My hands were free.

"What's your name?" I asked.

I had never picked up her name at our initial encounter at the camp over a year ago. I made no attempt to run as I waited patiently for her answer.

"It's Nadia."

I watched her slide my knife into her homemade belt and walk out of the cluster of trees until I lost sight of her in the darkness. I attempted to push myself off the ground using the tree as support, but my legs were like jelly, and I immediately fell back to the ground. Why did she let me go? She was no fool. Although she had stolen all my money, the woman could have easily extorted more out of me, knowing full well that I was being funded by the American military.

Her decision to release me was not the act of a shrewd Gypsy. Her slight compassion was not unlike a bone tossed at a dog in the village after killing a rat. Within minutes, I quickly grabbed the dirty pillowcase that held my radio transmitter and headed back to the Reichinger compound. This was a textbook case of my cover blown to pieces. My instructors back on The Farm would find me foolish if I didn't abandon my mission.

I ran across the grit of stripped wheat fields and thought about my second encounter with this exotic Gypsy woman. Now that she cut me loose, I found her even more intriguing than I had at our initial meeting at the Gypsy camp. She had sold me a broken-down horse and robbed me a year later, but I wanted to know more.

I sensed that information gathered from people in this village increased in quality as the war crept closer to Theresiafeld. My radio transmissions now took on even more importance, but my cover was blown. If I left Theresiafeld, I would never see this Gypsy woman again. If I stayed, my life would remain in her hands through the duration of my intelligence-gathering operation. What if she changed her mind and turned me in to the German authorities at a later date? She was an opportunist, and the thought of her trading information for money crossed my mind. I continued running, but I knew I had to decide whether to leave or to stay in the southern Banat.

Partisan battalion command outpost,
southern edge of the Yugoslavian Banat
October 1944

The communist soldiers scattered their wounded under makeshift tents off the gravel road for a brief respite from their grueling march. Each soldier's ethnic identity was hidden from view under a green cap patched with a red star, the insignia of the Yugoslav Partisans. Like vultures ripping flesh from abandoned carcasses, the Partisans picked over dead German soldiers on the battlefield, confiscating any equipment found useful. Armed with confiscated German MG 42 machine guns and fresh ammunition, the former guerrilla fighters now operated more as a professional military machine with each passing month. The fascist ideology that pounded the Banat with a hammer under German occupation, now felt the communist opposition growing like a cancer with each passing month.

This mixed bag of Serbs, Croats, and other nationalities toting fresh military equipment suppressed their kneejerk loyalty to their own ethnic group during a time of war and joined the collective consciousness of the communist ideology. Committed to driving the German occupation out of Yugoslavia, these freedom fighters scattered along the field were the military arm of the Communist Party of Yugoslavia (KPJ).

"How many Chetniks did we pick up?" the Partisan battalion commander asked.

"About fifty. We're back up to three hundred men," the Partisan soldier said.

Unlike at the start of the resistance against German occupation, the Partisans now had the upper hand in the Yugoslavian Banat.

Vanko, the communist battalion commander, had seen his numbers dwindle over a year ago in guerrilla fighting against German stronghold positions. Chetnik soldiers under the leadership of Mihajlović were granted amnesty by the Partisan leader, Josip Broz Tito. Provided these soldiers switched sides and joined the Partisans, their disloyalty of collaborating with the German military would be forgiven. Replenishing his killed soldiers with these Serbian nationalistic fanatics was a shot in the arm for the recently promoted battalion commander. The brutality of these former Chetnik soldiers was second to none and would be needed for a final push to drive the German military out of Yugoslavia.

Vanko had been in the business of killing now for several years and was more committed to the communist ideology than ever before. The dogma caught a spark with him shortly after a random mortar shell from German artillery ripped through his family's straw-roofed home. Shrapnel from the blast pierced the abdomen of his mother, who suffered in excruciating pain for several days before eventually succumbing to death from infection. He had caught a lucky break by being on the opposite side of the building, and Vanko managed to walk away from the attack unscaved. It was the tipping point that had pushed Vanko to link up with Tito's fledgling resistance movement against German occupation. At first he was an inexperienced guerrilla fighter, learning military tactics with each raid against German positions. By the simple trick of not dying in combat, he had moved up the ranks, eventually in charge of his own battalion.

As the bastard son of a Serbian merchant, Vanko had passed through many German villages as a boy. He had taken any work he could find to help his mother pay for food, learning how to read in his spare time. He envied the German communities in Serbia with their modern conveniences such as indoor plumbing and automated farm equipment. This casual envy of a poor child swelled into rage when the war escalated to inhuman levels in Yugoslavia. The communist ideology that Vanko fanatically embraced would correct the economic inequities that existed across the Banat, transforming the plains into a utopia for the poor and downtrodden. In Vanko's mind, the German forces committing atrocities against Serbian villages stood in the way of equality for all its citizens. These crimes of war needed to be punished tenfold under the red star.

"Take the pain, comrade!" Vanko yelled out his orders as a medic poked the sharp end of his surgical needle through a Partisan soldier's neck. Blood squirted out as the communist surgeon attempted to sew up the wound ripped open from German shrapnel. "Take it!" Vanko yelled again.

Over the rustling of the makeshift canvas tent, screams of agony from the young Serbian soldier howled across the plains of the Banat. The raki, a powerful alcohol made from distilled plums, was all out, forcing the medic to perform the surgery without anything to help ease the soldier's pain. It was another example of the endless shortages Vanko's band of communist freedom fighters endured while fighting the German occupation in Yugoslavia.

"Can he be moved?" Vanko asked.

"Maybe tomorrow," the medic said.

"I want him up as early as possible. They're on the run now, comrades. We have them on the run!"

Vanko seemed unaffected by the suffering of the wounded man who lay on the operating cot passed out from the agony of the surgery.

At first, Vanko's attacks against the German war machine had seemed futile. In the early years of resistance, he had seen many of his poorly equipped comrades die on late-night raids. With each attempted bust of German stronghold positions, the communist leader grew more desensitized to suffering. Retreating to the mountains to regroup and strike again decreased in frequency as the victories piled up. The tide had now changed for his band of Partisans. It felt good to have the upper hand against the German military in Yugoslavia.

"Tito's taken Belgrade!" The radio operator yelled out. His skill set at operating the B2 radio supplied by British reconnaissance improved as they pushed further north into Yugoslavia. The parachute drops of equipment from the British Long Range Desert Group (LRDG) were hitting their mark. Redirecting the allied war effort further north to help communist Partisans added muscle against the retreating German military.

"We've taken Belgrade!" Other Partisans took up the shout, spreading the news of Tito's recapturing of the Serbian capital through the scattered ranks. Rifles fired into the air. Two Serbian soldiers near Vanko's location began a ceremonial dance with their arms locked at the shoulder.

Amid the celebration, Vanko thought back on his military career over the last several years. At first, he had felt uncomfortable trusting someone who wasn't Serbian, but slowly Vanko had grown to respect the Croatian communist leader, Josip Broz Tito. This leader of the Partisan movement possessed a unique talent for keeping his men disciplined, even during the dark early days when they had to escape to the mountains to flee the German onslaught. Vanko respected the old man's deep philosophical belief in the communist movement.

"We need our directive," Vanko said. "Get command on the radio and find out what our next target is and where they want us."

He stared at his radio operator. The young man screwed his Morse key to the lid of his spare parts box and tapped out a message. "Push north and wait for further orders," the radio operator said.

"We're running low on everything. Do they have a supply drop?"

The radio operator stuck his ear back on the headset.

"Looks like we're on our own."

Vanko was used to confiscating provisions from surrounding villages to aid in the struggle. In his mind, there was nothing wrong with taking civilian property for the good of the Partisan cause. As soon as the communists were in control of Yugoslavia, everything would belong to the people anyway.

"Come with me," Vanko said.

The young radio operator followed Vanko into a green, canvas tent and watched his commander roll out an oversize map on the tiny, fold-up table. The Russian and Partisan forces were now in control of Belgrade, and the push north was on. Vanko needed a good location not far from his makeshift camp to provision his men with additional food and clothing as they continued pressing the Germans out of Yugoslavia.

Vanko ran his dirt-covered finger across the map, noticing several tiny villages north of his temporary camp. "How far is one of these towns from our location?" he asked.

The boyish radio operator waited for a moment, measuring the estimated distance over the map with his keen eyes.

"I'd say about 40 kilometers from here," he said.

"We're packing up and moving out in one hour," Vanko said.

"That's a good day's walk. Our men are exhausted. I don't think the wounded can make it."

"They're going to have to. We'll pick up food and supplies at one of these towns once we get there," Vanko responded.

He turned away from the fold-up table and gazed northward across the flat, sandy soil. It was barren and lifeless, without a tree in sight. His wounded, starving men would have to march another day, but he showed no outward sympathy for their pain. The only thing that mattered was winning the war against the Germans.

"Let's move out, men!"

Vanko's orders were final, and the patched tents and salvaged equipment of his communist fighters were packed up without dissent. The informal power Vanko wielded over his Partisans meant that no one questioned any of his decisions, no matter how harsh the order. Within a half-hour, the wounded were placed on stretchers, and the temporary camp faded into the wind as the battalion began a slow march north.

Partisan boots marched through the mud while sporadic gunfire and shelling could be heard in the distance. The military front continued to push out of Yugoslavia.

Vanko heard a desperate voice shout from behind him. Some of his wounded men were falling behind. "Hurry up!" Vanko shouted.

He stopped the march to wait for his comrades to catch up. "Pick them up; it's only a few more hours!" he instructed harshly.

The Partisans, injured from a raid several days ago, stumbled across the damp, uneven soil to the worn-out stretchers that would carry them the rest of the way.

The impact of shells rocked the damp soil. He could feel the noise pulse through his green military jacket as his men repositioned themselves closer to their battalion commander. The raid several days ago against a German fuel depot had resulted in many of his men being killed. When the battle had ended, Vanko, though unscathed, was surrounded by body parts from other Partisan soldiers. When shots from German guns rang out, standing close to Vanko was now considered good luck.

As the march northward continued, his second-in-command caught a glimpse of harvested wheat fields, signaling the outskirts of a village somewhere in the distance. "There it is!" he shouted.

It was a large stretch of land, chopped clean of brown wheat. Vanko pushed his wounded men onward as a church steeple in the distance came into view on the passing of a storm cloud.

The young Partisan recovering on the stretcher from the surgery performed only hours ago, burst out in a high-pitched shriek as his body shook violently for several seconds.

"Get the medic over here!" someone cried.

The Partisan soldiers placed the stretcher on the sandy, wet soil as the medic ran his fingers alongside the wounded soldier's neck.

"He's dead, *komandir*."

The young communist could not endure the hardships of travel so soon after the surgery, and now he was dead.

"Leave him here," Vanko instructed. His outward appearance showed no signs of remorse at the news of the young freedom fighter's death. In Vanko's mind, the young soldier had died for a noble cause. He would send more to their deaths if need be. The people of a free Yugoslavia would benefit from the sacrifices made today, and that future freedom would make all the pain and suffering worthwhile.

"Get on the radio and find out if there are any anti-Communists in this village that we need to get rid of," Vanko said.

The radio operator dropped his steel box covered in black crackle paint and hooked up the power leads to his transmitter and receiver.

"We have something, komandir," the operator said.

"What?"

"There's a war criminal. Someone working for German intelligence."

"Get the info on him so we can hunt him down while we're here."

It was Vanko's policy to root out all enemies of the Partisan movement in territory he conquered, and collaborators to the German military were the first to face his firing squad.

Vanko stared down the gravel road at the village in the distance. His eyes followed the wall of the large building to the dark clouds in the sky, staring at the sharpened point that balanced a cross overhead. He could tell by the shape of the steeple and the modern roofs on the neat rows of houses that the village was definitely German. As the bodies of dead Serbian soldiers under his command began piling up from the constant raids, Vanko's hatred swelled against the entire German nationality. He once split a German civilian in half with an ax for refusing to give up more grain so Vanko could feed his starving troops. As the violence escalated to inhuman levels across the plains of the Banat, his socialistic vision of full equality for all ethnic groups in the new Yugoslavia included fewer Germans with each passing day. Vanko's blackened teeth peeked through his thin lips, and his jaws clenched at the thought of so many dead comrades. The death of ethnic German civilians born and raised in the Banat paled in comparison with the thousands of Partisans killed in action against the German military now on the run. In his mind, these Partisan deaths had to be avenged.

"What are your orders, komandir?"

The storm clouds above him turned a shade darker while the battalion commander stood motionless, staring down the gravel road leading into the Banat German village.

"What's the name of this village?" Vanko asked.

His radio operator pulled out the tattered map from its leather sheath, unrolling it over his knee as he scanned the dots marking the villages north of Belgrade. Vanko stared at his subordinate, waiting for a response. "Theresiafeld, komandir."

Vanko's teeth clenched tighter as he heard the name of the village coming out of the radio operator's mouth. Unlike other villages whose names had changed to Serbian after World War I, Theresiafeld had slipped through the cracks, still claiming its German label from the days of old when the Banat had been under the control of the Austrian Empire. The mere sound of the Germanic name disgusted this fanatic communist leader.

"Take a good look in the distance, comrade," Vanko said to his assistant. "German control of this village is about to come to an end. Theresiafelders' tra-la-la days are now over."

✝

Yugoslavian Banat
October 1944

"Look at it, my friend," Johann Reichinger said. "It's beautiful."

We stared over the dry field where the green, marshy swamp once stood. It had been more than a year since the canal project was completed, and I had made the decision to stay on another season with my employer, helping out during the harvest of his wheat crop.

"This ground should do well for years to come," I said.

"Yes, it should."

With the green nemesis that had killed his wife now drained off the land, Reichinger seemed more relaxed. As I stared at the man cursed with a spinal deformation, I admired his sense of serenity during this chaotic wartime environment.

"I love looking at the view from up here."

"It is something."

Reichinger made a ritual of riding to the top of the hill just before sunset to stare at the new addition to his significant land holdings. We continued chatting on the hilltop as the sun faded. I caught a last glimpse of the church steeple of Theresiafeld, towering over the orderly rows of whitewashed houses that broke up the free flowing movement of the surrounding pasture.

"So what's your plan?" Reichinger asked. "Are you going to take your dinars and grain or stay on another season?"

"Don't know yet," I said.

As was the custom, Reichinger's workers would be released after the last puff of black smoke snorted out of his massive threshing machine and faded into the wind. The seasonal workers would be given enough surplus grain to make bread until Reichinger rehired them in the spring. Unlike the others, he wanted me to stay on the estate, helping out with some routine maintenance projects that came with managing a large farm. I think he enjoyed my company to the point that it was worth spending the extra money to keep me around over the winter months.

"Are you going to mass tomorrow?" Reichinger asked.

"Probably not," I said.

"If you change your mind, let me know. We'll ride in together."

Reichinger attended mass every Sunday. I rarely felt compelled to ride into town for Father Peter's religious services. In my mind, our priest was a spy, and the idea of listening to him preach seemed absurd.

I watched as Reichinger pulled the leather reins on his muscular stallion, limping alongside his horse to get a better view of his dry field from the steep edge of the hill. Before the canal was completed, Reichinger never liked to be seen off the back of his horse. By remaining on his mount while barking out his orders, the largest landholder in Theresiafeld concealed his hobble, protecting himself from mockery by his work crew. Now that his canal was completed, Reichinger's insecurity at his physical handicap seemed to wash away like the murky, green water that had covered the land around him.

"I'm heading back," I said.

I dug my heel into the side of the broken-down stallion, Mercy, and began a slow trot back to the estate, leaving Reichinger on his hilltop to savor his accomplishment a moment longer in solitude.

As I forced my stubborn animal to continue moving forward, I thought about how much I had changed as a person in the last several years. My view on life and the war had evolved as I grew accustomed to living among these ethnic German minorities of the Banat. I became ever more integrated into this tight-knit community, and my role as a spy became less important to me. The number of coded transmissions sent out of my radio faded like the water running into Reichinger's new canal after a hard rain. I even caught myself on several occasions withholding valuable information from the Allies for fear that my radio transmissions would hurt the soldier sons of families that were close to me. I didn't want my side to lose the war, but I wanted life in Theresiafeld to continue as it had for the last two hundred years.

With the labor of the wheat harvest behind me, my thoughts drifted back to my encounter with Nadia, the Gypsy woman. I had decided not to abandon my mission, even though the woman knew that I worked for the Allies. I gambled that her hatred for these Germans, especially Reichinger, would be enough to prevent her from selling me out to the German military. I hoped her nomadic band of Gypsies would make their way through Theresiafeld one last time before the war ended, giving me an opportunity to form some kind of relationship with her. I fantasized about her leaving a nomadic life and returning with me to America where the social pressures against marrying a Gypsy would not be as great.

The next morning, I struggled to pull my head out of the oversized pillow crammed with goose feathers. I tried to motivate myself to wake up and climb out of my bunk to dig up my radio equipment and send a transmission.

"Are you going to do it?" I said to myself.

I laid there for about an hour, fiddling in between my fingers with the lucky gold coin my father had given me. In my mind, I reviewed the cipher learned back on The Farm to send my coded messages. It was no longer second nature to me given my sporadic activity using the transmitter as of late.

"Well, are you?" I said again.

I slammed my fist against the wooden frame, reluctantly climbing out of bed to send the coded transmission. I gave Mercy a rest this Sunday morning and walked to my concealed radio, delaying the inevitable torture of having to send information that might hurt my friends in Theresiafeld. I had missed enough transmissions over the last couple of weeks, and I knew if I didn't send some useless piece of information to the European desk back home, I risked being recalled from my location in Theresiafeld.

I made my way across the trampled grass that shriveled up at the ends, signaling the start of fall. Giving up the coded transmissions altogether and continuing on with the Hans Mueller cover entered my mind. I could handle being perceived by my countrymen as a traitor, but the idea of never seeing my father again was too painful to allow me to abandon all ties to America. I pushed the idea from my mind as I continued walking.

There! In the distance! I dropped to the hard ground. My heart began pounding as I slithered behind a large bump along the pasture. I could tell immediately from the green cap and ammunition belt rolling over his shoulder that it wasn't a local from the village. As he adjusted the machine gun slung over his shoulder, I could see the Partisan soldier moving closer to my hidden location. I poked my head above the brown, trampled grass and gazed at the communist creeping ever closer to my location.

The radio announcements still proclaimed the glorious victories on the Eastern Front for the German army, but in reality Yugoslavia was losing ground to the Partisan resistance movement. The man in front of me was one of Tito's communist rebels, probably a Serb. The Partisans were in Theresiafeld, territory that only yesterday I had thought was still controlled by the German military. I couldn't believe my eyes. The Germans were losing more ground in Yugoslavia than I had realized. I lay in the dirt, confused and trying to recall some distant memory of mission training back on The Farm.

I allowed myself to calm down. At first, I wanted to stand up out of the grassy field and turn myself in to this lone Partisan soldier, but I dismissed the idea almost immediately. The communist and I were technically on the same side of the war, but our intelligence network didn't inform the communists about American agents in Yugoslavia, probably because they didn't trust them. The stories I heard from young German soldiers returning to Theresiafeld on leave frightened me. These Partisans were capable of incredible acts of violence against civilians. I doubt this Partisan soldier would believe my story anyway if I told him I was an American spy.

I slithered out of the Partisan soldier's path and pressed my body into the soil as a drizzle of rain dampened the surface of the pasture. As soon as the soldier's side-cap disappeared over the open field, I leapt to my feet and sprinted toward Theresiafeld. Many of the people in our village were in the lone church, attending mass. I needed to give them fair warning about the arrival of communist Partisans.

Upon reaching Theresiafeld, I crept along the edge of a whitewashed building and dropped my exhausted body under the acacia tree on the edge of the main gravel street. My eyes followed the ruler-straight road in the distance, alarmed by the sight of several armed men in green uniforms standing on the steps of our Roman Catholic Church. I was too late. The Banat German families began filing out of the church.

"Move to the right."

"Forward."

"Move to the right."

As the terrified Theresiafelders moved down the cement steps of the church, the Partisan soldiers separated the men from their women and children, pushing the males like a herd of local farm animals into the adjoining school building.

"Father, don't go!" Renate screamed.

"No!"

I watched as Reichinger's hand was ripped from his daughter. Renate continued screaming as the Partisan grabbed my employer by the shoulder and forcibly moved him away from his family. As women and children were corralled together, I wanted to do something, but there were too many Serbian soldiers and only one of me.

For what seemed like an eternity, I watched from a distance behind the lone acacia tree. The women and children returned under force to their rows of homes while the last adult male faded out of sight into the school building that adjoined the church. Within minutes after the streets were clear of German civilians, the males filed out of the building under the watchful eye of machine gun–toting Partisans. The confused locals worked their way down the road to the open pasture surrounding Theresiafeld.

"Keep moving!" the Partisan soldier said.

"Move it!"

As the marching continued, I followed the group from a safe distance along a ravine running parallel to the gravel road, relying on detached contact skills I had picked up at The Farm. I knew most of the men being escorted at gunpoint. From the safety of the gulley, I continued stalking them for several kilometers as the forced march veered into an open field. I could still visualize my first encounter with each one of these Theresiafelders, a card game, the butcher shop, Kirchweih.

"*Stani*!"

The apparent leader of the Partisan task force, clad in a thick green jacket, yelled out a command in Serbian, pushing the group of Banat German males at gunpoint toward a low point further out along the outlying grassy field. Within minutes, a large truck approached the location, loaded to the hilt with additional soldiers and supplies.

"Take one!"

"Go!"

As the terrified Theresiafelders moved past the rear of the truck in single file, a soldier began passing out shovels for what appeared to be some kind of forced work detail.

From my hideout tucked off the open pasture, I could see the upper part of the German villager's bodies, moving back and forth, throwing fresh dirt onto the elevated, damp surface next to them. Their moving bodies disappeared farther from my view as their digging continued.

I tensed up as the German men stripped their bodies of their church clothes and tossed them in front of the freshly, dug ditch. My eyes followed the band of naked Theresiafelders standing in a row parallel to the newly made gulley. I focused on my employer, Reichinger, whose crooked upper torso angled toward the young Viennese priest standing next to him. His status in the community as a priest meant nothing to these communists as he endured the naked humiliation along with the rest of the Germans. My body started shaking as I watched Reichinger make a sign of the cross as he tossed his black, French boots onto the loose pile of clothing in front of him. I could see the Partisan soldiers begin checking their machine guns as they repositioned themselves in front of the row of naked, male Theresiafelders.

Rat!-tat!-tat!-tat!-tat!-tat!-tat!-tat!-tat!-tat!-tat!-tat!-tat!

My fingers clawed into the wet, sandy soil of the ravine as the bullets sprayed out of the Partisan machine guns. The noise of the machine guns pounded in my ears as the naked bodies of men began toppling into the freshly dug trench on top of one another.

Another quick check confirming the amount of ammo left in their machine guns, several soldiers approached the edge of the trench line.

Rat!-tat!-tat!-tat!-tat!-tat!-tat!-tat!-tat!-tat!-tat!-tat!-tat!

I could see tiny droplets of blood popping out of the trench from my ground-level view where I was hidden in the ravine. The confirmation round sprayed over the civilians reassured the savages that their victims were dead.

Only an eerie silence remained, as the last puff of smoke from the guns faded into the rain. My body continued trembling from witnessing the brutal act. Within minutes, the Sunday clothing of the dead Theresiafelders was loaded on the truck and hauled away. I tried to control my trembling as I pushed against the side of the gulley. The Partisan butchers covered the bloody bodies in wet dirt and retraced their steps along the gravel road to Theresiafeld.

I peeked out of my hideout at the mass grave. With the Theresiafelders now covered up with a loose layer of damp dirt, there was no visible sign that a machine-gun-style execution had taken place only moments ago. I doubt anyone would be able to find the bodies, unless I pointed out the exact location to them.

"Murderers!" I whispered as my head burrowed into the soil, still trembling in fear. "I didn't sign up for this!"

I had aided these followers of Tito with my radio communications over the last year and was rewarded for my services with the execution of my friends from Theresiafeld. These so-called freedom fighters, my allies in the war, had betrayed me. I was filled with guilt, disgusted at the thought of being associated with these

Partisan murderers. My last glimmer of loyalty to the Allies and the war effort died with these ethnic Germans now buried in the ditch. Nearly everyone I knew during my stay in Theresiafeld was cut down by machine gun fire before my eyes. Reichinger, Father Peter, all dead, and there was nothing I could do about it.

"Calm down," I said to myself. "Get control of yourself."

As the slow drizzle of rain increased in intensity, the dirt covering my clothing turned to mud, caking my quivering body as I made my way back to the road. My mortal sin of not attending mass this morning became my saving grace, giving me the privilege of living another day.

"I've got to warn the others," I said.

I moved along the wet, gravel road, putting more distance between me and the trench of bloody victims. I thought about Renate and her mother. I needed to tell them what had happened and get them out of Theresiafeld.

My legs were weak as I struggled to move without shaking. I was the only one in Theresiafeld who knew of the revenge-killing rampage. As the rain continued, I struggled to move through the damp soil toward the Reichinger compound. I had to warn Renate.

I waited till dark outside of Reichinger's compound, which was now filled with small puddles where only weeks ago brown wheat had grown. By the time I returned to Reichinger's place, several trucks were parked in front of the compound. Multiple, thieving Partisans stamped with their red star insignia sprawled across the property, looting whatever they could get their hands on. The Partisan trucks now loaded with pilfered goods stolen from my dead employer's farm drove off through a mist along the open field. It was now or never. I needed to get inside and tell Renate what happened to her father, hopefully convincing her to leave Theresiafeld with me. She was a spoiled, little rich girl, ill equipped for the events now taking place in Partisan-occupied Theresiafeld. Maybe it was guilt at using her and her father to gather information to help these communists that drove me. As the trampling over this village by my supposed allies in this war effort continued, I felt a sense of moral duty to help her in some way.

I moved along the exterior wall surrounding Reichinger's compound, pulling myself over the top and splashed along the wet ground below me. The sounds of Serbian spoken in low voices and an occasional scream could be heard as I moved along the dark shadow of the wall, careful to move undetected with little sound. I could hear several voices chattering in Serbian. The soldiers remaining behind moved about freely, using Reichinger's ransacked estate as sleeping quarters for the night. I crawled behind the workers quarters, waiting patiently for some kind of plan to pop into my head as drops of rain dribbled off the roof, covering my face and hair. My espionage training on The Farm didn't include many combat skills. If caught by one of these seasoned Partisan killers, I probably couldn't put up much resistance and would be forced to surrender.

"Thug!"

"Thug!"

The sounds of broken glass smashing against the roof of the workers' quarters echoed across the Reichinger compound. Over the sound of rain hitting the ground, I could hear an object rolling off the back of the roof from above me. As it dropped along the ground, I stared at the lit flare glowing along the wet soil.

"They're going to burn the place," I said.

I rolled away from the worker's quarters to get a better view of the flames coming from the top of the roof. I could see bottles of Valmer's wine flying through the air and crashing on the shingles. The alcohol fueled the flames above me. As drunken laughter filled the damp air near the front of the burning building, I used the distraction to head behind the main house of the Reichinger family.

I crawled away, cutting my hands as they pressed against the damp soil now filled with broken glass from countless raids to Reichinger's wine cellar. The order and neatness I had grown accustomed to on Reichinger's estate was now gone. In its place stood a mess of discarded furniture and broken bottles from the communist raiders.

Once at the main house, I pushed myself off the wet soil with my bloody hands and stood in front of my dead employer's bedroom window. I could see the disorder, wooden furniture tossed in every direction. My eyes moved toward the elevated bed, balancing high on sturdy wooden legs in the corner of the room.

"My God!"

Amidst a sea of goose feathers ripped out of pillows and blankets, the naked body of Reichinger's wife lay motionless over the torn blanket stained red with blood. I scanned across the dark room. I could see the bloody incision carved deep along her throat, and her lifeless eyes stared at the ceiling of room. She was another rape and murder victim from one of these Partisan drunks ransacking the Reichinger estate. I dropped my shaking body to the wet soil below the bedroom window and crawled away from the atrocity. It was pointless looking for survivors. I needed to concern myself with my own safety and figure a way out of Theresiafeld.

As I crawled away from the main house, I could see the fire in the distance. Several Partisan soldiers gathered around the flames, singing Serbian folk songs as they held several bottles of the local brew in each fist. My location near Reichinger's private horse stables was hidden from the glossy eyes of the Partisan soldiers, who continued their celebration around the fire. It appeared the soldiers were the only people still alive on Reichinger's plundered estate, allowing me relative ease of movement while I made my final escape. Before abandoning Theresiafeld for good, I wanted to steal one of Reichinger's stallions and avoid walking out of Yugoslavia. Except for my father's lucky coin snug in my boot, my money and personal belongings were now burned to ashes, thanks to the Partisan soldiers, but at least I could have transportation out of the village.

I started digging furiously with my fingers in the wet soil, ripping out dirt from along the edge of the horse stable. I was fortunate that the stable was the only building on the Reichinger property without a cement foundation, allowing me to carve out a hole under the exterior wall. After digging a sufficient-sized burrow, I squeezed my body as hard as I could under the small opening and slipped under the wall of the horse stable.

If I could steal one of Reichinger's prized stallions under the noses of the drunken Partisans, I could ride to the safety of the west, away from the advancing communist troops. As far as I was concerned, I was no longer an American spy, but a Banat German civilian trying to escape the onslaught of these murderers in control of Theresiafeld.

"No! Get away from me!"

I rolled my dirt-covered body through a cracked door in one of the horse's stalls, as a familiar German voice rung out over the interior of Reichinger's private stable. I scrambled over Reichinger's stallion, brutally killed from gunshot fire, and hid behind his muscular, black frame.

"Renate!" I said to myself.

As her screams continued, I lifted myself off the hay covered in the horse's blood. I peeked over the wooden wall surrounding the stall in an effort to gauge Renate's location. I could see her struggling on the other side of the oversized stable, attempting to escape from the clutches of a drunken soldier pinning her frail arms across the ground.

Unlike her mother and father, Renate lived, being raped and beaten by the communist butcher in front of me. As the rape continued, the vision of the brutal slaying of my friends surfaced in my mind. I could see their frozen, lifeless faces rotting in the ditch. The hard work and sacrifice Theresiafelders had made over the years in building this community was now up in flames. I caught a glimpse of the rusty sickle displayed along the wall of the stable. The old, harvesting tool had been forced out of retirement this season when Reichinger's modern farming equipment was confiscated by the German military. I rushed to the metal sickle and pulled it from the nail hanging on the wall. As quiet as a farm mouse, I moved toward the Partisan with my makeshift weapon.

My foot moved over several loose eggshells mixed with debris scattered along the ground. The sound caught the ear of the half-naked soldier in front of me. His face turned toward me. I could see the startled look in his beady eyes as my sickle thrust downward into his chest cavity. I watched with delight as the life drained from this young communist in the process of raping Renate. A feeling of exhilaration came over me like I had never felt before in my life.

I was still filled with rage after witnessing the slaughter of civilians that afternoon. I wanted revenge, revenge for the death of my friends. I would not classify myself as a particularly violent person, but the events leading up to my brutal killing of this communist had turned me into something I had never imagined possible. My instructors back on The Farm abandoned their effort to harness my killer instinct during training, eliminating me from potential undercover service as an assassin. I accomplished what my instructors failed to do, as blood from the chest cavity of the Partisan butcher dripped off the edge of the rusty sickle, oozing over the empty horse stall.

"Renate!" I said. "We've got to get out of here."

"Leave me!"

She didn't recognize me at first in the darkness of the stable. I rolled the dead perpetrator off of her and forced her shivering body off the hay.

"Listen to me. You've got to run with me, leave Theresiafeld. It's the only way."

"Don't touch me!"

The confused, spoiled girl ran out of her father's private stable, past the iron gate toward the surrounding dark pasture. I covered the dead Partisan with loose hay in an attempt to hide his mutilated, bloody body from the eyes of his drunken comrades. I knew the Serbian soldiers around the fire would come looking for him now that Renate had stormed out of the compound.

The wind thrashed outside the stable, causing a dinner bell used to gather farm workers for their evening meal to ring out. The sound of the bell shaken by the powerful wind caused a horse across from me to bang his hoofs against the wooden barrier of his stall.

"Mercy!"

The broken-down animal I had purchased from Nadia was still alive, startled by the noise. Unlike Reichinger's other prize stallions in his private stable, Mercy was lucky enough to survive the gunshots of drunken Partisan soldiers having some sport with a wealthy farmer's collection of fine horses.

I dropped a saddle over the back of the animal and hopped on top of it. As the dinner bell continued ringing out from the raging wind, a strange vigor returned to the step of my animal as it raced into the rain and galloped out of the compound. I could hear the sounds of startled Partisans shouting out. The drunken soldiers caught a last glimpse of Mercy's ragged tail swaying in the wind like the coarse, black hair of a Gypsy. The rain intensified as I flew past the iron gate, galloping onto the wet, muddy plains covered in darkness.

I changed my horse's direction and headed toward the newly dug canal, hoping to lose them as I continued forcing the animal forward. I hoped to make it to the canal before the old, tired legs of my animal lost their temporary spark of greatness. Mercy continued carving his hoofs into the mud as I approached an old well in the distance. I could see the outline of a torn dress on a figure leaning against the stone wall surrounding the well. It was Renate, terrified in the confusion, retreating to her familiar oasis during the difficult times in her life. I pulled back on the reins of my stallion, coming to a sliding stop in the mud. Her eyes popped out at me, still terrorized from the rape.

"Renate!" I shouted. "Climb on quickly. The soldiers are coming! Quickly! There's no time!"

I stretched out my bloody hand, motioning her to hop on. Renate's life had been sheltered up to this point from the cold realities of war. She gazed in the distance as parts of her father's home continued burning. Her life as the pampered daughter of a wealthy farmer in Theresiafeld was now over.

"We're going to die! Jump on!"

Renate shook her head frantically, turning her body away from me as she stared into the well, trying to escape from the insanity she was now surrounded by. I couldn't wait any longer. I turned my horse toward the canal in the distance as Partisan soldiers caught a glimpse of us with one of their confiscated lanterns.

As I rode away, I glanced back at Renate leaning against the well. The spoiled girl stared into the dark abyss of her familiar retreat, looking for an answer to the terror she now faced. As the soldiers splashed through the mud toward her location, Renate, in one last feat of courage, allowed her body to fall over the stone wall into the watery depths below. The cold reality of the brutal situation was too much for her naive, sheltered mind to handle, so her body gave up the struggle and drifted below the water's surface.

Several of the Partisan soldiers rushed past the well and continued their pursuit of me. As the rain increased in intensity, I could see Reichinger's canal in the distance. Shots continued firing from behind me. I kicked my legs deep into the side of the faltering animal, pressing the horse onward.

"Oh, no!"

The weathered stallion lost his footing against a stone camouflaged under the mud. Its bulky body tripped and hurled me through the air.

As I hit the surface, I became disorientated. I needed to regain my composure if I wanted to live. Several additional shots fired. I tried to shake off the violent jolt as I scrambled along the muddy surface. I was protected from view by a dark blanket of sky covering the former swamp area. I snaked through clumps of wild grass now budding out of the ground, attempting to regain my bearings.

"He's back farther!"

The sounds of Serbian voices could be heard moving closer to me.

I was exhausted and badly bruised from the fall, but I crawled on, trying to put more distance between me and the communist soldiers. The rain increased in intensity, disorientating me in the empty field of grass as to which direction to move. I could feel the earth begin moving around me as the uneven ground filled to capacity with deep pockets of muddy rainwater. I was trapped like an animal, and my body shook in fear of being captured by the approaching communist soldiers. The rain continued pouring buckets of water over my drenched body as I lay frozen in the muddy soil. Which way do I need to crawl? I needed to rest for a moment, but there wasn't any time. I planted my face in the water below me, paralyzed from confusion. The water crept past me as my tears mixed in with flowing rainwater. I prepared to die as sporadic machine gunfire whizzed over tips of grass surrounding me.

Suddenly, it hit me. As the rainwater drifted past my muddy face, a second burst of energy filled my tired body, and I forced myself to move. Using the slow, natural flow of the water as a navigation tool, I began crawling through the sludge, following the flowing water as it moved across the muddy surface of the sporadic grass blades. I followed the flow of the water until I heard the faint sounds of a waterfall over the rain and Serbian voices. I continued toward the sound of the waterfall, letting my mud-covered body fall over the watery edge into the drainage canal that I had built with my crew last year.

The long process of digging the canal out of the sandy soil was intended to increase the usable farmland for my dead employer. It was now my salvation from the approaching Partisans as the rainstorm flooded the drainage canal, carrying my exhausted body off the Reichinger property. I struggled to stay above the water and grabbed a broken tree limb that fell into the canal, using it as a float. I pushed myself along the flooded canal, moving farther away from the sounds of the Partisans in the distance. I was mentally and physically drained of all energy, but I was alive. Alive, amidst a sea of destruction in this tiny German community trapped in the Yugoslavian Banat.

Yugoslavian Banat
October 1944

The dirt clumps brushed along Father Peter's face, moving in different directions as the sound of thunder could be heard from above him. The weight of the dirt against his limbs prevented him from repositioning his naked body in the wet soil. His fingers felt the cold touch of another man's skin stretched out alongside him in the shallow grave. Father Peter continued wiggling back and forth, enabling him to lift his head out of the mud. The repositioned wet soil created openings over the young priest's eyes, allowing him to distinguish debris restricting his vision from the darkness covering the open pasture.

Pushing away the lifeless arms of victims draped in every direction around his naked body, Father Peter focused on the view from above him. He could see the stars reappear as a storm cloud floated away like smoke from a local farmer's cigarette. In the cold and bloody dirt, the young priest tried recalling the horrific experience of being machine-gunned into a ditch. Confusion on whether being alive or dead took hold of him. Was he in hell? He was not a good priest while alive, and it only seemed logical that he would end up in hell.

As the blood flow returned to his arms, he moved his limbs, swaying the dirt in all directions. Maybe he wasn't dead? It seemed like hours since Father Peter had heard the sounds of Serbian voices above him from his partially buried location. He wanted to attempt further movement but feared detection from a Partisan soldier who might still be lurking nearby.

How could he still be alive? The Partisans had lined the men up in a row and filled their naked bodies full of bullets. Father Peter closed his eyes for a moment and struggled to incrementally move his legs from their constrained position. Abandoning his fear, he pushed himself out of his temporary grave and let the cold, wet air blow against his naked body on the open pasture. He rolled his aching body onto his chest as the rain continued. Mud seeped into narrow crevices along the edges of human limbs. The long row of dead bodies stretched out like a black quilt splattered in dots of blood and skin-colored patches.

"Is anyone alive?" Father Peter asked.

He looked closely at the soil covering the victims, searching for any sign of motion that might indicate another survivor in the group. After close inspection of the trench, there appeared to be no hint of movement. He was the only one. In a trench of Banat Germans slaughtered in cold blood by communist soldiers, Father Peter was the only survivor.

The priest rolled onto his back and opened his mouth as wide as he could. He let the cool fall air flow into his lungs, unrestricted by the dirt and bodies that had covered him only moments ago. He was not in hell, but alive on an open field, several kilometers from Theresiafeld, his home for the last two years. By some miracle of God, he was still alive.

Father Peter ran his wet, dirty hands over his naked body, smearing blood over his skin. At first, he thought it was his own blood, but their appeared to be no bullet wounds. After careful inspection, it appeared to be the blood of other victims, for not a single bullet from the Partisan machine guns appeared to have penetrated his thin layer of Viennese skin. He dragged his naked body across the wet, sandy soil. Leaning his head into the long ditch, he stretched his arm into the open hole where only moments ago, his body had lain motionless

Father Peter's ability to focus slowly returned. He stared at the dead body of the individual who, only hours ago, had stood to the right of him before the shots blasted out of the Partisan machine guns. He recognized this man with the severely deformed spine from his church services on Sunday. Other than the party he threw upon his initial arrival in Theresiafeld, he had little contact with this wealthy farmer. Father Peter brushed the soil away from the dead man's chest and stuck his finger into the bullet hole that penetrated off center into his upper torso.

He tried to recall the shooting spree from this afternoon. The man he now stared at in the ditch had fallen on top of him after the first round of bullets fired at the row of German civilians. He knew the Partisan bullets missed him completely when the deformed man's body crushed him in the ditch. As several soldiers moved in closer for one last pass with their machine guns, the wealthy farmer's body must have acted like a human shield, protecting him from any further bullet wounds. As Father Peter continued poking his finger through the opening of the wealthy farmer's chest cavity, he surmised that the bullet ricocheted off his crooked spine, preventing the metal slug from passing through his body and entering his own. In a strange twist of fate, the spinal deformity of this man was his saving grace, allowing him the privilege of living another day. If any other victim had fallen on top of him, he surely would have been killed.

Father Peter scooped his hands through a puddle of water on the wet soil, cleansing his face of the blood and dirt caked over him from lying in the pit. Besides a few cuts and bruises as a result of his fall into the ditch, he was unscathed from this afternoon's incident. It truly was a miracle.

After regaining his composure, Father Peter walked along the pasture, staying a safe distance off the gravel road as he navigated back toward Theresiafeld. By staying off the main path, he hoped to avoid any encounters with Partisan soldiers who might like another opportunity to assassinate him.

After walking nearly an hour, his body collapsed from shock. He let himself rest on a fallen, isolated tree, cracked down the middle from a lightning bolt. Father Peter sat along the edge of the fallen acacia tree with his dirt-covered hands covering his face. He tried to make sense of the incident that had occurred this afternoon. Why did God spare him? Better men were lying dead back in that ditch, yet he was allowed to live another day.

A sense of guilt came over him at the thought of being the only person escaping the wrath of the Partisans. He suddenly became keenly aware of his own mortality and the finite nature of life. The priest's life up to this point had been a waste of precious time. He had twisted his religious vocation into some self-serving business, using the priesthood as an opportunity to improve his lowly position in life. The near-death experience from this afternoon had changed him somehow.

"My God, who am I?" he cried. "Please forgive me. Please forgive me."

He prayed aloud. Several tears fell from his bloodshot eyes, dropping in a muddy puddle filled with rain. It was the first time he had prayed in a long time, maybe ever.

Suddenly he heard the sounds of footsteps in the distance. Father Peter quickly dropped his naked body behind the fallen tree and lay on the ground in total silence. The Partisan soldiers were probably combing the surrounding pasture in search of fresh victims. As the footsteps grew louder, he crushed his naked body against the bark of the fallen tree, attempting to hide himself from the approaching soldier. He heard a pair of marching feet kicking fallen leaves over the October wind rattling the tiny, dead branches dangling on the fallen tree in front of him.

The individual was almost right on top of him. Father Peter's tension eased as he stared at a crying, young boy wandering aimlessly through the barren, wet pasture.

"Son."

The boy stopped crying, startled by the sound of his voice.

"Relax, son. It's me, Father Peter."

"Father Peter?" the boy asked.

"Over here."

He walked over to the broken tree as Father Peter moved out of his hiding place.

"Aaayy!"

The boy screamed in fear. Father Peter was completely naked, still partially covered in dirt and blood. The sight of his filthy nudity surfacing from behind a tree would easily frighten any boy his age. Father Peter grabbed him by the shoulders and moved him closer so he could take a good look at his face. The naked man covered in debris and blood recognized him as a server boy from his parish in Theresiafeld. The boy saw the familiar face under the dirt and calmed himself.

"Father Peter, you have to help me," the boy said. "I need to find my father. The Partisans are in our home, and my mother told me to run."

His Sunday clothing was torn in several places with socks soaking in blood from running across the sharp stones. He obviously didn't have time to lace up his shoes when the Partisans entered his home.

"Where did you last see your father?" Father Peter asked.

"This morning. The soldiers took him at church."

"Relax. I know where he is."

Father Peter didn't want to tell him that his father had died at the hands of a Partisan firing squad. His young age had saved his life this morning, returning him home with his mother after church services. The boy didn't join the rest of the male Theresiafelders lured to the outer pasture for a Partisan work assignment ending with their execution. A few years older and the scared youngster would be dead alongside his father in the ditch.

"Father, what are we going to do?"

They were both scared, but the young priest from Vienna felt an inner strength come upon him like he had never felt before. The overwhelming desire to improve his position in life was now replaced with a burning need to help this desperate child. The boy looked at him, longing for direction. It felt strange wanting to help him.

"What are we going to do?" the boy asked a second time.

The solution to this problem would normally come from one of the older, male leaders of the community, now lying dead in the gulley. Because of the mass execution this afternoon, Father Peter was now thrust into the role of leader in this community. After a moment of silence, he looked up and touched the boy's ice-cold cheek with his hand.

"We're going to leave Theresiafeld tonight," he said. "Run back to the village and spread the word that we're leaving."

"What about food, wagons?" the boy said.

"Never mind about that."

"Yes, Father."

The boy ran toward Theresiafeld to spread the word. The military front was moving west faster than he had originally thought. The priest figured if he could make it back to Austria, he'd be out of the way of these advancing communist troops and their anti-German mentality that had cost the lives of so many Theresiafelders this afternoon.

Father Peter prayed for a moment, using his own words and not some memorized lines learned at the seminary in Vienna. The struggle of finding a few sentences in prayer felt good. He felt like a priest maybe for the first time in his life.

After a brief, prayerful moment, Father Peter ran toward Theresiafeld, in the direction of his church to gather up some personal belongings. He was weak and cold, but he continued onward, eventually reaching the outskirts of the village. He sneaked along the edge of the main road, staring in the distance at the familiar Catholic church with its baroque architecture and tall, white steeple towering over the rest of Theresiafeld. He had grown to despise the building over the last two years. The simple church was like a prison, preventing him from returning to his beloved Vienna. Father Peter jumped off the edge of the road and ran toward the middle of the street, dropping his unclothed, shivering body behind a stone monument, a memorial piece dedicated to Theresiafelders killed in action during the Great War. The gravel road seemed abandoned as he crossed to the other side. Father Peter slid under the window of his residence that adjoined the church.

He cracked it open, slipping his naked body through the opening in total silence. The dark room was the sleeping quarters of a live-in servant who had quit a year ago, mentally worn out from hiding his drunken, psychotic behavior from the rest of the Roman Catholic community. Father Peter slipped through the servant's bedroom and entered the tiny kitchen, quickly scrubbing his body with some homemade soap in the sink. As the soap and cold water rushed over him, he felt good to be cleansed of the baked-on blood and dirt covering his loose skin. He despised the rank odor from this local, all-purpose cleaning bar, but given the brutal events occurring earlier today, the annoying smell seemed insignificant in comparison.

The young priest put on some old clothes and shoes that he used when working on his tiny garden adjoining the church and grabbed one of his large, leather suitcases that he brought from Vienna. Lumbering into the main church with his suitcase, he scanned the wooden pews for any sign of intruders. The place seemed eerily quiet as he moved across the altar toward the adjoining sacristy. Father Peter opened the empty, leather suitcase and filled it with gold chalices and other church property. He thought the items might prove useful to sell for food or clothing on the way to Austria.

"Check the building, comrades!"

Father Peter was frozen in fear. The Partisan soldiers entered the church. If they recognized him from this afternoon's shooting spree, they'd kill him for sure. As the Serbs rummaged through the main church, he dropped a last golden trinket in his leather case and moved toward the door of the sacristy to check on their position.

"Oh my God," he whispered.

Father Peter could see across the main church Partisan soldiers wandering through the hallway, pilfering through various items in his adjoining bedroom and kitchen. He had hidden a radio transceiver in one of the cabinets, and if it were discovered, the Partisans would torture him for information. He wanted to go back and grab the radio equipment. He felt it would be useful in monitoring Partisan troop movements or maybe to sell it on the road as he navigated the remaining survivors from his village out of Yugoslavia. It was too late. Father Peter needed to leave his church if he wanted to stay alive.

He moved toward the rear of the sacristy, attempting to open the window and escape out the back. He tried sliding the window open, but it froze half way up in a locked position.

"Damn this thing!"

Despite all his strength pushing on it, the window was permanently jammed, probably from lack of use.

The Serbian voices moved closer to the sacristy. "Over on the other side."

"Yeah, check back there."

Father Peter could hear the footsteps approach his location. The stubborn window was only half-open, but it would have to be enough if he wanted to escape from the thieving communists. He could hear the soldiers' voices grow louder as they made their way toward the sacristy. He climbed out the window and reached back inside, grabbing the oversized, leather suitcase by the handle, attempting to squeeze it through the tiny opening.

"Come on!"

He desperately needed the leather suitcase filled with gold and other valuables. The fine piece of luggage was given to him as a gift from his benefactor, Tante Anna, and he was determined not to leave it behind. The young priest could hear the door to the sacristy open as he gave one last powerful tug to force the suitcase through the cracked window.

As the Partisans entered the sacristy, the suitcase fell back on the interior floor, and his body dropped to the wet surface of the adjoining cemetery. A graveyard void of any Theresiafelders drafted in the German military and buried in some random pit somewhere on the Eastern Front.

Father Peter moved along the shadow of the wall, away from the partially opened window. He could hear the thieving band of Partisan soldiers, rummaging through the valuables in his suitcase on the other side of the window.

He moved away from the exterior wall of the sacristy and returned to the center of the gravel road behind the stone monument. Peeking from behind the stone memorial, he took a last look at the tiny baroque church, with its white steeple towering over the neat rows of whitewashed houses surrounding Theresiafeld. For some unknown reason, he would miss this church. He wanted to have one last chance of saying mass there.

Father Peter wondered about the future of this village now that many were dead or running, trying to escape the onslaught of the communist Partisans gaining momentum in Yugoslavia. He repositioned his body in search of a safe exit. His body, free of bullet wounds, would soon join the harvested wheat and confiscated machinery that had abandoned this village over the last year. Who knew what the future held for Theresiafeld, given the anti-German environment now boiling over in Yugoslavia. Leaving this tiny village would have elated the young priest several weeks ago, but now it saddened him. Father Peter's brush with death that afternoon had changed his life. He was no longer angry with God for sentencing him to service in Theresiafeld and thanked him for sparing his life from the onslaught of the Partisan machine gun fire.

He glanced across the gravel street. It was now filled with scattered puddles from the rainstorm earlier this evening. From his kneeling position behind the monument, Father Peter saw no sign of stray Serbian soldiers wandering about as he sprinted to the opposite side of the street. He was leaving Theresiafeld with no money or food, only the old work clothes on his back. The golden chalices and artifacts collected in his fine, leather suitcase would be left to the thieving Partisans now looting his tiny parish.

"I guess it's good to leave some baggage behind every now and then," he said to himself. Ducking under a branch from an acacia tree hugging the gravel thoroughfare, Father Peter headed toward the pasture for his rendezvous with the other Theresiafelders.

Yugoslavian Banat
October 1944

I dragged myself out of the icy water, pushing myself along the rocky shoreline in total exhaustion. My body shook like the tail end of Reichinger's threshing machine, hobbled together from old parts not confiscated by the military. Had I stayed in the cold water any longer, I would have frozen to death. My body collapsed from lack of energy under a cluster of trees not far from the river's edge. I felt a sense of relief at successfully escaping last night's wrath from the Partisan soldiers. The drainage canal I had built for Reichinger over a year ago had dumped me into a tributary that fed into the Danube River, allowing me to float away from Theresiafeld virtually unharmed.

I covered my shivering body with fallen leaves crammed together in jagged clumps, providing some protection from the chilling effects of the October winds. I was starving, but rest was my first priority as my clothes slowly dried under a makeshift bed of leaves.

Now that Partisan soldiers had ransacked Theresiafeld, I hated myself for betraying these Germans, using them for information. I wanted to leave Yugoslavia immediately and forget I had joined the war effort as a spy. I would love to spot some American soldiers who could rip me out of the Banat for good. My conversations with other returning soldiers in Theresiafeld suggested no contact with Americans on the battlefield, at least not in Yugoslavia. I could risk turning myself in to the Russians who were forcing the German military westward, but I feared repercussions from the communists who were unaware of American undercover operations taking place in Yugoslavia.

The sound of wind rustling against my blanket of leaves blocked out the blasts from mortar rounds in the distance, and I drifted off to sleep. For a little while, I could put the chaos in Yugoslavia on hold, and try to recover psychologically from yesterday's bloody turmoil.

As the afternoon sun turned my dripping, wet clothes into damp rags, my desperate need for sleep faded away, replaced by a powerful craving for food. I pushed the leaves off my body and began walking through the intermittent trees along the river, looking for anything that might be edible. Unable to find a single nut or mushroom to eat, I pulled a leaf from a low branch and bit into it as my desire for food grew more uncontrollable. I grew uneasy as I marched along a thin, dirt path snaking through the trees. The idea of staying on this trail seemed dangerous, considering Russian or Partisan troops might be using it as well, but I figured it might lead to a small village nearby where I could beg for some food. Having no compass or map to guide me, I gazed upon the sun peaking through the tops of trees all around me, making sure I wasn't headed back in the general direction of Partisan-occupied Theresiafeld. Although returning to Theresiafeld to recover my radio transmitter seemed tempting, the risks were too great. I accepted the fact that I was on my own from now on, without the help of Allied support on the other end of a radio, guiding a lost American to safety. I felt my father's gold coin tucked deep in my damp boot as I walked along the trail. My foot pressed against the surface of the coin, providing a strange sense of comfort from the loneliness I now felt without the companionship of other Theresiafelders.

"Stay focused," I reminded myself.

I moved farther away from the river, northward along the winding dirt road. I regretted not exploring the plains and rivers outside the general area of Theresiafeld. My lack of curiosity now cost me in terms of my ability to navigate through this empty wilderness.

Suddenly, I could see a smoke cloud drifting like a white balloon across the open sky above me. At first, I considered turning back, but the desire to satisfy my raging hunger drove me closer. Maybe it was a cooking fire? The thought of successfully begging some food from the owners of that fire seemed worth pursuing. I maneuvered toward the location of the smoke, creeping from tree to tree. I could hear voices as I moved in closer.

"How much longer till we get back?" a voice asked.

The voice was German! I increased the pace of my shuffle toward them.

"I'm familiar with this area. My father sent me here one summer to live with a Croatian family to learn the language," another voice responded.

I couldn't see the faces of the strangers from my hideout behind a tree. It felt good hearing the sounds of Germans as the group continued chatting around the campfire. Maybe they could part with some extra food, sharing their surplus with someone of the same ethnic kinship, at least on paper.

"Hello!"

I shouted out loud. I wanted to give away my hiding place before approaching any closer. I could hear the sounds of a bolt-action rifle make a clicking noise as a bullet dropped into the firing chamber.

"Can I come closer?"

Their bodies shuffled over the leaves as they repositioned themselves upon hearing my call through the woods. With the war going on, everyone was on edge, especially when a stranger like myself approached an open campfire.

"Who's there!" the voice shouted from the camp. "Hands in the air and come out!"

I followed his orders and placed my hands behind my head, slowly walking toward the location of the campfire. As I moved into the clearing in the woods, I could see three young men dressed in patched, German uniforms. I twirled my body around, so the boyish looking soldiers could see that I wasn't hiding any weapons. They were probably in their early twenties, a few years younger than I, and by looking at their faces, I could tell they were more nervous than I was.

"I haven't eaten in two days," I said. "All I want is some food."

As their rifles lowered a bit, I hoped my Volkdeutsch dialect and outward appearance gave off a stench of familiarity to the German soldiers. My white collared shirt and ragged, dark pants added to the presentation that I was from a local German village. I squatted down alongside the fire, as the last of the frightened, German draftees eased his rifle away from my face.

"Where are you from?"

The soldier sitting next to me was the first to open his mouth. He moved his arm in front of me, offering a cigarette from his crushed paper carton.

"Theresiafeld," I said.

I pulled the cigarette out of the pack and leaned in front of the open fire to light it. His beige uniform was practically in shreds. A ragged leftover that had seen better days when the Germans had controlled Northern Africa.

"And you?" I asked.

"My friend and I are from Liebling," he said. "Leo is our lone *Siebenbürger Sachsen* in the group."

"Thanks for the cigarette."

As their metal can of rations warmed in the flames, I glanced at the Saxon across from me. The kid looked ridiculous in his uniform, as if he were pretending to be a soldier when he should be still in school. The Siebenbürger Sachsen was an ethnic German whose descendants probably arrived in Transylvania before the Austrian Empire controlled the Banat territory. Like most ethnic Germans around his age from the Banat, he was now a draftee in the SS Prinz Eugen division, even though his family hadn't been on German soil probably since the twelfth century.

"How old are you?" I asked.

"Nineteen," the young soldier said. "I was drafted right after I finished my final exams at the gymnasium in Hermannstadt."

His home town now had the Romanian name, Sibiu, not Hermannstadt. In the company of only Germans, a town or village usually was referred to by its name when the Banat territory was still part of the Austrian empire.

"Isn't that a little young?"

"We're needed as cannon fodder for the German war machine," he answered.

The soldier cracked a cynical smile, and his boyish features and tiny body looked almost childlike in his patched-up, brown uniform. The soldier's ragged clothing showed how desperate the situation was for the German military, struggling to supply their men with adequate provisions.

"Are you on leave?"

They waited an uncomfortable length of time before responding to my question.

"Yes, we're on leave from our unit."

"I hope you're not headed back to your village."

"Why?"

"In Theresiafeld most are in hiding or running west from these Russian and Partisan soldiers."

"If we don't go back to our home town, where are we supposed to go?" the Siebenbürger Sachsen asked.

The young soldier was either naive or in denial at how serious the situation was. As I stared into his boyish face, he seemed primitive, not battle-hardened like soldiers I knew returning from service on the Eastern Front. Maybe it was his eyes that seemed different. The haunted, lifeless eyes were missing on the young soldier. A look I recognized in the face of Fetter Matz's son after returning from Russia on leave last Kirchweih.

"Head west with me," I said. "It's too dangerous to travel back to Romania."

"It's like an accordion in the Banat now," the soldier said. "Russians are squeezing against our troops retreating from the west and the Americans on the opposite side."

"Where are the Americans?"

I risked revealing my cover by asking the question, but I needed to navigate in the general direction of the advancing American military.

"I heard they're moving through Germany," the soldier said.

"If you risk being captured, wouldn't you rather it be the Americans?" I asked.

From what I had seen of the brutality in Theresiafeld, I figured the American military would treat these German soldiers less harshly than the communists now in control of Yugoslavia.

They looked at one another for a moment as an uncomfortable silence fell across the campfire. It was obvious they were hiding something. The young Sachsen finally broke the silence with a slight nod of his head to the soldier in rags lying across from me. It was the go-ahead gesture that I could be trusted with some dark secret they held under the remnants of their patched-up uniforms.

"We've got a plan," the soldier said.

"What is it?" I asked.

The soldier huddled toward me, guarding against the possibility of someone lurking behind the trees, overhearing the words of treason about to roll off his lips.

"The war's going to be over soon. Germany's lost. We all know that. We're going to wait it out and hide back in our village."

"Aren't you afraid of being picked up by the German military police? You'll be shot if you're caught deserting."

"That's why we're keeping off the main roads."

I grabbed the boiling, metal can out of the fire, ready to satisfy my ravenous hunger, and thought about the risks these men took in heading back to Romania. If stopped at one of the checkpoints without the proper paperwork, they could be shot for abandoning their post.

"How'd you sneak away from your unit?"

"We were at an isolated position not far from Niš south of Belgrade. Our division held off Russian troops as the Wehrmacht pulled back through Greece. We were put under a commander who must have been as old as my grandfather. He was ripped to pieces by a grenade explosion, so we abandoned our post and headed home."

As the need for additional German soldiers grew more desperate, the rigorous standards of entry into the SS Prinz Eugen had dwindled like the German victories on the battlefield. The image painted by this young soldier of his dead commander wasn't even close to the idealized image of a tall, blue-eyed candidate volunteering from the Volkdeutschers to serve in German uniform.

"I don't blame you for leaving, but you're headed in the wrong direction. Things are getting bad."

"I don't believe you."

As the young soldier recited his tale, I could tell he was in total denial of how serious the situation was in the communist-controlled Banat. I wanted to convince him that his plan was flawed, but it was clear he didn't believe me.

"These Partisans are on revenge killings now against Germans. Your parents' wagons are probably rolling out of the Romanian Banat as we speak. Why don't you head back to Austria with me?"

"Are you crazy? My family's not going to abandon their home," the Sachsen said. "The war will be over soon, and life's going to go back to the way it's always been."

I watched as he rolled up the torn, brown sleeve of his uniform and pressed his lit cigarette over the fleshy part of his upper arm, burning off a tiny tattoo. The engraved marking on his skin, given to all new recruits in the SS, signified his blood type in case he needed a transfusion for a battle injury. I had heard rumors that anyone captured by a Partisan soldier wearing a *blutgruppe* tattoo would be classified as a war criminal and summarily executed. Enduring the excruciating pain of burning off his blood-type tattoo made for good insurance if captured.

I didn't want to press these young kids into anger by disagreeing with their decision to return to their home towns in the Romanian Banat. Their views on how things would return to normal after the war ended were shared by many back in Theresiafeld, including my dead employer, Reichinger. As I continued eating their rations, I wondered how these young guys would operate in a new Banat home run by communists. Would they be allowed to continue farming like their fathers and grandfathers? What kind of discrimination would take place against this ethnic minority since they had challenged the communist onslaught and backed the German military during the invasion?

"Which direction are you going?" I asked.

"We're headed towards the Timis River," the soldier answered. "It's not far from here." An idea suddenly struck me. I could follow the river north for a while, walking at night to avoid Partisan troops and slowly guide my way out of communist territory.

"Do you mind if I tag along for a while?" I asked.

I didn't have a weapon or any food, so it seemed like a good strategy to join this group of soldiers who seemed to know the area better than I did.

"I guess," the soldiers said.

After packing up their equipment, the boyish German soldiers and I marched eastward, staying off the roads to avoid any contact with German military checkpoints. Used to hard work on the Reichinger farm, my legs seemed in relatively good shape as our group walked a good ten kilometers through the late afternoon, calling it quits at the grassy banks of the Timis River.

"We'll camp over there," the ragged, young soldier said. "The high grass should be good camouflage."

We dropped our bodies in the field of tall, brown grass, sprawling out across the open area as the sound of the flowing water lulled us to sleep. Unwavering in their commitment to return to their villages in Romania, the soldiers and I would part company in the morning.

The rifle barrel banging against my forehead startled me awake.

"Up!" a voice barked at me.

"Ouch!" I screamed.

"Up! Up!"

I opened my eyes and stared at a large, bearded man, partially blocking the rising sun in the distance as he towered over me with his machine gun. His rough, wrinkled face contrasted with that of the young draftees of the Prinz Eugen SS.

"Stand up," he repeated

The boy soldiers and I forced ourselves to stand as other machine gun–toting soldiers surrounded the grassy field.

My first instinct was to run, but I soon realized it was pointless, given the number of communists carrying weapons now watching us. Mixed in with the Russian uniforms, I recognized the green jackets of Partisan soldiers from my brutal encounter with Tito's so called "Freedom Fighters" back in Theresiafeld. I could hear a few of them chatter in Serbian, scanning the ragged uniforms of my traveling companions as their faces clenched with rage.

I could see the hatred in some of their eyes as we moved out of the grassy field with our hands in the air. Serbs had taken heavy casualties against the German military occupation, and I feared the repercussions of being caught on the wrong side of the war in this field. The communist resistance movement in Yugoslavia had dragged on for some time, and the savage killings now crested to a violent pinnacle of barbaric behavior. One atrocity by the German military against Serbs was returned tenfold by Partisan soldiers against Germans. My slippery escape from the communist soldiers back in Theresiafeld now seemed like a fleeting victory to me.

I walked out of the tall, brown grass, now under captivity by my technical ally in the war. I was now a prisoner and would most likely end up like my friends back in Theresiafeld, shot in an open field along this river without a gravestone to mark where I was buried.

"The war is over for you, *Schwabo*."

The bearded Partisan spoke in a broken German, sending a blow to my kidney from the butt end of his machine gun causing me to drop to my knees.

"The war is now over for you."

Yugoslavian Banat
October 1944

The tiny, dark-skinned man entered the crowded Serbian inn and made his way toward an unoccupied wall in the corner. He leaned against a rickety, wooden support beam while his black eyes scanned through the haze of smoke at the mixed bag of Partisans and Russians singing in celebration. His outward appearance gave off a look of mixed Gypsy or Mongol background, blending in nicely with the multitude of ethnic groups present among the drunken communist rabble. Hiding in the chaos of Yugoslavia was easier than the British undercover agent had anticipated before starting his mission. With the German military in retreat, the euphoria of victory coated in a layer of hard liquor provided additional cover while carrying out his latest assignment in the Banat.

His false front as a peasant refugee of Gypsy background was not all that different from his humble beginnings. He had been born into a poor family of Limbu ethnic identity in Nepal. His Tibeto-Mongolian subgroup didn't practice the Hindu caste system, freeing him of any societal constraints to pursue a career of his own choosing. He was attracted to the meritocracy of serving as a Ghurka in the British Indian Army. Through hard work and discipline, he had climbed through the hierarchy, advancing to the elevated rank of subedar, a viceroy's commissioned officer subordinate only to British officers serving in a Ghurka regiment. His high intelligence and exemplary service record made him a natural recruit for special assignments by the British Secret Intelligence Service, MI6.

His current assignment in the Banat was to remove or confirm dead an intelligence asset that the Americans had lost contact with in the recent past. His superiors wanted no trace remaining of their network of spies now that the communists controlled Eastern Europe. The last remnants of their intelligence-gathering network needed to be swept away, with their communist allies remaining forever in the dark about their espionage activity.

He slid his arm under his weathered, dark jacket and rubbed his thumb over the small, sharp notch near the handle of his curved blade. Touching his *kukri*, the knife of all Ghurka soldiers, gave him a feeling of comfort before beginning an operation.

He made his way around the maze of soldiers, showing a photo of a man to anyone wearing a red star, hoping one of them might recall the face. The Ghurka knew from his intelligence gathering that some of the Partisan communists in the building had been present at the last known location of this American OSS agent.

Refugees were on the move everywhere. Another poor, displaced person seeking the whereabouts of a man in a black and white photo was not out of the ordinary. A Partisan soldier pointed his finger in the direction of a wooden plank held up with old truck tires as legs.

"Who is he?" the Ghurkha asked.

The Ghurka gazed at the battalion commander leaning against the makeshift bar sprinkled with empty shot glasses.

"He is a battalion commander," the Partisan said. "His name is Vanko."

"Did any soldiers under his command move through Theresiafeld?" the Ghurkha asked. "The man in the photo is from that village."

"I'm the political commissar recently assigned to his battalion," the Partisan said. "We can ask him."

"Victory comrades! Victory to the death!" the Partisan commander yelled. The Ghurka slid a step back, adjusting his position as the Serbian commander shouted in his face. His loud, baritone voice sank into the dirt floor and straw roof of the Serbian inn.

"The old man has pulled it off!"

Vanko slapped the Ghurka on the back and raised his shot glass of *slivovitz*, toasting his communist leader, Josip Broz Tito, for overthrowing the German occupation in Yugoslavia. In one giant gulp, Vanko swallowed the clear, plum brandy, in an attempt, the Ghurka suspected, to deaden the pain of all the killing he had done over the last several years. A high-pitched sound from Gypsy violins began playing in the crowded inn. The tiny, dark stranger attempted to communicate with this drunken communist leader, but he paid no attention. The Partisan battalion commander followed the rotating heads of his comrades, staring at the Gypsy woman who sprang onto the dance floor.

"She's beautiful," Vanko said.

"Some of our comrades don't seem to think so," the political commissar standing nearby responded.

The Ghurkha watched the political commissar whisper in Vanko's ear as the sound of Russian and Partisan soldiers clapping in unison thundered over the inn. He seemed irritated by the distraction of a meddling stranger as he gazed at the blue-eyed woman contorting her body to the music.

"Who?" Vanko asked

"This man here," the political commissar responded.

Vanko took another look at the tiny, half-breed Gypsy standing in front of him. The stranger seemed barely aroused by the partially clothed woman performing her version of "The Snake Dance."

"I'll never understand these Gypsies," Vanko said.

"I know what you mean," the commissar said.

The Partisan battalion commander pounded back another round of clear, hard liquor. The Ghurkha could tell the communist commander standing in front of him was hardened from battle. His dirt-covered boots and ripped, bloodstained jacket gave off an impression of a seemingly unlimited ability to tolerate suffering. The long, hard battles against German strongholds in Yugoslavia were now over. The communists had driven out the German military occupation, enabling centralized planning to take a foothold in the fertile soil of the Yugoslavian Banat.

"He wants to see if you recognize someone in a photo," the political commissar said.

The clapping and singing of communist soldiers only increased in intensity as the political commissar moved closer to Vanko, attempting to force the disinterested commander to listen to the Ghurkha's request.

"Let me see the photo," Vanko said.

The political commissar waved to the tiny man, motioning him to hand over the picture. Vanko grabbed it out of his hand, once again displaying annoyance at being disrupted from his Gypsy entertainment.

"Don't recognize him."

After a quick glance at the photo, he strained his neck, struggling to see over the crowd as the Gypsy woman continued her exotic dance.

"He is from Theresiafeld. Are you sure?" the political commissar asked.

The Ghurka noticed that the reference to the German village seemed to irritate Vanko. He looked angry at recalling the memory and after glancing at the old photograph a second time, he handed it back to the stranger.

"Come on! One more, one more!"

Ramming his empty shot glass against the wooden counter top, Vanko shouted in Serbian for another round of slivovitz. He pushed the Ghurka's small form out of the way as the innkeeper approached with another round. It was obvious to the Ghurka that gathering some information from this Partisan commander was a waste of his time, and he walked away.

"Wait a minute!" the commissar shouted.

He waved his arm, signaling the Ghurka to halt his retreat. The young communist, whose boyish, wrinkle-free face could have been used on a poster to promote the new worker state in Yugoslavia, walked across the dirt floor and grabbed the tiny stranger by the shoulder.

"Let me take another look at that picture."

The Ghurkha studied the facial expressions of the political commissar. He looked for some signal of deception that would indicate a reluctance to share any information that might lead to the whereabouts of the man in the photo.

"I'll tell you this much," the political commissar said. "I believe Vanko's battalion passed through Theresiafeld to load up on supplies before moving on to another location. If this man is from Theresiafeld, he probably ran away like the other German civilians when the front moved through."

"I heard rumors that several civilians were killed," the Ghurkha said.

"Why would they do that?" the political commisar asked. "These German villages scattered across the Banat can be folded into the brotherhood of our new socialist state. We need them to provide leadership in agriculture for the emerging collectivized farms."

The Ghurkha could sense a naive commitment from the inexperienced commisar in his vision of a communist utopia. Unlike Partisan soldiers who had fought against the German military occupation, his political role had isolated him from the bloodshed. He could sense a general disinterest from the young man when it came to issues regarding hideous acts of violence committed by Partisan troops against civilians. These human rights violations were a minor distraction from the greater socialist good now being molded into the newly formed worker state of Yugoslavia. The political commisar's detachment from events that might have unfolded in Theresiafeld would not be helpful in the Ghurkha's mission to locate the lost spy.

"Are there any Germans still in Theresiafeld?" the Ghurka asked.

"Maybe," the commissar said. "Many of the single women with no children in some of these German villages were rounded up and put on trains bound for work camps in Russia."

"Thank you for your time," the Ghurka said.

The Ghurka's frustration grew as the evening went on. After asking around for several more hours, the stranger left the rowdy group of drunken communist soldiers and headed up the rickety, wooden steps to his room for the evening. His search for the man in the photograph would have to wait until morning.

"Rom," a voice called.

As he approached his room for the night, the man turned his dark-skinned face toward a room across the hall, where a toothless Gypsy peeked through a wooden door.

"Rom so?" the Gypsy whispered again.

The Ghurka knew the word from his knowledge of Sanskrit, the root tongue of Nepali, the language spoken by all Ghurka soldiers.

"Yes, I am Rom," the Ghurka answered.

The word meant "brother" or "man." Only a Gypsy was Rom; the rest of humanity was less than Rom and could never truly be trusted. The two individuals of dark complexion stared at each other, acknowledging they were brothers because of their common ethnic origin.

"Rom, come closer."

The stranger waved his dark hand in the air, motioning the Ghurka to enter his room.

"What do you want?"

The Gypsy set his violin on the table, motioning with his finger for the man to take a seat. The Ghurka pushed the costumes covering the wooden surface of the chair to the side, struggling to understand the man's speech that whistled through the gaping holes through his front teeth.

"We heard you are looking for someone?"

"That's right."

"Maybe we can help you."

The Gypsy must have seen the Ghurka inquiring around the Serbian inn. It seemed none of the Partisan soldiers remembered seeing the man in the photo when they had rampaged through Theresiafeld. This Gypsy entertainment group must have caught a glimpse of the photo and recognized him from somewhere.

"I am willing to pay for information that might help me locate him," the Ghurka said.

He didn't want to disclose too much to this group of vagabond entertainers. He knew the Gypsy desire for money and thought he could appeal to their practical nature.

"How much is he worth to you?"

The voice of a female came from behind him. The Ghurka turned his head abruptly toward a dark blanket hanging on a string, used as a makeshift dressing room for the entertainers. The woman revealed herself from behind the blanket. She moved toward a dim light coming from an old, rusty gas lantern hanging on the wall. It was the blue-eyed Gypsy woman, who had performed earlier in the evening.

"Let me see the photo," she said.

She tied a last knot on her long scarf decorated in a colorful pattern around her waist and grabbed the photograph from his hand. As she looked at the face, she hid all expression that might indicate some emotional attachment to the man in the picture.

"You still haven't answered the question," the Gypsy woman asked. "How much is he worth to you?"

"Name your price."

The woman didn't say a word as she continued staring at the black and white photo.

"What tribe are you?" the Gypsy woman asked.

"What do you mean?"

The tiny Ghurka squinted his eyes as he struggled to understand the Romani language coming out of the exotic woman's mouth.

"What tribe are you?"

The Ghurka waited before responding to her question.

"Sinti."

The undercover British agent watched as the Gypsy woman widened her blue eyes at the sound of the tribal name. As someone born in Nepal, he possessed some limited knowledge of the Romany language, given their common Sanskrit root.

"That is the tribe of my childhood," the Gypsy woman said. "I am now part of the Lovari tribe and travel with them across the Banat."

The Ghurka sensed a crack in his cover. His attempt at bonding with this group of nomadic entertainers by sharing a mythical background had been a mistake. He was not a Sinti, and any further attempt at playing that role could blow his cover.

"Sit down, and have a beer with me," she said.

The Gypsy woman grabbed a small, metal bucket from the wooden table and handed it to the stranger.

"I am a Lovari Gypsy, my friend. Normally our tribes don't get along, but Europe has enough people fighting. Internal strife among the Rom can be put aside for the moment."

The Ghurka took an uneasy sip of beer out of the bucket. He was no fool and could tell she wanted to put him at ease in order to gather some additional information.

"I recognize this photo as a man that worked for a wealthy farmer in Theresiafeld," she said.

The Ghurkha was surprised that the Gypsy woman's information confirmed what limited background he knew of the American's cover. He took another sip of alcohol and paused for a moment to gauge his next line of questioning.

"As I already stated, I'm willing to pay for information that might help me locate this individual," the Ghurkha said.

"Let's assume I know where this man is," Nadia said. "Would you be willing to give me, say, one hundred dinars if I told you?"

The Ghurkha pulled out a roll of Yugoslavian dinars from his pocket and counted it out on the table. Her face lost all expression. The Ghurkha could see she was caught off guard at the large amount of paper money presented to her for such a small piece of information. As he waited for her response, he could sense the Gypsy woman concocting some new plan in her mind.

"Let me explain why I called you up here," the Gypsy woman said. "I've been unable to locate a woman who is very special to me. I think this man in the photo might know what happened to her."

"Who is the woman you seek?" the Ghurkha asked.

"She's the daughter of a wealthy landowner in Theresiafeld. The person you're looking for worked on her family's farm."

"If I knew any information about the woman you ask about I would be happy to share it with you as part of the exchange."

The Ghurkha was reluctant to lie to this Gypsy woman and share with her some false ideas about where this daughter of a farmer from Theresiafeld might be located. Her knowledge of villages and contacts across the Banat region gave her the upper hand in this game of deceit he now played.

"Do you have any information on the whereabouts of the man in the photo?" the Ghurka asked.

"My contacts in this part of the Banat are vast. With enough money, I can find him for you."

"It sounds like you don't have any information to give to me. Thank you for your time."

The Ghurkha rolled up his dinars and headed toward the door. He was by nature a loner and wasn't interested in forming any kind of a partnership with the woman.

The dressing room door slammed shut as the Gypsy woman blocked the man's path.

"You little liar! You're no Sinti! I ought to turn you in to the Partisans right now!"

Her eyes turned a deeper shade of blue as she pushed the tiny man back toward the wooden chair.

"I know this man in the photo. His name is Hans Mueller, and he's a spy working for the Americans!"

The Ghurka did not startle. He measured his response before responding to her threat to turn him in to the Partisans still entertaining themselves downstairs. He couldn't believe this Gypsy woman knew of the undercover operations taking place in Theresiafeld.

"How long have you known this man in the photo?"

"About a year," she said. "He paid me to get some information for him on several occasions."

Although possible, the Ghurka was not aware that the American in the photo had been using subagents for information-gathering purposes in Theresiafeld. He did not trust the Gypsy woman and assumed she was lying in an attempt to appear more trustworthy. She probably hoped her words would make him more inclined to help her locate this daughter of a wealthy farmer from Theresiafeld.

"Why did you help him with information gathering?" The Ghurkha asked.

"Years ago, my mother and I were forced off the farm of a wealthy landowner who I know for a fact hired the person in the photo. I despise this farmer. The idea of getting paid to undermine the military allies of some wealthy German from Theresiafeld seemed worth it to me at the time."

The Ghurka new from his American contact at the Office of Strategic Services that radio communication with agent John Miller stopped several months ago. Based on the Ghurka's limited knowledge of the man, he had sensed an increasing sloppiness in his espionage operations. In his mind, it was not unreasonable to assume that the American intelligence officer planted in Theresiafeld had forgotten to disclose his use of this Gypsy woman to gather information. He was sure the American would have abandoned his mission if he had thought that the woman now towering over him would double-cross him.

"Look, we don't trust each other; that's obvious," the Gypsy woman said. "Using your money, I can hunt down this person for you, but I'm only doing it because I believe he might know what happened to the daughter of this wealthy landowner."

"Why do I need you?" the Ghurka asked. "I can bribe people without your help."

"I know many *Marime*, unclean Gypsies who are no longer nomadic like me. Many of them joined up with the Partisans when the Germans invaded Yugoslavia. You're not Rom. They won't trust you, but they'll trust me."

The Gypsy woman was right about one thing. It would be easier using her contacts than trying to run down every lead on this American spy trapped somewhere in Yugoslavia.

"You're willing to help me locate the American, all to find some information on a woman you're looking for?"

"Yes."

The Ghurka was an independent operator, committed to military service and his assigned mission for MI6. The idea of working with someone else, even someone as attractive and resourceful as this woman, didn't particularly appeal to him.

"How do you know he's still alive?" the Ghurkha asked.

"I heard a Chetnik commando unit shot a number of male civilians in Theresiafeld including the wealthy farmer the American worked for. The person you're looking for was not in the group."

"What about this dead farmer's daughter that you seek," the Ghurkha said. "Do you think she is still alive?"

"A Roma from Theresiafeld told me her mother was raped and killed when the Partisans entered Theresiafeld and took control of their farm. The daughter's body was never found, so she must have run away."

"You must want her real bad."

"You have no idea."

"What's your name?" the Ghurka asked.

"Nadia."

"I expect this conversation to go no further than this room, Nadia."

The Ghurka threw out some words in Sanskrit. His native Indo-Aryan language from Nepal borrowed many words from the ancient tongue. It was the root language of the Gypsies, before their tribes left India and wandered into Europe. Nadia, whose Romani language was similar to the Sanskrit, could understand some of it as he spoke. The two continued discussing different strategies on how to recover this lost spy floating somewhere on the open plains of the Banat.

Although their exterior appearance of dark skin and jet-black hair gave the impression of a common ancestry, their backgrounds were completely different. Nadia was a street-smart Gypsy, wandering through villages across the Banat, surviving through trade with the agrarian settlers who lived there. He was a trained Ghurka soldier in the British Indian army and now employed in the services of MI6 to extract an American spy before the communists managed to penetrate his cover.

In a simple gesture to seal their alliance, the Ghurka officer stretched out his hand, holding a pack of cigarettes between two of his dark fingers for Nadia to grab one. The Gypsy woman gripped his outstretched hand, stealing the entire pack of cigarettes as she pulled away, quickly slipping them into a pocket, hidden between two pleats in her long skirt.

"If we find him, do I get my cigarettes back?" the petite Ghurka soldier asked.

"A Rom never cheats another Rom," she said.

"But I'm not Rom."

"That's why you're never going to get the cigarettes back."

An unstable alliance between the Gypsy woman and the Ghurka soldier had now begun. Armed with Nadia's network of contacts and the Ghurka's financial resources, the two of them could hunt for the lost American trapped somewhere in the Banat.

Nakovo Labor Camp,
Yugoslavian Banat near the Romanian border
December 1944

It had been several months since I was separated from the boy soldiers serving in the SS Prinz Eugen. After being captured by the Partisans along the river's edge, the deserters from the German military were sent to prison in an abandoned milk factory in Kikinda. My association with them immediately labeled me as a collaborator with the Axis belligerents and a promoter of the fascist ideology. The stigma I now carried with me forced me into residence at Nakovo, a holding pen of slave Germanic labor and other non-slavic threats to the new communist ideology. It was all part of Tito's grand central plan at confiscating private land and corralling ethnic German civilians into labor camps across Yugoslavia.

"Let's move it!"

My fellow Theresiafelder said as he pushed me along to hurry up. He was now a prisoner with me. Too young when the war started to be a draftee in the German military, this son of a farmer I had known back in Theresiafeld was now a prisoner with me in the Nakovo work camp. As survival from starvation and disease took priority, German civilians trapped in this labor camp morphed into beings like the gang members I'd heard of on the streets back in New York. Shared values and traditions that came from a common German ethnic identity splintered into loyalty based on your village of origin.

"Come on already!" he said.

"I'm going! I'm going!" I responded.

I shoved a last morsel of cornbread into my mouth and followed the other prisoners toward the front of the work camp. The cup of black coffee and tiny square of cornbread would be my only meal for the day unless I managed to find some work with one of the Serbian farmers.

"They're going to get a better spot in front," he muttered in a worried voice.

"I'm right behind you!" I answered, hurrying him on.

These slave drivers looking for cheap labor arrived at the front of the prison camp at dawn. It was a great deal for these Serbian farmers. They only paid Banat German prisoners in food, allowing them to keep their wage expenses as low as possible.

"Push yourself toward the front!" he shouted.

"I know," I said.

Rushing past the other starving prisoners, I battled for a good position along the row of onlookers, allowing the Serbian farmers to inspect the selection of human farm animals available for the day. I stuck my bony chest out, hoping to give off an impression to a potential agri-slavemaster that I was capable of hard physical labor.

"We're going to be passed by again," my fellow prisoner said.

"I can't believe it."

The last of the Banat German prisoners were plucked from the masses by the Serbian farmers and allowed to pass through the row of Partisan guards out of the Nakovo work camp. I abandoned my position in disgust as the last farmer handed his paperwork to the guard, showing he had made his payment to the state for the privilege of hiring German slave labor. The lucky, chosen few would receive food from their temporary employer in payment for backbreaking labor while the rest of us would starve another day.

As I struggled to move my weakened legs, I placed my hand over my forehead to check the condition of my fever. It had worsened through the night. Another couple of days without food, and I risked being too weak to work. Maybe it was better that way. A quick death from sickness seemed better than gradually starving to death in this prison camp.

"Move out of the way!"

"Excuse me," I said.

Partially delirious from the fever, I almost fell under a wagon wheel rolling through the gravel street. Nakovo was a vibrant German village before being converted into a labor camp for the communists. Limbs dangled from the edge of the wooden wagon as prisoners collected dead bodies from the rows of former houses now converted into overcrowded prison barracks. The body count on the back of the wagon rose to more than six a day as the inhumane conditions in Nakovo grew to horrific levels.

I watched as several women tossed the naked body of a young boy onto the back of the wagon, He had been too young for military service in the German army but old enough to be corralled into this labor camp. He was one of the unlucky who were born an ethnic German minority under Serbian communist control. A mysterious plague that gripped the camp had taken the young boy's life, and from the looks of it, would soon be taking my own.

"Hans, do you see that?" My fellow Theresiafelder, caged with me in the Nakovo labor camp, pointed toward the open pasture.

"What?" I said.

Beaten down by fever and hunger, I found myself struggling to remember and respond when someone called out the name given to me on The Farm. Avoiding the confusion in my mind as to my identity grew more difficult with each passing week in Nakovo. Oscillating back and forth from John Miller, the OSS undercover agent to Hans Mueller, a farm worker from Theresiafeld now became a problem under the threat of starvation and disease.

"There."

I struggled to focus. The fever blurred my vision, preventing me from seeing what my fellow Theresiafelder stared at from across the clearing.

"Is it a Partisan?"

"He's not dressed like one."

I followed with my eyes along the whitewashed fence of one of the converted prison barracks, struggling to focus on the image of a man walking across the flat, empty pasture. His tiny figure grew more vivid as he moved closer to the camp. His face was hidden under a dark hood as he navigated toward my location. It was no accident that the hooded stranger timed his approach while Partisan soldiers focused their attention on the wagon loaded with dead Banat German prisoners, rolling past them on the other side. The daily ritual of mass burial of dead prisoners in a ditch not far from camp was the perfect distraction for the Partisan guards. The stranger moved in closer to the camp.

"What's that in his bag?"

The hooded stranger carried a large, cloth bag in his hand, moving along the edge of the last row of barracks.

"He's got bread, Hans! Quick!"

We hurled our weakened bodies in the direction of the hooded stranger as he tossed out rolls of bread to the swarming band of prisoners in front of us. As the oval pieces popped into the air, hands of desperate prisoners flew in all directions, trying to grab a roll to satisfy their ravenous hunger. As the wagon of dead bodies rolled farther away from the front of the prison camp, I could see several Partisan guards focus their attention on the mob of prisoners gathered behind the whitewashed building.

"This guy's crazy," I said. "He's going to get killed!"

"Let's get some bread before the Partisan guards get to him," my friend said.

In a frenzy, the starving prisoners continued clawing at the hooded stranger, attempting to grab one of the bread rolls as hundreds of additional prisoners moved closer to his location. The swarm ripped at him, hoping to snatch a small loaf from the generous stranger before he emptied his entire cloth bag. As the begging herd of German prisoners knocked one another to the ground like hungry wolves competing for a scrap of meat, I could see a bloated man in a green uniform moving across an abandoned soccer field toward us. I caught a glimpse of his unshaven, angry face as he moved in closer to the hooded stranger. I was starving, but the fever burning inside me robbed me of any desire to compete with other prisoners in the frenzy for bread. My desire to die and end my suffering seemed to be greater than my longing for life-sustaining food coming from this tiny, hooded man.

"What the hell are you doing!" the bloated Partisan screamed.

The mob of prisoners scattered like cockroaches as the Partisan soldier moved in closer. I distanced myself from the approaching guard, having given up on any attempt at grabbing one of the rolls of bread. I could see the black eyes under the dark hood of the compassionate stranger. He gave me a look of pity, seemingly unconcerned about the final approach from the angry guard. The wooden cross hanging around his neck swayed back and forth as the last of his life-giving bread emptied from his cloth bag. I could see the guard's clenching jaw as he moved the final steps to the stranger's position. In one last feat of compassion, the black-eyed stranger removed a last loaf of bread hidden under his dark robe and tossed it deep over the heads of the other starving prisoners. It rotated through the air as its trajectory bent in my isolated direction. The small bread roll landed practically on my worn-out boots. I quickly scooped it off the dirt floor and placed it in my pocket.

Boom! The butt end of the Partisan guard's rifle smashed across the hooded face of the charitable stranger. With the bread roll safely tucked in my pocket, I moved in closer to this tiny man who now lay motionless along the dry grass. A powerful blow to the head was his reward for calming one last prisoner's ravenous hunger.

"What's a matter with you!" the guard screamed.

"I'm a Jehovah's Witness, comrade," the stranger said. "I only wanted to give some bread to the prisoners."

His broken Serbian was difficult to understand as he spoke through a swollen lip and battered cheek.

"If you ever do that again, I'll kill you!"

The stranger lay motionless while his blood dripped along the grass. Several soldiers saw the confrontation and made their way toward the location of the beating.

"Don't ever give food to the prisoners again. Do you understand?" a young Partisan said. "Get out of here!"

The Jehovah's Witness received a brutal kick to the abdomen from the Partisan soldier before crawling across the open field and away from the Nakovo labor camp. I leaned against the converted barracks wall, watching in disbelief at the tiny stranger's ability to tolerate with dignity the beating received from the Partisan soldiers. In the labor camp, I had seen many civilian prisoners cry and scream after receiving lesser beatings. This tiny Jehovah's Witness didn't make a single sound as his crawling body vanished behind the trees toward the Romanian border in the distance.

"Everybody move back!" the bloated guard ordered. "I said, move back!"

The Partisan soldier flourished his machine gun at the prisoners, and they scrambled back to their assigned barracks. I watched the lucky few who had managed to grab one of the bread rolls begin wolfing down their hard-fought meal, trying to satisfy the never-ending hunger that was a part of daily life in this work camp.

As I scrambled away, I stuck my hand into my ragged pants pocket and etched a sign of the cross into the bread with my index finger, saying a quick prayer for the Jehovah's Witness whose generosity now satisfied some of the brutal hunger in the prison camp. I had not been a religious man during my stay in Theresiafeld, but over the last several months, my spirituality had deepened with the rising body count of dead Banat Germans tossed onto the wagon for burial outside of the camp. The bravery of the tiny stranger, willing to risk his own life in a simple act of generosity, lifted my belief in the compassion of mankind. With my bread loaf secure, I felt a temporary respite from my state of depression, a relief from the lingering fever I carried around the prison camp.

Like many evenings before, I drifted to the front of camp, past a large building that had been used for commercial purposes when Nakovo had thrived as an agrarian community. The building now doubled as the camp commander's office. I glanced through the window of the building, scanning the sparsely furnished interior room. I stared at the radio transmitter sitting idle on a table in the corner. I would fantasize about breaking into the building and sending a coded message to my contact person about my imprisonment, hoping my government could negotiate a release for me. From my position near the window, the receiver and transmitter of the apparatus seemed similar in appearance to the suitcase radio that I had used to send my ciphered messages from the cluster of acacia trees back in Theresiafeld. With some fiddling, I probably could operate the equipment and tap out a quick message. A simple short phrase that the Fox was a prisoner in the Nakovo labor camp would be all that I needed.

Revitalized from my encounter with the gutsy Jehovah's Witness, I broke off a morsel of the bread roll hidden in my pocket as I walked back to my assigned barracks. The feeling of food in my mouth lifted me temporarily from my depression. I was reluctant to devour the entire roll, hoping to ration the food over the next several days. I let my filthy, sickly body stretch out on the hard wood floor of the prison barracks and thought through my plan again. I needed to create an opportunity for myself, and breaking into the camp commander's office seemed the logical opening. I scanned the faces of other prisoners wrapped in old clothes and blankets lined up in rows along the floor around me. As the death toll rose, the once-crowded barracks now offered additional space for the survivors. Tiny bugs irritated me through the night as their legs, covered with bacteria and disease, crawled over the loose skin on my face and hands. I could feel the fever draining energy from my body, but I was determined to harness enough strength to attempt a break-in to the commander's office before sunrise. My lack of nourishment impaired my ability to concentrate and plan tonight's mission in my mind. After several hours of struggle, my body temporarily stopped trembling from fever, and I drifted off to sleep.

"Ahh!"

A temporary bout of maniacal confusion rattled me awake, and I realized I was still alive in my barracks full of diseased and starving German civilians. I flicked a bug off of my sweaty face and watched as it crawled under the plank wood floor. If I wanted a way out of the camp, I had to fight off the fever and implement my plan. I reviewed my old cipher learned back on The Farm and climbed over several half-asleep prisoners, slipping out the door to the gravel streets of the camp.

Creeping along the walls of the barracks, I quietly moved down the narrow, dark streets toward the commander's headquarters. As I ran from barracks to barracks, ever closer to my final destination, the evening's cloud cover gave me some added protection from the Partisan guards wandering the gravel roads of Nakovo. Hopefully, once I accessed the radio, my contact on the other end would recognize the encrypted message and make some kind of effort to negotiate my release with these communist allies. If I were caught using the transmitter, I dreaded thinking about what punishment I'd receive from the guards. I was a desperate man. If I didn't get out of here soon, I would probably die of starvation or sickness. I had to get to that radio. It was my only hope.

I dropped my body to the soil directly below the glass window of the commander's office. As I looked up and down the gravel road, I couldn't see any Partisan guards patrolling near my location. For the moment, it appeared I was alone in the darkness of early morning. I pressed my shivering body against the window, trying to force it open. The bulky radio transmitter lay on a wooden table in the corner of this neglected building. I continued pressing against it, but it wouldn't budge. It was locked from the inside.

I dropped to the ground and began searching along the barren soil for something to break the glass. Stubble from old bushes lining the edge of this building were ripped out, leaving me free to claw along the open area, in search of a large rock to break the glass. As I looked for a stone, my hand occasionally brushed against a thin blade of grass. I quickly pushed it in my mouth to satisfy my hunger.

I found a smooth stone and banged it against the surface of the glass window. Crack! The high-pitched sound echoed off the crumbling exterior of the whitewashed building but caused no damage to the smooth glass surface. Nervous from the loud sound, I huddled below the window in preparation for a second attempt. Crack!

With all my effort, I smashed the smooth stone a second time against the glass and heard the shattered pieces fall on the wooden floor covering the interior of the makeshift camp headquarters.

I moved my hand through the jagged edges of the broken glass window, reopening the old hand wound I had sustained from the shattered wine bottles covering the ground of Reichinger's farm the night I had escaped from Theresiafeld. After several failed attempts to locate the latch on the window, I managed to unlock it and push it open, crawling off the main gravel road and inside the building.

The office of the building seemed unusually disorganized. For most Banat German businesses back in Theresiafeld, the room I was now standing in was always impeccably clean and highly functional, a far cry from its current condition.

I brushed my bloody hands along the surface of the radio equipment, looking over the tuning knobs that stuck out along its dark surface. The transmitter appeared to be a short-wave radio, capable of sending long-range messages like my suitcase radio back in Theresiafeld could. I tapped the Morse key several times, simulating the act of sending a coded dispatch of my whereabouts. I knew I had to move quickly if I wanted to get back to my barracks before daybreak.

"What's the new rotation?" I heard Serbian voices ask from outside my broken window.

"I don't know," the Partisan said. "Let me check something out."

The soldier stopped speaking as his footsteps grew louder, approaching the broken window where I had entered. Other voices grew louder as the patrolling guards approached the commander's headquarters. It was still dark outside. Maybe the Partisan soldiers would dismiss the shattered glass as another example of the routine disrepair of this village. I pushed my body against the interior wall, attempting to conceal myself from a guard potentially looking through the broken window.

"Wait a minute," the guard said.

From my hideout along the interior wall next to the window, I caught a faint whiff of the soldier's filthy breath coming through the jagged hole of the shattered glass, as he inspected the disturbance. My heart pounded. I feared for my life as I crushed my body tighter against the interior wall. The Serbian voices faded from the location of the broken window, and my body relaxed as the sound of guard footsteps moved away, seemingly unconcerned about the disturbance.

Suddenly, I could hear the sound of keys jingling like bells connected to a horse during the Fasching festival back in Theresiafeld. Someone fiddled with the lock on the office door, attempting to find the correct key connected to his chain. Risking detection from another guard waiting along the gravel road, I moved away from the wall and poked my head outside the broken window. The guard was moments away from unlocking the door. I quietly slipped my sickly body through the broken window and made a mad dash for my barracks. The fever and hunger that drained the energy from my body were now secondary concerns, as I sprinted along a side street, hoping to make it back to my barracks undetected.

"Halt!" a Serbian voice said.

As I turned the corner into the final stretch back to my barracks, I skidded along the loose gravel, grinding to a halt. A bloated Partisan guard pointed his Italian bolt-action rifle at my face, staring at me in disbelief. For a moment he didn't know what to do, but he quickly regained his composure and moved closer toward me. I raised my hands in the air, hoping he wouldn't fire his weapon.

"Schwabo!" the Partisan said. "To the ground!"

I dropped to my knees with my hands over my head as the guard shouted for several of his Partisan comrades to approach me. The egg-shaped Partisan soldier aiming his rifle at my head was known in the camp as particularly ruthless. Many of the prisoners had received beatings from him even for the most minor offenses. Rumor had it the chubby Partisan had a son killed in the war fighting against the German military. The guard's anger at losing his son now manifested itself as endless beatings for the helpless civilians now held captive.

I screamed, covering my face as the bloated Partisan clubbed me with his rifle. Unlike the boyish, German draftees I was captured with back at the river, a civilian such as myself received no protection under the rules of the Geneva convention. The Partisan soldier was free to inflict as much cruel treatment on me as he felt desirable. After several final kicks to my head, the ruthless soldier and one of his comrades picked me off the ground and dragged me along the main street. I was completely disorientated from the beating, but they pushed me through a deserted building with its front door ripped from its hinges.

"Get in there, Schwabo!" the Partisan said.

The door in the rear of the building was opened. With the butt end of his rifle, he hammered me one last time in the back, forcing me through the interior door against the back wall of the building.

"No!"

I screamed as my body rolled down the stairs, splashing into a pool of shallow water at the bottom of the wooden steps. The door at the top of the staircase slammed shut, and darkness returned to the flooded basement. I struggled to get to my feet, wading through the icy water that went up over my ankles.

The morning sun began to rise over Nakovo, as a break in the clouds allowed a thin beam of sunlight to sneak through a crease in the wooden floorboards above me. I repositioned my body in the flooded basement, allowing the beam of light to shine directly on my face. I was thoroughly bruised, and my head injury made it a struggle to keep my balance above the water line. The tiny ray of light provided some semblance of comfort as I stood in the icy water, struggling to stay conscious in the dark isolation of this basement.

As I cried, I let my hand, still bleeding from breaking the glass, wander into my pocket, touching the small roll of damp bread grabbed yesterday afternoon from the generous, Jehovah's Witness. I had forgotten that it was still there. I had wanted to devour it as a reward for completing a radio transmission, but that had ended in failure. I was in a world of hurt, the abyss.

"My God, please let me die," I said.

Whatever will to live and fight another day was now gone from my being. I removed the small loaf of bread, struggling to open my injured jaw to take a bite out of it. I would at least satisfy some of my unbearable hunger before dying of sickness in this icy prison. As I fixated on the stream of light squeezing through the wooden floorboards from above me, I placed one end of the bread roll into my mouth and struggled to find the energy to chew. I had no intention of rationing this limited food source any longer. It would only prolong my endless suffering and delay my inevitable death.

As I took a second bite into the small loaf of damp bread, I could feel my lips and tongue press against something strange. At first I thought it was a tiny worm or insect that made its way inside the bread, ruining the last meal I would receive in my young life before dying in this basement flooded with icy water. I pulled the object out of the roll with my bloody finger. It was not a worm, but a tiny piece of paper folded up into a square.

Using the ray of light from above me to guide my fingers, I slowly began unfolding the tiny square. As it opened, I noticed some markings along the surface of the paper, which I couldn't make out in the dark abyss of the basement. I lifted the tiny slip of paper over my head, directing it over the ray of light creeping through the wooden floorboard from above me. The beating I had received from the Partisan guards had caused my right eye to swell up, impairing my ability to see the handwritten letters on the slip of paper. I closed my swollen eye completely and focused on the writing with my one good eye as best I could. Using the dim lighting from above me as a crude reading lamp, I looked closely at the English words in disbelief. THE FOX HAS A FRIEND.

Outside the Nakovo Labor Camp,
Yugoslavian Banat near the Romanian border

December 1944

Nadia and the Ghurka soldier working for British intelligence crawled toward a cluster of pine trees in the distance. Through a combination of bribes and calling in favors from several non-nomadic gypsies serving with the Yugoslav Partisans, they had managed to hunt down the location of their American target trapped inside the Nakovo labor camp.

They stared over the flat, open pasture leading up to the former village of Nakovo. Nadia could see the subtle changes of the former German village now converted into a labor camp under communist control. Her clan of Lovari Gypsies had visited Nakovo before the war, selling horses and sharpened knives to the local German farmers. The whitewashed buildings in the distance were now converted to prison barracks. Their exterior appearance seemed in disrepair, scarred from lack of private ownership under the new communist model of central planning. The camp looked lifeless; thousands of malnourished prisoners crammed into makeshift barracks surrounded by motionless Partisan guards. No fence surrounded Nakovo, only a contingent of machine gun–toting Partisans prevented escape across the Romanian border nearby.

"This is as close as we can get," Nadia said.

"How much longer is it going to be?" the Ghurka asked.

"Relax. They'll be here soon," Nadia said.

The Gypsy woman and the Ghurka hid behind the pine trees waiting for the sound of a hand-picked group of Lovari Gypsies to begin their entertainment diversion on the other side of the labor camp. The tiny Ghurka let his hand wander under his jacket. Clasping the curved blade of his kukri eased some of his stress as he thought about the mission ahead. Using a wild band of nomads as a distraction while extracting an American spy trapped inside the camp seemed risky. Trusting outsiders was not in the Ghurka's nature. He was used to operating alone, relying on no one but himself to carry out an objective established by MI6.

"I can't believe I'm doing this," he muttered to himself and shook his head, grazing his dark-colored cheeks through a patch of dry grass on the surface of the pasture where he lay. If MI6 knew he was using Gypsies to spring an American agent from captivity, he might risk being demoted from his Subedar officer rank, degrading the elite reputation of Ghurka soldiers.

"Are you sure the commander is gone this weekend?" the Ghurka asked.

"Positive," Nadia said. "That *marime* I bribed with several packs of cigarettes back in Kikinda wouldn't lie to another Rom."

"Marime" was a term used to describe non-nomadic Gypsies like the soldier she had bought some information from several days ago. This Gypsy Partisan guard had told her that the commander would be absent from the Nakovo labor camp tonight, creating a window to extract the American spy trapped inside.

It was a partial lie telling the Ghurka that information bought from the Gypsy soldier back in Kikinda could be relied upon. From her point of view, the guard was a non-nomadic Gypsy and therefore unclean, not someone who could be completely trusted.

"Can you hear it?" the Ghurka asked.

"It's starting," Nadia said.

The darker tones of Gypsy violins could be heard over the drunken voices of soldiers bellowing out an old, Serbian folk song. The entertainment diversion was in place. It would only be a matter of time before the Ghurka could sneak into the camp and extract the American trapped inside.

"It looks like several more are moving away."

"Yes, I see it."

From an isolated, electric bulb on a pole near the entrance of the camp, several men in dark green Partisan uniforms could be seen moving toward the opposite side of the camp, joining the entertainment in progress sponsored by the small group of Lovari Gypsies.

"A *raatze* can smell slivovitz a kilometer away," Nadia said.

Whenever a Gypsy used the word raatze referring to someone of Serbian background, it never came off as complimentary.

"Slivovitz. It seems like everybody drinks that crap in Yugoslavia," the Ghurka said.

"Not me," the Gypsy woman said. "Lovari Gypsies drink beer, not slivovitz."

They could see a bottle of the clear, plum brandy rotate through the band of Partisan guards. Nadia watched her adopted tribe begin intoxicating the communist soldiers, hopefully giving the Ghurka a slight edge in yanking the American out of Nakovo without getting caught.

The Gypsy woman kept her blue eyes on the lookout for any stray guards wandering near their hidden location behind the pines. As the drinking binge orchestrated near the front of the Nakovo labor camp dragged on, it would only be a matter of time before her nomadic friends gave the final signal.

"If only we had gotten that message to him sooner," the Ghurkha said. "We could have grabbed him before he was locked up."

The tiny man ran his hand over the hidden bruise on his dark face, placed there by the bloated Partisan guard. The Ghurka's cover of a Jehovah's Witness passing out bread to starving Banat German prisoners had resulted in his target prisoner receiving the hidden message in the bread roll a day too late.

"We could've paid the fifty dinars to the state, and we'd have him already," Nadia said.

"Don't remind me. I can't believe we're going through all this."

Before the American spy was locked up in the abandoned building, the Gypsy woman and the tiny Ghurka were planning on renting him out as a day laborer. With his imprisonment in solitary confinement, the overall mission of pulling him out of Nakovo had become more complicated.

"That's the signal, Ghurka!"

After waiting under the pine tree for nearly two hours, the faint sound of a high-pitched howl shrieked over the singing and clapping near the front of the labor camp. The screeching sound was the go-ahead signal for the Ghurka to start the operation. Nadia trusted her Lovari Gypsies to make the call for when to start the breakout.

"You're sure your people can get us out of here after I grab the American?" the Ghurka asked. "That guard back in Kikinda said Hans is in pretty bad shape. I may have my hands full carrying him out of there."

The tiny man had a general mistrust for women and questioned whether Nadia could truly defend herself against an attack from one of these communist guards.

"Just worry about getting that gadjo out of the camp," Nadia said. "I'll cover your back."

Nadia's eyes turned a darker shade of blue as the Ghurka prepared for the long crawl over the open pasture. The street-smart Gypsy woman found it somewhat arrogant that this undersized creature would think himself more capable in outmaneuvering these Partisan soldiers than she was.

Nadia grabbed a chunk of the Ghurka's black hair.

"Have no illusions, Ghurka. I will hold up my end of the bargain."

He cracked a partial smile. His mistrust of the woman eased a fraction as he listened to her words of inner strength. The Ghurka took a quick look in both directions and began crawling across the dry grass toward the first row of abandoned homes that were being used as prisoners' barracks.

Once on the other side of the open pasture, he pushed his stunted frame against a deep crack carved along the wall of the first building at the edge of the camp. His black eyes glanced down the ruler-straight row of converted barracks, keeping a lookout for any random patrolling guards that lingered along the abandoned gravel streets.

Except for the faint sounds of drunken laughter and Gypsy violins coming from the other side of Nakovo, all was dead silent near his location. Leaping off the ground, the Ghurka crept along the walls of confiscated homes. He had studied the layout of the civilian camp over the last several weeks and knew, from Nadia's intelligence gathering, the exact location where the American was being caged like an animal. Navigating from memory, the Ghurkha jumped over a collapsed street sign and turned the corner for the final stretch to the solitary confinement building where the American spy was being held.

"There it is," he said to himself.

He crept along the exterior wall of his targeted building and turned through the opening where a wooden door had been ripped from its hinges.

The Ghurka methodically scanned the interior of the structure. It was used as a holding cell for disruptive prisoners like the American spy. He pulled out a bulky, metal flashlight from the cloth bag strapped to his belt and used it to scan the interior. It appeared to be an abandoned butcher shop with an empty display counter parked on the opposite side of the room. Metal hooks dangled from the ceiling, now free of the smoked meats and sausages once available for sale in this community.

"Where are you, American?" the Ghurka murmured to himself.

The light from his flashlight moved slowly along the interior walls of the abandoned butcher shop, checking for any sign of the lost spy. Maybe it was the wrong building? Suddenly, the Ghurka stopped his beam of light along an opposite wall, directly behind an empty display case. He traced his light over a straight crack that separated a door from the interior wall of the makeshift prison. He could see the fresh, metal brackets carved into the wall, holding an old, wooden beam along the front of the door.

"Got it!"

The tiny British agent moved behind the barren display case and pressed his ear against the cold wood of the interior door. Not a single noise could be heard coming from the other side. He moved his flashlight across the rest of the walls, soaking the contents of the abandoned butcher shop into permanent memory. Once the Ghurka's methodical analysis was complete, he lifted the wooden barrier away from the door.

Using every ounce of energy, his arms pushed against the door, but it wouldn't budge. Within minutes, the Ghurka abandoned the attempt and leaned on the ground, sifting through his bag of tools in search of some device to pick the lock. After locating a thick metal pin in his dark bag, the Ghurka inserted it into the large keyhole and fiddled with the lock. He rotated his head back toward the entrance of the building, keeping a lookout for any guards that might be drifting along the gravel road outside the abandoned butcher shop. The Ghurka, a veteran of working with even the most intricate of locks, felt the crude mechanism within the keyhole unhook, allowing the old wooden door to open freely.

His black eyes followed the light from his bulky flashlight down the flight of stairs toward the basement. The entire floor seemed to move in front of him as the Ghurka made his way down into the cellar. He placed his foot in a pool of dark, murky water covering the entire basement floor, gauging its depth as he entered the freezing, cold water. He struggled to balance himself as the water line crawled up his pants leg, stopping below his knee.

There, in the far corner of the room his flashlight revealed the head and shoulders of an unconscious prisoner propped against the basement wall. The individual kept his eyes closed as the light continued shining into his bony face, hovering in a curled up ball above the water line. He moved in closer, meticulously analyzing the facial structure of the unconscious man for signs of familiarity. The American seemed different in appearance than his black-and-white photo. He seemed haunted, thinner.

"Wake up!" he hissed, smacking the American's red skin where it hung loosely over his cheekbones. The bony prisoner didn't flinch. The long, dark fingers of the Ghurka moved along the American's narrow neck, finding a weak pulse still throbbing in a body burning with fever.

"Come on. Wake up!" He smacked the man forcefully across the face once again.

"No—" the American groaned as his eyes flickered in rapid motion. "Go ahead. Kill me, Partisan. I want to die."

"Do exactly as I tell you American, and we'll both live to see another day."

In a tremendous feat of strength, the Ghurkha grabbed the American by his wet, black jacket and pulled him to a standing position, propping his lanky body against the basement wall.

"Who are you?" the American said as he partially regained consciousness.

"I'm a friend of the Fox."

The Ghurka moved his dark hand around the American's narrow waistline, carrying his lifeless body as he plowed through the icy water to the narrow stairway. After pulling the American up the staircase, the Ghurka leaned him against the wall and methodically placed the wooden barrier back to its original position over the interior door. He knew if he managed to get the American out of the camp, there was a good chance the Partisan soldiers wouldn't discover he was missing until morning. This would give him time to put some distance between them and Nakovo while the band of Lovari Gypsies shuttled them off to safety across the Romanian border.

"Try to balance yourself. I need to check something out."

He felt wired from the high-pressure situation, but he tried putting the overpowering stress out of his mind. He peeked through the opening of the abandoned butcher shop and looked down the side street. No guards seemed to be around as the high-pitched sounds of Gypsy violins near the front of the prison camp bellowed out the crude entertainment distraction.

"What am I going to do with you, American?"

The Ghurka looked back at the half-dead man leaning against the wall. He was in worse shape than he had originally thought. The British intelligence officer faced the overwhelming task of carrying this sickly creature across the labor camp to the wagons waiting nearby.

"Maybe I should kill you, American."

His orders from intelligence were to pull the American out of Yugoslavia or to confirm he was dead. Slitting the American's throat and letting him die as Hans Mueller, a prisoner trapped in this camp for German civilians, would accomplish his mission all the same. As the war in Europe had begun winding down, the alliance with the Russians had eroded, creating new potential problems if undercover American spies were discovered in communist-controlled territory.

The Ghurka released his hand from the kukri blade strapped along his belt as the devious thought of killing the American quickly passed. Although a practical alternative to carrying him across the compound, he feared repercussions from the Gypsy woman waiting nearby. Her network of contacts working for Tito might tell her how the American spy died in the camp. Betraying the woman might result in his own life being taken in an act of vengeance from this street-smart nomad. Besides, if he killed the American, Nadia would probably have no interest in helping him escape from this communist-controlled jungle he operated in.

It was clear that Nadia wanted this American spy released from the camp, maybe even more than the Allies did. The Gypsy woman was convinced the American had information regarding the whereabouts of another woman she desperately wanted to locate.

"Let's go," the Ghurka said.

He tossed the half-dead man over his right shoulder. His lanky frame was awkward to carry, but he hauled him through the dark streets of Nakovo anyway. Struggling to keep his balance under the dead weight, the Ghurka retraced his steps, moving from barracks to barracks, trying to avoid detection from the Partisan guards. Once he arrived at the last barracks along the edge of the camp, the Ghurka dropped the body of the young American to the ground. He was exhausted from the hike across the gravel streets. Through the darkness, the Ghurka could see the open pasture, leading toward a patch of pine trees in the distance.

The Ghurka placed his hand over the forehead of the American, checking the status of his dangerously high fever. He was fading in and out of consciousness. If he didn't get some medical attention soon, all this effort would be a waste of time.

"How are we going to do this?" the Ghurka asked himself.

The rest of the way to safety would be across open terrain. His presence could be easily detected by Partisan guards wandering through the pasture along the perimeter of the Nakovo prison camp. The Ghurka needed to stay low to the ground to avoid detection by one of the soldiers floating around the exterior of the camp. He needed to figure out an efficient way to drag the unconscious American without being discovered.

The Ghurka removed some string from his cloth bag and wrapped them around the American spy's wrists, binding the end of his arms tight together. He then placed the American's tied arms over his own thin neck and dropped to the ground, crawling along the dirt pasture dragging the American underneath him. The sweat poured down his neck, dripping into the American's irritated face as he crawled over the open pasture toward the location of Nadia, hidden behind the pine trees in the distance. It was a slow, grueling process.

"Nadia," he whispered as he drew close to her hiding place.

She jumped off the ground and ran toward the dragging mass of bodies, grabbing the American by his bound arms and yanking him behind the tree like a dead animal.

"Is he alive?" she asked.

"Barely," he replied.

The Ghurka's chest expanded and contracted like a balloon, throbbing in exhaustion from carrying his cargo across the open pasture.

Nadia stared at the extracted prisoner. With his tremendous weight loss and ragged clothing, uncharacteristic of a typical Banat German worker, his outward appearance seemed completely different from when she had met him in Theresiafeld.

"Let's move it," the Ghurka said. "I'll carry him to the caravan."

"He's too heavy. Let me do it," Nadia said.

The muscular Gypsy woman couldn't believe this petite creature marked up with soil stains around the knees of his pants had managed to carry the American this far.

"No. Do as I tell you."

The Ghurka officer of Subedar rank sounded his command, still struggling to catch his breath from the exhausting ordeal of dragging this lifeless body stretched out in the dirt. He lifted the unconscious American over his shoulder and followed Nadia toward the rendezvous point, where the Lovari Gypsies had hidden their caravan of covered wagons.

"Let me have him," Nadia said. "I'll carry him the rest of the way!"

"Don't stop moving; we're almost there," the Ghurka said.

The Ghurka's simple act of endurance and strength forced Nadia to dismiss her opinion of him as a frail human being who would be unable to survive the rigorous hardships of nomadic life across the plains of the Banat.

"Oh no!" Nadia whispered, turning back to the Ghurka and grabbing him by the shoulder. "Can you see him?" she asked.

The Ghurka turned where Nadia pointed. He could see a bloated Partisan guard strolling near the clearing where the open pasture sloped upward. His presence along the hill created an illusion that the guard was larger, more formidable in size. It was the same heavy-set Serb who had beaten him up when he attempted to sneak a message to the American.

"We're going to have to cross over that open area to get to the wagons," Nadia said.

"Is there a way to go around?" the Ghurka asked.

"It's open area in all directions. He'll see us. We have to go through him."

"Wait here," he instructed.

The Ghurka dropped the sickly American to the hard ground near a lone tree in the pasture, totally insensitive to any pain caused by the fall. Nadia watched as he pulled the curved dagger from his cloth bag, crawling like a snake along the grass toward the location of the fat Partisan guard. She pulled the unconscious American to her chest as the sound of an owl rustled a branch above her head, frightening the superstitious Gypsy woman. When this "bird of the dead" took flight, a cold sensation drifted down Nadia's spine, bringing back memories of her mother, a woman of Sinti Gypsy background who feared the owl as a bad omen.

The tiny, slithering Ghurka moved like lightning up the slight incline of the pasture, creating an opportunity to ambush the bloated communist, now urinating on the open field with his baggy, green pants in a pile over his ankles. The Ghurka drew his kukri from its leather scabbard and charged the soldier. It was the first time in the Banat he had unsheathed his Nepalese knife. The Partisan soldier pulled up his green trousers and turned his thick upper body toward the oncoming Ghurka who was charging at him like a mad man. The communist soldier barely had time to adjust his Italian rifle as the Ghurka lunged at him, knocking the startled guard to the sandy soil. The two of them rolled along the ground, struggling to control the curved dagger in the Ghurka's tiny, dark hand.

"No!" Nadia gasped.

She abandoned the American and ran toward the two men grappling each other on the ground in a fight to the death. Almost at the scene, Nadia watched in disbelief as the Ghurka held his own against an enemy twice his height and weight. As the two warriors struggled for possession of the Nepalese dagger, the Ghurka managed to release his other hand from the clenching grip of the Partisan soldier and drive his index finger into his enemy's right eye socket.

The fat Partisan shrieked in agony. The Ghurka managed to free his hand wielding the kukri and lunged forward. The heavy weight from the end of his curved blade gathered momentum as he drove it into the enemy's chest cavity. Within seconds, the communist lay motionless on the ground, covered in blood.

"What kind of demon are you?" Nadia asked.

She was at the scene of the brutal hand-to-hand combat. Nadia watched the Ghurka crawl off the bloody, lifeless body of his victim and couldn't believe the animal-like tactics he had used to kill his enemy.

"Let's move out before someone finds us," the Ghurka said.

She sensed no fear in him as the stunted warrior's mind instantly returned to the mission at hand. The Gypsy woman couldn't believe this stranger from Nepal was capable even of defending himself, but armed with his bent blade, he was a disciplined assassin, capable of deceiving the most cunning Gypsy about his true physical deadliness.

"I see the *vardo*," Nadia said. "We're almost there."

The exhausted Ghurka stumbled the last stretch to the waiting Gypsy caravan and dumped the sickly American in the dry, warm interior of the last covered wagon.

"Let's move out," he said. "We'll meet the others at the rendezvous point over the Romanian border."

The black-eyed Lovari Gypsy on the lead wagon started his horses. Other wagons joined the caravan, following the rolling wheels crushing a set of wide lines through the dry soil away from the Nakovo labor camp. Nadia placed the unconscious American on a set of pillows as the wagon bobbed along the uneven ground.

"My God, you're burning up," she said.

The American was deathly ill from a fever that was draining his body of all energy.

"This will help, gadjo."

She tied a small piece of string around the ring finger of the American and recited a few incantations. Nadia had learned the Gypsy ritual from her mother. The string circling around his digit would prevent the sweat from draining out of the American's frail body and destroy the fever within him.

The American, disguised in a ragged version of Banat German clothing, awoke from his unconscious state and glanced at the blue-eyed Gypsy woman leaning over him in the back of the wagon.

"Where am I?" he asked.

Under the influence of the deep fever, he wasn't certain that it was the same woman he had become infatuated with during his time in Theresiafeld.

"Nadia?" he ventured hesitantly.

"I have you, gadjo. You are safe with me."

The dangerous mission was accomplished. The line of decorative, Gypsy vardos rolled away from the Nakovo labor camp and across the Romanian border.

✝

Linz, Austria
December 1944

Father Peter pushed his band of German refugees farther down the road. Worn out boots followed the grooves cut into the gravel road as far as the eye could see. Like bread crumbs leading the way to safety, the parallel lines carved out from the endless stream of wagons showed the path westward out of communist-controlled territory.

The starving orphan yelled out toward Father Peter's location near the front of the traveling pack of Banat Germans clothed in rags.

"What is it, son?" Father Peter asked.

A gaping hole stuck out of the young boy's Sunday dress shoes, worn down from the long walk out of Yugoslavia. He looked up at the priest with his cracked lips, dried out from dehydration. He was the same child Father Peter had met outside of Theresiafeld the day he survived the Partisan firing squad. The boy's father wasn't as lucky as he, shot down by communist butchers into a ditch along with many other men from the village.

"Can you see that up the road?" the boy asked

The boy's mother was also dead. She had been struck down several weeks ago by a fever on the long journey by foot out of the communist-controlled Banat. He was now alone in the world, carrying only the belongings his dead mother had left him, moving forward into an uncertain future like the rest of his exhausted traveling companions from Theresiafeld.

"It looks like a soldier," the young orphan said.

Ahead of them stood a lone soldier leaning against a small wall of sandbags flattened out from the pounding of rain.

"Hold up a minute!"

Father Peter shouted to his band of refugees to move off the road and approached the checkpoint alone. The soldier moved his rifle toward the priest's face as he moved in closer. He was too exhausted to be afraid.

"Don't shoot!" Father Peter said in German. "It's all right. I'm Austrian."

His uniform was clearly German military, easing some of his concerns that he would be trying to get some help from a Russian soldier.

"I'm a priest in desperate need of help. My group's been on the road for weeks and we're almost out of food."

The soldier was probably no more than eighteen years old, another unlucky replacement in the dwindling German military.

"I'll let you cross over the checkpoint," he said. "There's a refugee camp set up in Linz. They probably can take you there."

"Do you think the Germans will hold this part of Austria from the Russians?"

"Doubtful, Father. We're losing ground fast."

"How many ethnic Germans have crossed the border?"

"I've noticed a decrease in the numbers. You're probably some of the last civilians to get out."

As the window of escape began to close behind them, his band of Theresiafelders had barely made it out of Yugoslavia alive. After witnessing the atrocities in Theresiafeld, he did everything possible to avoid Partisan or Russian soldiers on the road. He feared they might act out of vengeance against German civilians as they walked ever westward out of communist-controlled territory.

"Get your people to Linz," the German soldier said. "Pray to God the Americans get there before the Russians."

The Wehrmacht soldier pointed down the road past his checkpoint. It was clear he preferred letting a ragged Austrian move farther along in hopes he would take his hunger problems on to Linz.

"Let's move it quickly!" The priest yelled back to his fellow travelers.

As the sun dried mud into caked layers over Father Peter's boots, the starving Theresiafelders moved past the checkpoint toward Austrian territory still under German control. When he was serving at the tiny church in his Banat village, the priest had longed for the day when he could return to Austria. Now that Father Peter was back, the feeling of triumph was somehow missing, replaced by a deep concern for the welfare of these Banat Germans refugees from his village.

The group struggled along, walking for days and begging for food along the way before arriving at the outskirts of Linz. Several German soldiers directed them past their army barracks toward an abandoned government building used to house displaced individuals streaming out of eastern Europe. They walked the last several kilometers to the building, ashamed by their outward appearance under the stare of local Austrians who were obviously disgusted by the responsibility of housing additional refugees like them.

As the Theresiafelders entered the government building now used to house displaced individuals, the refugee coordinator gawked at them.

"Keep moving forward," the Austrian bureaucrat said.

The group was a cluster of ripped dark clothing tied together with the pots and blankets they had used to stay alive on the road out of Yugoslavia. Free of the cold wind blowing outside, the sound of several children coughing could be heard as it echoed off the interior walls.

"Who are you?" the Austrian bureaucrat asked while he looked the man over. The priest found it odd that he addressed him first, considering he wasn't the oldest nor was he wearing any priestly clothing.

"My name is Father Peter."

It was obvious he had been given the monumental task of coordinating refugee movement, trying to squeeze more displaced civilians into a building already bursting at the seams with other refugees arriving from the Banat.

"Where are you from?"

"My group is from Yugoslavia, a German farming village near Belgrade."

Father Peter spoke of his desperate situation with a thick Austrian dialect, hoping it would buy a starving priest some extra help in treating his group of exhausted Theresiafelders.

"We'll assign your group to some space in this building and get you something to eat."

After scribbling something on his paper, the bureaucrat passed out some empty, old bowls chipped along the edges of the rim. The sound of cast iron pans clanking against old spoons dangling off of leather belts could be heard as the refugees seated themselves.

Through the window, a group of wagons could be seen unloading supplies as each of them was shoveled several scoops of hot chicken soup. Father Peter gazed down the long row of tables as the band of broken, humiliated Theresiafelders sipped on bowls of soup in total silence. This was their reward for navigating under his leadership. Some donated food and shelter for the lucky few that managed an escape from the chaotic environment that now stretched across the Banat.

"What are we going to do, Father?" the orphan boy asked.

"Don't worry. We'll make it," Father Peter said.

The starving orphan continued lapping up his first full meal in days, but his innocent question weighed heavily on the priest's mind. What are these people going to do? Stripped of their land and possessions, the once proud, almost arrogant, group of Theresiafelders were a thoroughly broken people. With their labor, they had supplied generations with the bread consumed on tables across the Austrian empire. Never in their worst nightmares could they have imagined returning to where their story of emigration had begun hundreds of years before, begging for something to eat.

Over the following months, Father Peter remained with his fellow villagers in the abandoned government building, trying to help them establish some semblance of order to their uprooted, chaotic lives. The German military eventually surrendered in May, and Austria was divided into sectors. Thanks to the luck that seemed to be with him since he had avoided the Partisan gunfire, Father Peter's random decision to head to a refugee building in Linz happened to land him in the American sector when the war ended.

Unlike the sector of Austria under Russian control, Linz under American occupation seemed to provide additional opportunities for the enterprising Banat German refugee. Father Peter's old skill set at negotiating surplus cash from well-to-do families back in Vienna now morphed into negotiating with local Austrian contractors hunting for cheap refugee labor willing to wield a hammer. Fueled with some American money and a greater degree of liberty in the American sector, Father Peter helped many of the ex-farmers not killed in Theresiafeld land some work from the business class of Linz. As the reputation of hard-working Banat Germans grew among Austrians, the portion of food stamps allocated to their ration cards multiplied. With each passing day of sweat on a construction site or pushing a broom for food, his Theresiafelders' daily caloric intake increased, driving the immediate threat of starvation from their minds.

Over the passing months, the overcrowded conditions of the refugee housing complex became more manageable for Father Peter. Wire stretched along the walls of the building, allowing blankets to be draped over as makeshift barriers for semi-private living space. The priest's temporary accommodation was no more than the length of a simple cot surrounded by thin walls of cloth. His presence in the building enabled him to intercept a multitude of problems that came along with the psychological train wreck of a displaced people.

He heard someone with a thick Austrian accent call out, "Father Peter!" and pushed a dripping wet shirt hanging from a makeshift clothesline to the side to scan the area looking for the source of the voice.

"Over here!" he replied and waved his hand in the air, motioning the elderly priest in the distance to approach him. He swerved through the mass of refugee humanity who were busily attending to daily chores across the converted government building. The elderly priest's clean, well-groomed clothing stuck out like a sore thumb amidst the poorly clad expellees scrambling all around him.

"One of the American military officers told me a priest was living here. Why didn't you come by my parish and tell me you were in this God-forsaken place? I would have found some better housing for you."

Father Peter had been pegged by the American military early on as someone useful to help with the refugee problem in Linz. Entangled with a multitude of challenges, he hadn't had time to cultivate relationships with other clergy in a city overcrowded with refugees.

"I felt I could do more good by remaining here," Father Peter said.

He could tell the elderly priest found his passion for helping these Banat German refugees somewhat ridiculous. It was obvious the elderly priest's compassion for their situation was tempered somewhat by the nuisance in dealing with such a massive influx of humanity pouring over the Austrian border into his hometown.

"Why don't you come back to my parish, and let me get you some decent clothing."

"Sure."

Father Peter still wore the same rags he had smuggled out of his tiny parish the night he left Theresiafeld many months ago. Not a day had passed that he didn't think of the dead men lying in that ditch covered in mud. Father Peter still couldn't believe that he had survived the mass execution. It had been the pivotal moment in his life that changed his way of thinking forever.

"I don't know how we're going to find any more space to house all these refugees," the elderly priest said.

He followed the old priest out of the refugee housing complex toward his parish.

"Many are Germans, like us," Father Peter said. "Don't you think we have an obligation to help them out?"

The two priests cut around a corner, heading past a makeshift trading stand where a young boy was bartering cigarettes for an old pair of shoes.

"These so-called Danube Swabians, or whatever they are, have crammed into every corner of Linz. The people in my parish are disgusted at having to take them into their homes."

"We'll have to make do."

As they walked toward his church, the priest complained about the problems associated with housing such a massive number of refugees. Father Peter was surprised that he didn't agree with the elderly priest. The gift from God at being the lone survivor from an onslaught of Partisan gunfire had filled him with a seemingly bottomless well of compassion for the Banat Germans' desperate situation.

"What are your plans now that you're out of that mess in Yugoslavia?"

"At first, I had thought about returning to Vienna, but I've changed my mind."

"Where then?"

"I'm going back down there."

He looked at Father Peter as an outside observer views someone psychologically damaged from the stress of war.

"You're kidding, right?"

"The Roman Catholic Church needs a presence in Yugoslavia more than ever now that the communists are in control."

Father Peter had thought his life was over when he had faced the bullets of a firing squad of Partisan soldiers. He had emerged from the ditch outside of Theresiafeld free of his former twisted ambitions and released from his fear of death. The priesthood was no longer a tool to better his humble beginnings, but a true vocation, a calling to help the suffering and downtrodden. Father Peter wanted to return to the communist-controlled Banat and try to provide some religious presence in the oppressive situation down there. Maybe he would be killed or imprisoned, but he was not afraid.

"I almost forgot to mention something," the elderly priest said. "That American officer who told me where you were wanted to ask you a few questions."

He slipped an old key through a metal hole on the giant, wooden door to his ancient Roman Catholic church and moved inside. The interior of the building was ornately decorated with fine religious paintings and sculpture. Excluding the missing votive candles along the corners, it was a far cry from the appearance of his simple church in Theresiafeld.

"What do you think he wants?" Father Peter asked.

"Who knows," the elderly priest said. "It's probably another one of the endless questions about German refugees, trying to flush out war criminals. Let me write down his name and address."

The priest looked through the interior of a messy, paper-filled drawer in his ornate wooden desk. He tore off the bottom portion of an old piece of paper, hoping to save the upper portion for a future note in a city rationing precious paper.

"The American officer said he wanted to see you right away. His office is not far from here."

Father Peter's only interaction with American military personnel during his time in Linz had been in coordinating food and clothing rations for refugees in the overcrowded city. The tone of urgency regarding this meeting seemed different.

"If you want to see the American, you had better leave now. Wouldn't want you to miss the curfew and not have you back at your beloved refugee barracks."

He stretched out his wrinkled hand and forced the address of the American officer into Father Peter's palm. He could see the elderly priest was mildly entertained that an Austrian priest wanted to remain in the poor living conditions of the crowded housing facility. Father Peter changed into some of the surplus priestly clothing pulled from his extensive wardrobe. It felt good to drop the old rags he had worn through the brutal days and nights of his long walk out of Yugoslavia. For the first time, he looked like a priest from the outside as well as in.

As the curfew put into place by the American military drew closer, the crowds on the streets of Linz began thinning. He continued making his way toward an ornate building now occupied by American soldiers.

"Excuse me," Father Peter tried to get the attention of the man at the front desk. He cocked his typewriter back forcefully, waiting to hear his question before starting another line on the letter he was typing.

"I'm looking for this man," Father Peter said. The young priest pointed to the scribble on the slip of paper given to him by the elderly priest. He didn't want to say the name out loud, fearing he would mangle the pronunciation with his thick Austrian accent. The soldier pointed with his finger to the rear of the office and quickly returned to hammering out another line of text on the clean, white paper clinging to his typewriter.

"Yes, can I help you?" the officer asked in German when Father Peter approached his desk.

Although Father Peter understood, the American's German came out of his mouth like several sticks of gum were shoved inside.

"I'm Father Peter. You wanted to see me."

"One minute."

He moved his finger along a list of names in a notebook. After several minutes, he stopped and looked at the priest with confidence.

"Where are you from?"

"Theresiafeld, in Yugoslavia."

"Yes."

It almost felt like he knew the answer to that question before Father Peter had opened his mouth. It appeared even his priestly clothing didn't sway the officer from assuming everybody lied to him.

"Were there any German military officers in your group when you left Yugoslavia?"

"No."

Father Peter could tell the American wanted to separate the refugees who served in a command position in the German military, hoping to flush out additional war criminals who had managed to slip through the cracks. Several older men in his group had served a short time in the Yugoslavian army before the war broke out, but the young priest decided not to voluntarily give up that information.

"Come with me, Father."

Without saying another word, they shuffled out of his office and into another building. As they walked along the street, Father Peter began to go over in his mind the last several years in Theresiafeld. He grew a little nervous, recalling various military activities in his mind. He was fully aware of certain events in his tiny agrarian village that American military officers might question. Activities that might have proved detrimental to the Allies' war operation.

They entered a building used as a prison by the Americans for anyone captured in an SS or Wehrmacht uniform. A routine ritual in Linz was that service in the German military resulted in thirty days in prison before being released. The revolving door of an American prison holding cell gave returning draftees from the Banat an opportunity to put on some weight while serving out their short incarceration. Upon their release, the lucky ones found relatives still alive in a refugee camp somewhere in Austria who they could later link up with.

They walked down the long corridor of prison cells and stopped in front of a numbered jail matching the American officer's markings in his book.

"Do you recognize this man?" the officer asked.

Father Peter looked at the man lying on the fold-up cot, fiddling with a deck of Hungarian cards with the few remaining fingers still attached to his hand.

"Yes, I know him," he said.

"Who is he?"

"I don't know his name, but he's from Theresiafeld."

"Was he in the German army?"

Father Peter stopped for a moment before responding.

"No, not to my knowledge."

"Did you ever see him with this man?"

The officer pulled out a black and white photo of a man Father Peter recognized immediately. It was the young man he traveled with from Vienna, upon his initial arrival in Theresiafeld. He seemed different in the picture. He had an outward appearance of sophistication that he had lacked when Father Peter had known him in his farming village.

"No."

"Are you sure? Look again."

The interrogator waited for the priest's response, not convinced he had given the photo enough thought before his initial quick reply.

"The man in the photo is Hans Mueller. He worked for a large farmer who lived outside my village. I never saw your prisoner with him."

He continued drilling Father Peter with questions about Valmer, but his responses gave him no satisfaction. As the interrogation continued, Father Peter grew more interested in the man in the photo, but he feared asking the frustrated American officer any questions about him. After nearly an hour, he gave up the pursuit and slammed his book shut directly in the priest's face.

"Father Peter, you're free to go now," the officer said.

"Out of curiosity—" Father Peter began.

"I said you're free to go, Father."

Without uttering another word, the American officer motioned him out of the prison. As quickly as his feet could move, Father Peter motored through the abandoned streets of Linz back to his refugee housing complex, right before the mandatory curfew kicked in. He had withheld a tremendous amount of information from the American officer, but in his mind it was the right thing to do. The war was over, and the activities in Theresiafeld should be nothing more than a thing of the past.

As he eased into his rickety, old cot for the night, Father Peter wondered about Hans Mueller, the man in the photo. Over the next week, he tried recalling the man in the photo's activity in Theresiafeld, but he found nothing that would be of interest to the Americans. Father Peter had never wanted to develop a friendship with the hired hand of Reichinger or with anyone else in Theresiafeld, but he now regretted that decision, given the American officer's interest in him.

Father Peter sat on the cot in his sleeping quarters, repairing a ripped shirt with some thread and needle when he heard a voice ask, "Why did you lie?"

He dropped the damaged shirt and looked at the fold in a blanket hanging on the wire. The dark blanket forming a makeshift wall to his bedroom in the overcrowded refugee facility was disrupted. There standing along the edge of the rope was the Theresiafelder he had seen as a prisoner of the American military over a week ago.

"What do you mean?" Father Peter asked.

"Why didn't you tell the Americans everything about me?"

Valmer stared at the priest as he ducked under the rope and entered his sleeping quarters. He knew Valmer had done some contract work for the Abwehr, the intelligence-gathering agency of the German military. His travels across the Banat as a kupetz in his wine trade had enabled him to gather human intelligence that might prove valuable to the Wehrmacht. In one of Father Peter's drunken states, he had even agreed to let him store his radio transmitter in his church, in case the Partisans ever took control of the village. While under intense questioning from the American military officer last week, he had made the decision to protect Valmer's dark secret.

"Why did you help me, Priester?" Valmer asked again.

"What's the point? The war's over. You might have been executed as a spy if I had told them what you were up to in Theresiafeld. Enough people in our village have been shot or tortured. We don't need you to join the others."

"Your generosity is appreciated."

"How'd you get out of prison so fast?"

"The Americans released me based on your compelling testimony, I guess. Having the hard-earned tax money of Americans funding free meals for a poor kupetz from Yugoslavia seemed like a waste of money to them."

He bowed sarcastically before Father Peter in an amusing gesture of humble gratitude at withholding information from the American military.

"What's the American's interest in that man who worked on Reichinger's farm?" Father Peter asked.

An evil smiled cracked along the edge of Valmer's face. Valmer moved in closer before responding to his question.

"Hans Mueller was a spy working for the Americans."

A look of shock crossed Father Peter's face at Valmer's words.

"I can hardly believe it."

"The Abwehr had known of the existence of a mole in Theresiafeld for some time. I was given orders to root him out."

"What lead you to Hans being an agent for the Americans?"

"Believe it or not, at first I thought it was you, Priester, but I dropped that idea after witnessing your behavior in Theresiafeld."

It was Valmer's kind way of stating that a priest that drank too much was not the normal behavior of an American spy wanting to avoid attracting attention to himself. Father Peter peeled the blanket back, glancing to see if any refugees lingered nearby, eavesdropping on their conversation through the thin makeshift walls.

"Who knows how I figured out it was Hans. Maybe it was the way he talked. He used certain out-of-date words in conversation that nobody said anymore. It was as if someone plucked him out of the Banat as a child and stuck him back there years later. Maybe it was his card playing. No Magyar plays fuchser as bad as he did."

"Why didn't you turn him in to the Germans?"

"By the time I figured out he was an undercover agent, the Germans were losing the war, and the Abwehr had folded up. I figured the communists would take control of Yugoslavia, so I sold my land and abandoned Theresiafeld for the west."

"You are a clever cat," Father Peter said.

Valmer looked at him and laughed. The German spy's old-fashioned clothing advertised his Banat German heritage relative to the more modern attire of the natives of Linz. He seemed more orderly in appearance, not destitute like the other Theresiafelders in the refugee housing complex. Valmer had managed to get out of the Banat before losing it all, which made him a little smarter than the others from Theresiafeld scrambling in fear across the Austrian border.

"What's your plan?" Father Peter asked.

"I went into growing grapes years ago only because I managed to win some land in a card game," Valmer said. "I figure since I've been lucky with that, I might as well stick with it."

"Where you headed?"

"I'm going back to my original homeland before my family abandoned France for the Banat. I'm joining some other families who have a chance to farm again in a small town called La Roque sur Pernes in southern France."

Unlike most of the destitute Banat German farmers trapped in the refugee camp, Valmer seemed confident in his ability to remain in farming. Most Theresiafelders had mindlessly backed the Germans through the war, but Valmer had fought off the groupthink devotion and shrewdly sold off his land, enabling him to walk out of the Banat with enough money to remain in farming.

"Going back to France. What's wrong with Austria?" Father Peter said jokingly.

"The Austrians have their hands full with enough refugees. They don't need another descendant of French colonists from the Banat to house and feed. Besides, when they talk behind my back, I can't understand a word they're saying."

The Banat German dialect was different from the Austrian way of speaking, adding to the stress and miscommunication between the two groups in the overcrowded city of Linz.

Valmer and Father Peter continued chatting, going through the laundry list of the survivors they knew from Theresiafeld in a form of group therapy. An occasional joke thrown in the mix brought a brief respite from the atrocities recollected over the last year. In some strange way, Father Peter respected this shrewd gambler from Theresiafeld. He had maneuvered through the difficult conditions across the Banat, coming out clean and safe in the American sector of Austria. Valmer was a survivor who had managed to make it through the hard times without losing it all. He was the idealized image of Father Peter's former self before he managed to dodge the Partisan bullets and crawl out of the pit in Theresiafeld, forever a changed man.

"What are you going to do, Priester, now that the war is over?" Valmer asked.

"I'm headed back to the Banat," he said.

As he repositioned his three-fingered hand against the wire along the blanket wall, Valmer looked toward the ground and shook his head.

"You're not a bright man, are you, Priester?"

"Many Catholics are still in Yugoslavia. They need my help."

"Are any in the refugee camp buying into that stupid idea?"

"Some. Many have families still in the Banat. They're planning on going back."

"They're all fools, including you. We need to forget about our life down there and move ahead. Those days are gone forever."

"Don't you understand? I'm not like you. The church needs priests in the new Yugoslavia. I'm going to be there regardless of how hard things get."

In an authoritative manner, Father Peter sounded off about his compassionate position to the shrewd gambler from Theresiafeld. The priest truly believed in what he was saying, maybe for the first time in his life. With an arrogant smirk, Valmer smiled back at him. The concept of acting in a manner not consistent with his own self-interest was completely foreign to him.

"Come outside for a minute. I want to give you something," Valmer said.

Father Peter weaved alongside him through a cluster of refugees returning to the building barracks from their day labor jobs. They moved along the exterior brick wall toward the location of a horse and wagon. The priest could tell by the looks of his equipment that it was in excellent condition, not weathered from a long haul out of the Yugoslavian Banat.

"Where did you get the transportation?"

"Bought it right after the Americans let me out of prison."

Before the war ended, when the Germans still controlled Austria, any Banat German refugee managing to successfully escape from the Partisan onslaught in Yugoslavia had been rewarded by having his horse and wagon immediately confiscated by the German military.

"Jump on back here," Valmer said.

Father Peter hopped on the back of his wagon and helped him sweep aside a pile of old hay. Hidden under the straw was a large box, smeared with manure.

"What's that smell?" Father Peter asked.

"It's a combination of pig manure and sulfur," Valmer said. "I figure this should keep anybody away from my stuff."

Father Peter had seen corpses rotting on the side of the road as he had walked out of Yugoslavia. The rank odor from the animal manure covering his box smelled like a corpse mixed with rotting eggs. Father Peter gagged from the stench, covering his nostrils with an old, white handkerchief yanked from his pocket. Surrounded by farms, he had smelled plenty of manure back in Theresiafeld, but never this bad. Valmer smeared away a large clump of manure, exposing a keyhole near the center of the box. Unlocking the case, the priest could see a black Hohner accordion packed inside.

"Is this the right time for music?"

"Relax. I'm not going to start playing, Priester."

Manipulating the three remaining fingers not severed at his knuckle, Valmer unscrewed the front grill of the Hohner accordion. The handmade reeds providing the familiar musette sound were ripped out, replaced with several cloth bags hidden deep inside.

"I want to give you something for helping me out."

Valmer stretched out his crippled hand and handed him a carton of cigarettes. Cigarettes had replaced the German mark as the unit of currency in the black market underworld of Linz. The Banat Germans could not gain access to many needed supplies, now rationed under American occupation. Father Peter was a practical young priest and gladly took the cigarettes for distribution to other refugees who could use them in trade for rationed goods only accessible on the black market.

"Take this also. The Theresiafelders can use it to wipe their asses."

The priest took the worthless stack of old papiermarks he had wrapped in a rubber band. The old paper currency was left over from the hyperinflation days of the German Weimar Republic in the 1920s. Toilet paper was now hard to come by in the refugee camp, so the old paper notes made for a nice substitute.

As Valmer screwed the shell of his Hohner accordion back on, Father Peter caught a glimpse of the Hungarian gold coins and jewels crammed inside. The wise gambler's maneuver of converting farmland to hard currency before abandoning the Banat made for good insurance. Land formerly owned by Banat German farmers had been confiscated by the communists now in control of Yugoslavia. Valmer's entire net worth was hidden deep inside his Hohner accordion to begin the wagon journey for a new life in southern France.

"I can hardly believe it. Back to the Banat." Valmer shook his head in utter disbelief. The thought of returning to a communist country riddled with anti-German sentiment was unfathomable to a survivor like Valmer.

"My mind's made up," Father Peter said. "I'm going."

"I was always lucky in the Banat, Priester. Lucky at cards. Lucky to have my money. Lucky to be alive. But a smart man knows when to quit, and going back to the Yugoslavian Banat is pushing it too far."

"You may be right."

With his carton of cigarettes in hand, Father Peter jumped off the back of Valmer's newly purchased wagon. "I wonder if he made it out alive?" Valmer asked.

"Who?"

"You know, the American spy, Hans Mueller."

"I guess we'll never know."

Father Peter moved alongside Valmer's horse as he released the brake holding the wheel of his wagon in place. The curfew in place by the American military forbid anyone on the streets at night, but Valmer seemed unconcerned about the trivial regulation. With the destruction of the isolated German community in Theresiafeld, their lives were now on separate paths.

"Good-bye, Priester."

He stretched his three-fingered hand down from his perch, and Father Peter clenched it tightly in a last gesture of friendship. As Valmer shook his hand farewell, the animal manure concoction from the accordion case spread onto his own, covering his palm. The priest moved his filthy hand closer to his nose, gauging the power of the raw animal odor oozing off his skin. Valmer watched from his wagon as the priest squinted in disgust at the stench.

"Get used to the smell, Priester. All of us from the Banat now carry that stain for life."

Valmer cracked a last smile as his horse and wagon moved away from the refugee housing facility.

As Father Peter wiped the filth from his hand with his handkerchief, he thought about Valmer's last words. The Banat Germans now carried the negative stigma of backing the German military throughout the war. The error in judgment would probably result in brutal anti-German discrimination for those still alive in Yugoslavia for years to come. Father Peter would have to face those hardships when he returned to the Banat.

Father Peter remained in Linz for several more months, helping out where he could in trying to increase the quality of life for his band of Banat German refugees. Once he received approval from his bishop to return to Yugoslavia, the young priest packed a small bag of personal items and headed to the train station, determined to keep the Roman Catholic church alive under the communist authorities.

"Good-bye, Father Peter," a young boyish voice called.

Father Peter looked out the window of his railcar and waved back at the young orphan he had walked out of Yugoslavia with. His newly adopted parents and a handful of Theresiafelders came out to see him off at the Linz train station. It felt good knowing the people from his village respected his work in helping them cope with their difficult situation. He would be missed. Unlike Father Peter's first trip into Yugoslavia, he looked forward to returning and helping the survivors that remained behind cope in the new environment under oppressive communist leadership.

The man sitting across from him on the train fidgeted about, moving his hand through every pocket of his jacket in search of something.

"Shit!" he said.

"What's the problem?" Father Peter asked.

"I can't find my flask. I must have left it."

He continued fumbling through his pockets in a desperate attempt to locate his liquor bottle.

"Here."

Father Peter reached into his coat and pulled out the ornamental flask given to him years ago from his recently deceased benefactor, Tante Anna. It was one of the few items of value that he had managed to smuggle out of Theresiafeld under Partisan occupation. He hadn't taken a sip out of it since leaving Yugoslavia, but he kept it with him out of habit. The fidgety man took a large gulp of the vintage hard plum brandy he had grown accustomed to in Yugoslavia and handed the flask back to him.

"Keep it," Father Peter told him.

"What?" he asked.

"It's yours. I don't need it anymore."

Father Peter waved one last time at Theresiafelders gathered at the train station as his train headed east toward the Austrian border. He was on his way back to the Banat.

Romanian Banat

December 1944

Nadia angled the metal cup against my lips as the bad tasting fluid washed down my throat. "Drink some more, gadjo," she instructed me.

On more than one occasion, I had watched the blue-eyed Gypsy woman pick wild roots along the side of my covered wagon when we had stopped to rest the horses. The roots found their way into this vile-tasting medicinal tea I was now forced to consume in massive quantities.

"Move over!" The voice of the Gypsy leading our caravan could be heard over the pounding of raindrops hitting the cloth shell that bent over the wagon I recovered in. "Over! Over! Over!" the Gypsy said.

Our wagon splashed into the mud as we struggled to move away from an oncoming caravan of oversized wagons. I lifted the tarp protecting me from the harsh elements outside and glanced at the endless train of wagons passing in the opposite direction. The road came to life in sound as wheels rolled through puddles filled with rainwater. My eye was still swollen from the beating I had taken from the Partisan at the Nakovo work camp, but I could recognize the haunted, pale faces of Banat Germans tucked under dark blankets and coats rolling past me along the muddy trail. These ethnic German minorities were now on the move westward to Austria, trying to escape the Russian onslaught creeping farther into German-controlled territory. The square shape of the bulky wagons lumbering past me contrasted with the oval, sleek homes built for mobility that were waiting on the side of the road for their passing. Unlike the Gypsies I traveled with, these Banat Germans were out of their element. Forced into life as nomads on the backs of wagons built for work on a farm, these refugees continued westward, trying to escape the changing military front that had ripped a hole through the German villages of Romania.

"Go back to sleep, gadjo," Nadia said.

As I dropped the beige tarp covering the tragic spectacle of refugees on the run, I glanced back at the woman I had met in Theresiafeld. Why did she rescue me from Nakovo? What did she want from me?

"Why aren't we following those wagons?" I asked.

"We are meeting with other Lovari Gypsies." Nadia said.

"Where?"

"East, toward the Transylvanian Mountains."

"But—"

"You need to rest, gadjo. Go back to sleep."

As the sound of the last wagon wheel from the convoy of ethnic Germans rolled past me, our tiny caravan of Gypsies moved back on the muddy road, heading in the opposite direction deeper into Transylvania. Moving eastward, farther into Russian-controlled territory, made no sense, but I was too weak to ask any more questions. I let myself drift back to sleep, lulled by the rain tapping against the roof of the Gypsy wagon.

The next day, I awoke to the sound of our wagon shaking like the sharp bars beating against grain inside Reichinger's old threshing machine. I could feel my body sliding toward the back wall of the covered, dry wagon as the inclined road became more jagged with every passing kilometer.

"Where are we?" I asked.

I looked around the dry interior of my mobile hospital bed and noticed in the opposite corner the wrinkled familiar face of an old Gypsy woman. It was the same woman from my first encounter with these nomads when I had bought the horses for my now dead employer back in Theresiafeld. In my limited conscious state, the elderly, tiny creature would often climb in our wagon, keeping watch over Nadia until I fell back asleep. I could tell that my presence in such close proximity to her made the old Gypsy feel uncomfortable. I lifted the flap of my living quarters on wheels and noticed a horse limping along, tied to a piece of decorative scrollwork lining the edge of our wagon. Nadia walked alongside the injured animal, inspecting its movement as it hobbled along.

"Slow down the vardo," Nadia commanded.

Our sleek train of covered wagons shifted to a slow crawl up the incline. She continued shouting out orders as we moved along the bumpy road.

"Gadjo, you have to get up," Nadia said to me. "I'm sorry, but we have to walk the rest of the way."

The wagons came to a halt. I could hear the Gypsies shouting at one another in the secret language they alone understood. I slid out of the wagon that had served as my private bed over the last week and leaned against Nadia, trying to maintain my balance along the rocky ground below my feet.

"Can you walk, gadjo?" Nadia asked in German.

"I'll try," I said.

I began to move my feet. I was still weak and freezing cold from the fever, but I could move with some assistance from the woman.

Nadia placed a warm blanket over my shoulders as the group of Gypsies and I hiked up the side of the mountain. Through the foggy midst, I could see the jagged mountain peaks across the Transylvanian landscape. The view contrasted sharply with the smooth plains of the Yugoslavian Banat I had known as my home for the last two and a half years.

"Where are we hiking?" I asked.

"Our *vitsa* is joining other Lovari already at our winter camp hidden up this mountain," Nadia said. "You can rest there. The Wallachs won't bother us."

Apparently, the Gypsies felt more comfortable hiding from the military front in Romania rather than Yugoslavia. In the minds of my nomadic hosts, Romanians from the Wallachia were more docile creatures to deal with than revenge-filled Serbs from Yugoslavia.

"Try to concentrate on walking, gadjo," Nadia said.

We continued climbing up the uneven terrain. Under the influence of the fever, my weakened legs barely kept my rail-thin body moving forward, climbing ever upward toward the hidden camp tucked in the mountain. After rising along the near-vertical slope for a half-kilometer, I suddenly felt dizzy and collapsed into the arms of Nadia.

"I will carry him the rest of the way," a man said.

It was the familiar voice of the dark-skinned man who had appeared out of nowhere in my solitary confinement in the flooded basement back in the Nakovo labor camp.

"Hold on tight, John. Hold on."

As the petite stranger lifted me over his shoulder, it shocked me to hear my American name spoken out loud in English. He carried me up the last stretch of the winding road edging along the side of the mountain. The small band I had traveled with over the last several weeks finally arrived at their hideout on a dirt-covered plateau, high in the Transylvanian Alps. I looked around the entire open area with my one good eye. I could see the semicircular, canvas tents randomly situated across a camp filled with nomads of various ages.

"Put him in there," Nadia said.

My liberator from the Nakovo labor camp carried me past the tents bubbling out of the plateau like beehives along the side of the Transylvanian Mountains. We entered the mouth of a dark cave that burrowed into a rock along the edge of the plateau.

"Here!" Nadia said.

The English-speaking stranger dropped me on a dark cloth near a fire, and I fell asleep almost immediately from the exhausting climb. As I lay on the warm blanket near the hot ashes of the fire, the dream returned of a wagon full of early German colonists moving along the plains of the Banat toward their new home. The dream would start off peacefully, but then twist into a horrific nightmare. I could see the face of the Partisan I had killed in Theresiafeld laughing at me. Stripped of my ragged clothes and shoes, my body collapsed on a pile of rotting corpses on the back of a wagon of death. I would see the wagon wandering up and down the streets of Nakovo, gathering up new victims, an endless supply for the daily camp ritual of disposal in a mass grave. The image startled me awake as Nadia approached through the darkness from the other side of the cave.

"You must fight the demons, gadjo," she said.

I was partially unconscious, but I could hear her voice as she adjusted the string around my ring finger, hoping it would help me fight off the fever.

"I'm trying," I said.

"Fight hard if you want to win."

The process of sleep interrupted by periodic nightmares continued through the next week as my fever battled with the disgusting fluids the Gypsies forced down my throat.

I awoke to what sounded like a dog lapping up a bowl of water. I lifted myself to a sitting position and watched several Gypsy children flick their tongues along the surface of the fluid inside their small metal cups. The piping hot tea boiled in their cups, and small puffs of steam faded into the damp air of the cave.

"Gadjo, gadjo," they called as they stared back at me.

The children could see by my fair skin that I wasn't in their clan of Lovari Gypsies. Even at a young age, Gypsy children knew the difference between Rom, a member of their group and an outsider like myself. They continued prancing around my blanket, shouting the name given to all non-Gypsies, until out of boredom they ran out the mouth of the cave. I climbed to a standing position off my blanket, bracing myself against the cold, jagged wall of the cave. It was the first time I had managed to move in over a week since arriving at this hideout, high up in the Transylvanian Mountains.

"How are you feeling, John Miller?"

Near the entrance of the cave stood the dark-skinned man who had rescued me out of Nakovo.

"Who are you?" I asked.

He brushed his black hair to the side and walked toward me.

"I am a friend of the Fox, who else?"

He looked up at me and smiled. The man's features gave an outward appearance of being of mixed Gypsy ethnicity, but his English accent told the story of a different background.

"Who are you?" I asked again.

"I am a Ghurka officer working for MI6 British Intelligence. We had a hell of a time locating you. At first, we thought you were killed with the other German refugees in Yugoslavia."

"I guess I was lucky."

I struggled to continue walking, using the wall of the cave to provide support.

"The war in Europe is coming to an end, my friend. Our alliance with the Russians is beginning to unravel. As you are well aware, we never told the Russians we were using undercover agents in Yugoslavia. That's why I was assigned the mission to pull you out of there."

"I can't believe how bad things have gotten down there. What's going to happen to all those refugees we saw on the road?"

"Don't know for sure. Tito's consolidating his power as we speak, and we're going to lose another country to the bloody communists. Those German civilians we passed on those wagon trains are the wrong ethnic group in the wrong place right now."

Unlike myself, the MI6 agent seemed to have little concern for refugees on the run from the onslaught of Josip Broz Tito and his Partisans. On the surface, he struck me as a far more effective undercover agent than myself, more focused on his mission, less introspective about all this killing.

"How'd you link up with Nadia, that Gypsy woman?" I asked.

"Some of these Lovaris were entertaining some Partisans at a Serbian village. I happened to be asking some questions about you."

"Nice combination, a British intelligence officer using Gypsy subagents."

The British agent laughed as he watched me wobbling along the wall of the cave.

"To be honest, I probably wouldn't have found you without her help. This tribe of Lovari Gypsies has an information network in place that rivals the British and Americans."

"What's the plan now?"

"I sent a radio message that the Fox has been grabbed. We're supposed to wait for further instructions on what to do. That'll give you some time to recover."

"Do you think we're in danger here?"

I looked out the mouth of the cave and glanced at the dozens of canvas tents and burning fires spread across the plateau along the edge of the mountain. I thought back on my initial contact with Gypsies when I had purchased the horses for Reichinger more than a year ago. I knew these black-eyed vagabonds didn't take to outsiders like myself. I grew dizzy and took a rest along the uneven surface of the cave.

"I don't think we'll have any problems since we came with Nadia," the Ghurka said. "Besides, I'm paying them. If they didn't want us here, they probably would have eaten us by now."

"Right," I said. I tried to laugh, but my ribs were still sore from the beating I had taken from the guard back at Nakovo.

"Rest easy," he told me. "I'll check on you later."

The mystery man, who had slipped me the note hidden in the loaf of bread back at the labor camp, moved out of the cave. I let my weakened body drop back on the blanket.

This MI6 agent and I chatted periodically over the next several weeks while I recovered from my fever. While we hid in the camp with the Lovari tribe, no further word from the Office of Strategic Services came over his radio transceiver as to our next move.

As my recovery continued, the Lovari Gypsies gave me less of the horrible tasting medicinal drink and weaned me to some kind of fatty stew made from hedgehog meat. In our hideaway in the Transylvanian Alps, I knew this group of nomads was strapped for food, but the fact I was an outsider didn't leave me with fewer rations than anyone else in the tribe. It wasn't at all what I had expected from a group of Gypsies, whose mere presence in

Theresiafeld conjured up images among the Banat German farmers of suspicion and deceit.

As strength slowly returned to my sickly body, I ventured farther away from the safety of my cave. I wandered around the canvas tents that stuck out like oversize soccer balls buried partially in the rocky soil. I grabbed a long stick of firewood from a pile and used it as a cane while I toured the hideout. My eye was still partially swollen, making it difficult to balance myself. I watched a Gypsy craftsman scrape the exterior gold foil off a floral design on his decorative vardo. His pride in displaying the wealth that had covered his ornately painted wagon was now on hold. Gold exchanged for food and clothing now took priority among desperate Gypsies in the war ravaged Banat. As the confidence in my legs returned, I walked farther along the perimeter of the camp tucked high in the Transylvanian Alps.

"Dammit," I said as I toppled over my walking cane.

I looked down toward the ground and saw a spring-activated snare piercing the old leather boot on my foot. Removing my worn-out shoe, I inspected the damage done by the contraption. Luckily, the device, used to catch small animals roaming the mountainside, had only scratched the surface of my skin and didn't cause much bleeding.

I twisted my boot back on, working the Hungarian gold coin towards the front with my foot. I was surprised it hadn't been stolen from me during my time on the road. A Lovari man about my age moved over to me and yelled at me in his native Romani. I was clueless as to what he said, but it was clear he was more concerned about the damage done to his homemade snare than the excruciating pain throbbing under my boot.

"Gadjo!"

I could see the blue-eyed Gypsy woman stroll up the narrow mountain trail we had used to arrive at the hideout. She led a team of horses tied along a thick rope. The wrinkly, old woman that Nadia often spoke to told me she had left the camp almost immediately after we had arrived. She had traveled to a nearby Romanian town, trading a few horses to buy provisions for the influx of new arrivals at the camp.

As she moved toward me, I could see several of her companions maneuver the horses near a tree by jabbing the claw of a hedgehog into the animal's rumps, forcing them to move into position. A small bell connected to the Gypsy's waist rang out several times, tricking the animals into associating the painful prick from the claw with the ringing of the bell.

"So that's how you suckered me into buying that horse," I said.

The ringing of the bell could, for a short while, make a broken-down stallion like Mercy, the horse I had purchased for Reichinger, appear like a healthy, aggressive animal. I laughed at how clever the horse-faking trick was to an unsuspecting buyer like myself.

"You're learning the secrets of the Lovari, gadjo."

"I doubt that."

"Are the demons gone within you?"

"My fever's down. This string on my finger must have done the trick."

She stared at me somewhat confused, not at all amused by my sarcastic remark at the way her clan heals the sick. She spouted out a few words in Romani to her companions as they abandoned the two of us for the main camp farther up the rocky incline.

As Nadia and I walked in isolation along a rocky trail along the ridge of the mountain scrounging for food, we spoke of the harsh conditions that civilians endured across the Banat and the uncertain future of Theresiafeld. Like the Banat Germans of Yugoslavia, Nadia was concerned about her vitsa, the clan that had adopted her as a child, and the continuation of her nomadic way of life under the communists.

"Why did you help the British intelligence officer pull me out of Nakovo?" I asked her.

I could tell she felt uncomfortable with the question as we walked along the ridge.

"There is a reason, gadjo."

"What?"

She waited several moments before responding to my question.

"I wanted to find out what happened to Renate."

It wasn't what I wanted to hear. I had hoped she was interested in me, but I guess I was still perceived as an outsider, taboo for a Gypsy woman to pursue sexually.

"You mean Renate Reichinger?"

I found it amazing that this Gypsy woman possessed an almost obsessive interest in the daughter of my dead employer back in Theresiafeld.

"Yes."

"You're not going to like it."

She stopped walking along the thin trail carved into the Transylvanian Mountain. She had a nervous look in her blue eyes, but I wanted to tell her the truth.

"The Partisan soldiers arrived on Reichinger's farm to steal some supplies. I grabbed the old horse you sold me and was in the process of leaving Reichinger's burning farm. I shouted for her to come with me, but she refused."

"What happened to her?"

I didn't want to answer the question, as Nadia stood there traumatized.

"Being raped by a Partisan was too much for her. She committed suicide by drowning in the well not far from her father's compound."

Nadia stopped and leaned against a large boulder that rose out of the damp soil. It was obvious she was devastated by the news.

"I'm sorry, Nadia, I did my best to save her. You have to believe me."

I put my hands on her muscular shoulders as she continued facing away from me against the large rock.

"I wanted to be there for her," Nadia said as she began to cry.

"We've seen a lot of death over the last several months. Why is hers so important to you?" I asked.

I could see her tears run down the surface of the boulder. During my time in Theresiafeld, I had seen the tears of a Gypsy woman used as a weapon to get something she wanted, but I could sense this was genuine mourning.

"She was my sister."

I wasn't sure I heard the words correctly as she continued crying.

"What?"

"She was my sister, and she never knew I existed."

I turned her muscular body gently towards me. The color of her skin was darker than Renate's, but the resemblance could be seen in her blue eyes filled with tears. They were the eyes of her father, Johann Reichinger. It was all becoming clear to me how this Gypsy woman's life was linked with this wealthy landowner from Theresiafeld. Reichinger forced Nadia and her mother off the estate after upgrading to his second German wife, a maneuver that would increase his standing in the community of agrarian separatists who viewed Gypsies with contempt.

"I understand now why you hated Reichinger, and I wish I could bring back Renate, but I can't."

I gazed at her as she calmed herself. Renate was the last family member who had stood a chance of not rejecting Nadia because of her mixed ethnic origin, and she was now dead. The loss of her half-sister tested this strong woman, used to dealing with the hardships of nomadic life. I wanted to comfort her, but deep inside my reasons were also self-serving. I was tired of my detached existence in the Banat, serving my country without family around me. I longed for a sense of familiarity like I had known back on the streets of New York, in my own neighborhood.

I moved her muscular frame closer to me and pushed my lips against hers. I was tired of being alone and on the run. It felt good to feel a sense of intimacy with someone. I had desired her for a long time and hoped she wanted me as well. I was an outsider to the

Lovari tribe, and I knew it was strictly forbidden to touch one of their women, but I didn't care.

"I want to be with you, Nadia. I want you more than any woman I have ever known."

"No."

She pushed me away and took a few steps in the direction of the hidden camp farther up the rocky slope.

"This is not our way, gadjo."

From my interaction with other men in the Lovari tribe, I knew the price was high if a woman from her clan was caught with a gadjo like myself. Nadia's nomadic group would perceive her as unclean and permanently exile her from the rest of the Lovari.

I waited a moment before heading back to the campsite, hobbling back with the assistance of my makeshift cane. I knew she felt uncomfortable after my sexual advance, so she melted in with the rest of the nomads a safe distance from me. I regretted my decision to tell Nadia my true feelings about her. It was difficult to read this woman who had saved my life back in Nakovo.

The only surviving daughter of Johann Reichinger avoided me over the next several months. I knew she must feel uncomfortable after my taboo sexual advance. I remained in the hidden camp through the late winter, regaining my strength by feasting on the small animals trapped in snares that the Gypsies rigged along the mountainside. Unlike my fellow Theresiafelders, who were on the run or trapped in a labor camp, the Lovaris managed to tolerate the harsh conditions in their secluded mountain camp surprisingly well. Life was difficult high in the Transylvanian Alps, but nowhere near the brutal conditions that existed in the new labor camps popping up around communist-controlled Yugoslavia.

During the early spring, the Ghurka and I finally received a radio transmission that the Germans were on the brink of surrender. The two of us would receive new orders soon. Then I would have to leave the camp and probably never see Nadia again. As I slowly returned to my former self, my desire for Nadia did not abate. If I wanted to keep her, she would have to leave her tribe and come with me back to America. It was the only way. With the communists in control of Yugoslavia, Theresiafeld as a vibrant German community was probably destroyed forever, and I knew I could never integrate into this tribe of Gypsies. The only way for Nadia and me to make it together would be to return to America.

Late one evening, I watched Nadia from the mouth of my cave as she sewed a patch over the ripped canvas, repairing a leak in her bubble-shaped tent. She would only talk with me while in close proximity with others. I wanted to break the ice that had formed over the last several months, but I was nervous. I moved toward her in a desperate attempt at communication, as she mended the rip in her tent.

"I've been thinking about us, Nadia," I said. "There's no way I can remain in the Banat. The freedom Germans like myself once knew in Yugoslavia is now gone forever."

I stared upward toward the peaks of the mountains, moving in and out of view through the spring fog, struggling to find the words.

"I want you to come back to America with me. We've only known each other for a short time, but I feel it's the right decision."

She stopped stitching her needle into the canvas and turned toward me.

"You're an educated man with a future in America. Why do you want me?"

I could sense a slight insecurity in the Gypsy woman because of her mixed ethnic background. The woman still carried the scars of being rejected by her father and forced off the Reichinger farm with her mother because of their lower position in Banat German society. I could tell the other members of her clan didn't feel the same insecurity being around a Banat German like myself. To the others, I was nothing more then a gadjo, a barbarian eating their food. I was not a true Gypsy. I was not Rom. Nadia was different. She was at least partially like me, an outsider of Banat German background.

"You and I are the same," I said. "We're both outsiders among the Lovari. I know you were treated badly by the Banat Germans in Theresiafeld, but a part of you is still one of them. Only in America can you be totally free of all these ethnic tensions."

"What are you asking?"

"My mission is completed. I want you to marry me and return with me back to America."

She stared in disbelief at what I was saying.

"This is a huge thing you ask me to do, gadjo."

"It's the only way we can be together."

"You don't understand what it means to be a part of the Lovari and the work I had to go through to be accepted by this vitsa."

"Do you want to be with me?" I asked.

"I have never been attracted to a gadjo before, but you are somehow different, and I don't understand why. In many ways, I wish I had never met you. You have complicated my life beyond belief."

"I want you to think about it. I'll be leaving soon, and I want you to come with me."

As I moved back to my cave for the night, I felt empty inside at the thought of losing her to these long-haired vagabonds surrounding the camp. I envied the sense of community she felt with her fellow members of this nomadic tribe. Her ties to this band of Gypsies were strong, like the relationship I had with my father, even though I hadn't seen him in several years. I lay down on my blanket near the ashes of the fire and thought about how difficult it would be to convince Nadia to leave this nomadic way of life and trust an outsider like myself.

Romanian Banat
March 1945

From an early age, Nadia had learned through the culture of her Romani people to mistrust outsiders. Her German father planted that seed in her years ago when he threw her off his large farm along with her mother. Coming from the constant and familiar surroundings of Theresiafeld, the painful transition to her nomadic way of life was not easy. It took years before her final acceptance among the Lovari clan was complete. As years of nomadic life went by, a certain emptiness always remained with her. She was adopted into her nomadic vitsa at the age of 15, shortly after her mother died. A woman of her Romani ethnicity would have normally been married by that age, but her outsider status made her somewhat less desirable among many of the families looking to arrange a marriage for their sons. She was now 26, an older woman with few options to find a mate among the already-married members of the Lovari.

She was not committed to roaming the rest of her life on a trade route in the Banat carved out by the elders of her vitsa before her birth. The taste of a more sedentary life always lingered in the back of her mind, but the thought of returning to a separatist village occupied by mainly ethnic Germans disgusted her. After meeting the Gadjo from America, the thought of embracing a third path across the ocean with someone who shared a common childhood pricked an old memory she carried with her. Many years ago, she had met a woman from another tribe that crossed into the Lovari's territorial trade route. The woman's talent on the violin was exceptional. Nadia had heard of the woman's decision to leave her vitsa and pursue her musical talent in America. The freedom to chose a path free of the behavioral constraints imposed by her Lovari elders intrigued her.

Growing up rejected by her German father, Nadia feared excommunication by the Lovari. Running away with the Gadjo would mark her with the stigma of being a permanent outcast among her adopted tribe. The thought of being abandoned in America by a Gadjo without the safety net of her Lovari clan frightened her. She did not trust her judgment in this difficult decision and needed outside council. Sharing this risky idea with Bibi, her elderly companion, seemed the right thing to do. Bibi was a *phuri dai*, a woman in her vitsa who carried great influence on matters dealing with women and children. She had grown close to Bibi over the years and always respected her judgment.

"Bibi, I need to talk to you," Nadia said as she entered the tent of her close friend.

The wrinkly, leather-skinned woman set the pipe she was smoking on a smooth, flat rock shoved in the dirt on the dry floor of her residence.

"What is it, my child?" Bibi asked.

Bibi was known in the tribe as a woman who possessed a powerful intuition for dealing with the personal problems that existed among the members of her community. It was a gift that other members of her tribe respected, especially Nadia. Although she was born a Sinti Gypsy and not a true Lovari, Nadia was forever indebted to Bibi for convincing the clan to adopt her after the death of her mother. She would always turn to the wise, old woman in times of trouble, finding her advice worth taking.

"I am considering leaving the Lovari," Nadia said.

"What for, my child?" Bibi asked. "You've gained the respect of everyone in our vitsa. You're no longer a Sinti. You are Lovari, accepted by all members as equal."

"It's not my Sinti past that I hear calling. It is the Banat German side that awakens within me."

The woman, whose face was carved full of lines from age, took another smoke from her pipe and thought for a moment. Bibi was the only member of the tribe who knew of Nadia's German blood. If it ever leaked to the rest of the vitsa that she was half-German, her fate would be sealed as an unclean woman, banished from the Lovari permanently.

"Do you love this gadjo?" Bibi asked.

The old woman had guessed why she wanted to leave her adopted tribe. Bibi had watched Nadia care for the gadjo during his illness. As the wheels turned of the vardo, doubling as a mobile hospital bed for the sick gadjo, Nadia's attention to his needs seemed to only increase. "I think I do love him," Nadia said.

"I remember how hard it was for you when you first entered our vitsa. Always forced to do the most menial tasks as we roamed across the plains of the Banat. I watched as other members slowly began to accept you. Are you sure you want to give that up?"

"I'm not sure. I sense it's the right thing to do."

"You are a clever woman, Nadia. You are good at making money for our vitsa. What if the gadjo leaves you? Then you will have nothing."

"I thought about this. I hoped you could help me. I don't want to be outcast from the clan if I go with the gadjo."

Bibi thought for a moment as she took another drag from her pipe.

"What you ask will require a calling of the *Kris*," Bibi said. "Are you prepared to accept their decision?"

Nadia's blue eyes gazed at the cracked lips of her friend. She didn't want to run off in the middle of the night with the gadjo, leaving her forever marked by the other Lovari Gypsies as an unclean woman. She knew she had to endure a formal trial by the male elders of the Lovari in their winter camp.

"The judgment of the Kris could go either way. Are you sure you want to risk it?" Bibi asked.

"Yes, I'm sure."

Bibi puffed another cloud of smoke into the dry interior of her bubble-shaped tent. She knew it was her position in the community as the phuri dai to deal in matters of marriage and women. She loved Nadia like her own daughter and only wanted the best for her.

"I will call for a Kris tomorrow evening. The gadjo is forbidden to attend."

"I understand, Bibi. Thank you."

As she left the smoke-filled tent of her friend, Nadia knew the judgment of the Kris would be the final word on marrying the gadjo. It was a long shot that the male elders of the Lovari would allow her to remain in good standing with the tribe and let her run off with a gadjo, but she had to risk it. Everything she had worked for as a member of the tribe was now in jeopardy. If the judgment of the Kris ruled against the marriage and she left with him anyway, Nadia would be perceived by her fellow Gypsies as unclean and never allowed to return.

If she didn't pursue the gadjo, Nadia knew she would lose her one chance at loving a man who accepted her mixed ethnic origin. By marrying the Banat German gadjo, the insecurity of being rejected by her father would be washed away. She had to take the risk and face the Kris.

Romanian Banat
March 1945

Bibi's wrinkly face stared into the black eyes of the *bandolier* of the Lovari tribe. The new leader of the clan sat in the center of the cave surrounded by the other male elders of the Lovari. As the phuri dai of the tribe, Bibi rarely appeared at a Kris. Only when an issue came up regarding women and children did she need to face the men of her tribe, crammed around the firelight.

"We have a delicate matter to deal with," Bibi announced.

"What is it, woman. Speak your mind."

The bandolier's loud, baritone voice echoed throughout the cave as the packed crowd of men silenced their voices to hear the phuri dai.

"A woman in our vitsa would like permission to marry a gadjo."

The shriveled-up, female advisor knew the rules of the Rom: women of their tribe were strictly forbidden from marrying outsiders. Even marrying outside of their vitsa needed approval and would only be allowed if the union created economic advantage for both clans. Bibi was the only one who knew of Nadia's dark secret of having a gadjo father. If word ever spread to the elders that she was of mixed blood, they would banish her from the Lovari immediately, especially now, after formally announcing her interest in marrying the American recovering in their camp.

"Is she missing an eye or a foot that makes her undesirable to any of our own men?" the bandolier asked.

A roar of laughter from the elders echoed off the rocky walls of the cave. Those gathered were the heads of various vitsa now joined together to ride out the winter. This *kumpania,* or gathering of vitsa in the mountain camp, shared a common Lovari background. The elders in attendance carried the weight of decisions that affected the entire tribe.

"The woman I speak of who desires the gadjo is too old for our men. With the shortage of food and money, it would be a way to relieve ourselves of this burden."

Nadia was far older than fifteen, the normal age when a woman married in the Lovari tribe. Bibi loved Nadia like a daughter and didn't intentionally mean to degrade her in front of the group. In order for Nadia to get approval from the practical-minded elders, she needed to paint a picture that it was in the tribe's best interest to unload this undesirable creature onto the foolish outsider, now recovering from illness in their hidden camp.

The bandolier turned his head along the edges of the cave and watched as the elders whispered in one another's ears. With the death of the former chieftain of the Lovari in a German concentration camp, he was now the newly elected leader of his tribe. Choosing the most profitable migratory path for his vitsa in a communist-controlled Banat weighed heavily on the bandolier's mind. With the risk of starvation growing as the winter food supplies depleted, matters dealing with women were the furthest from his concerns. The bandolier rubbed his fingers against the black hairs stuck against his cheeks and thought about how the other elders might react to his decision if he didn't allow the Lovari woman in question to marry an outsider. It was important for the inexperienced leader to choose wisely. He wanted the other elders who had elevated him to his leadership position as bandolier to grow in respect of him.

"Bibi, as the phuri dai, your opinion is always valued. What is your feeling on this matter?"

The new bandolier wanted to maintain a good relationship with this old woman appearing before the Kris. It was important for him to have Bibi's input on these delicate matters in order to gain her support for future decisions he would be forced to make. The ancient female advisor wielded a tremendous amount of informal power in the vitsa. Alienating her so early in his new role as bandolier would be politically foolish.

"I have seen the signs that her heart is with the gadjo."

"Does the gadjo wish to remain with our kumpania?"

"The gadjo will be leaving soon and wishes to take the woman with him. We will then be relieved of two additional mouths to feed."

The bandolier rotated the golden ring on his finger as he thought about what to do. Normally, he would not approve of the woman marrying outside of the Lovari, but times were difficult. Shortages in food and clothing for his people were jeopardizing the survival of their nomadic way of life. It was important he maintain a practical edge on his decision this evening.

"Call this gadjo before us!" the bandolier ordered.

Several of the younger men moved out of the mouth of the cave and grabbed the gadjo, who was resting in one of the egg-shaped, canvas tents. After bringing him back near the firelight, they could see the fear in his pale face as he faced the wrath of the Kris.

"I do not want him here!" an elder shouted. "Gadjos are forbidden at the Kris."

"Silence!" the young bandolier shouted.

The bandolier gawked at the gadjo with his black eyes tucked deep within a layer of loose skin. The harsh conditions over the previous winter had melted away the thick layer of fat that had once stretched over his cheekbones. The new leader of the Lovari broke through the crowd and lumbered toward the pale-faced outsider.

"I know what you think about us, gadjo," the bandolier said to the man standing before him.

As he spoke, one of the younger men's black wool clothing rubbed against the gadjo's shoulder. He translated the sharp-edged Romani words into a broken German so the outsider understood.

"You view us as savages, less than you."

"How can that be?" the gadjo asked. "I want to marry one of your kind."

"Years ago, before the Schwabos existed on the plains of the Banat, the *voivodes* controlled the land. The great landowners enslaved my people, forcing us to work to the point of starvation. We escaped from them, hiding in these mountains where the soldiers could not hunt us down. They called us *Netotsi*, wild men who eat human flesh."

The assembly grew dead silent as their leader continued lecturing. Only an occasional pop bursting from a log on the burning fire could be heard across the damp cave.

"When the German military took control of the Banat, we were again enslaved, forced into their concentration camps for being lazy and unclean. Once again, we learned from our past and hid in the mountains like the Netotsi of long ago. You see, gadjo, both of these groups are now gone, but we remain. The Germans who lived on the plains of the Banat are now dead or leaving, but the Roma remain. That is what makes us more powerful than you, Schwabo. That is what makes us better than you."

The bandolier moved closer to the gadjo's face. The tiny jewels hanging from a golden bracelet on the bandolier's wrist jingled as he squinted his dark, beady eyes through the gadjo's trembling soul. From his travels across Romania, the bandolier had moved through many Banat German villages. He knew first-hand the negative perception these German farmers had of nomads like him, and had learned through the years not to trust them.

"Do you love this Lovari woman, gadjo?"

"I know I am not Rom," he responded. "But I do love her."

The bandolier's facial muscles began to relax. "What can you give us in exchange for this woman?" he asked.

The practical-minded bandolier waited for a response from the gadjo standing before him. After a short pause, the leader of the Lovari tribe watched as the gadjo slipped off his worn, leather boot and pulled out a Hungarian gold coin.

"My father gave this to me for good luck," the gadjo said. "It's the last item of material value I possess. I give it to you freely in exchange for the love of this woman."

As the shiny, gold coin lay on the palm of the bandolier, he studied the piece carefully, making sure it wasn't a fake. Like all Gypsies, his love for gold and jewelry was only exceeded by a desire to live free and roam across the plains of the Banat as he pleased.

The bandolier fiddled with the gold piece for a moment and placed it in his pocket. The leader of the Lovari clan then pulled out a small knife from a tear in his pants leg and pointed it at the startled gadjo. He could see the gadjo was terrified as he took several steps back. In one swift motion, the bandolier slid the sharp edge of his knife over his own wrist, allowing the blood from his veins to drip onto the rocky floor of the cave.

"Stretch out your arm gadjo," the bandolier ordered.

He could see the fear in the gadjo's eyes as he moved closer towards him. The bandolier made a long, violent cut across the gadjo's wrist, watching his face closely with his black eyes, gauging his strength as he endured the pain from the incision.

"You are now *Phral,* young gadjo, a brother to the Rom."

The bandolier pressed his bloody wrist against the gadjo's bleeding wound as the crowd in the cold mountain cave howled like the wild wolves that roamed across Transylvania.

As their blood mixed together, the bandolier continued to stare into the gadjo's pale face. The blood oath was sealed; the gadjo was now an adopted member of this nomadic group of Lovari Gypsies, as Nadia had become as a young girl, after her mother died. The word of the Kris was now closed. The gadjo was officially no longer an outsider, but a blood brother to the Rom for life.

Romanian Banat

May 1945

I stayed with my adopted brothers of the kumpania of Lovari gypsies in our mountain retreat a few additional months. The chaotic situation across the Banat complicated matters for the male elders of the various vitsa, delaying their exit from their winter hideaway to pursue agreed upon trade routes still not finalized. My limited conversations with the leader of this band of Gypsies through Nadia as an interpreter had hinted at a number of concerns for his tribe. The uncertain future in his nomadic territory now controlled by communists along with the food supply challenges weighed heavily on his mind. Before abandoning their winter camp, a simple wedding celebration to lift the spirits of his fellow tribal members seemed practical.

"John and Nadia stand before me," the bandolier said.

I was no longer an outsider to the Lovari Gypsies surrounding the open area along the mountain ledge covered in fresh, green grass. As Nadia and I approached his elevated location, it felt good hearing my American, real name coming from this Gypsy leader. I was no longer a gadjo to him, a necessary condition if I wanted to take Nadia's hand in marriage.

"The *darro* has been paid by John to have this woman," the bandolier said.

He held up my father's Hungarian coin for all to see. The simple gesture was proof to all that were present that payment had been made to take Nadia as my bride. The bandolier moved his black eyes over Nadia, studying her to confirm my one gold piece was adequate compensation to take the woman as my bride. Nadia was way beyond the normal age of marriage and with her family all dead, no one was present to question the adequacy of my payment for losing a daughter.

The bandolier grabbed my wrist, still scarred from the ritual of acceptance as a blood brother to the tribe, and placed my hand into Nadia's.

"Be faithful to each other," the bandolier said as he smiled at us. "The *abiav* is completed. Let the celebration begin!"

Howls and applause from the male elders echoed off the rocks along the side of the mountain. The bandolier's simple gesture was all that was needed in the eyes of the elders to signify the two of us were married. I watched as Bibi tied a head scarf around Nadia's head. The scarf signified to all in her tribe that she was no longer a single woman. Nadia was now free to leave her vitsa with her husband, released of the stigma of being labeled unclean for wanting an outsider. I watched as the bandolier gave a quick glance at the phuri dai who had pleaded on Nadia's behalf to allow the marriage. Bibi nodded back to him, acknowledging his act of practicality at accepting the American as an adopted member of the Lovari tribe. The act of making the American a phral, a blood brother to the Gypsies, gave Nadia an opportunity to rejoin the tribe if he ever abandoned her.

That evening, several of the Gypsies poured what beer remained of their rations into several metal buckets as castanets and violins played in celebration of the new blood brother of the Lovari in his marriage to Nadia.

"I am one of you now, Nadia. I am no longer an outsider," I said.

I huddled in close to Nadia near the fire. As a blood brother to the Roma, my close proximity to her was no longer taboo and not to be feared.

"I know why you wanted the elder's approval in marrying me. You wanted to be able to return to your tribe if I abandoned you."

"That's not true."

The blue-eyed Gypsy woman was lying, but her face gave no indication of the deception. It was the blank facial expression learned through years of practice as a horse-faker in dealings with non-Gypsies.

"What Reichinger did to your mother will never happen to you," I said.

"My life is with you now, John, and not with the Lovari. I will go where you lead."

I knew the pain she carried with her from Reichinger's abandonment back at Theresiafeld. She was a practical survivor, and I couldn't blame her for wanting to protect her position among the Lovari. She wrapped her muscular arms around me as the small band of ragged-clothed musicians played through the night.

The next morning, I approached a tent some distance from the main Lovari camp where the Ghurka made his temporary headquarters. He was sharpening his kukri with a small auxiliary blade as several Roma children watched in close proximity.

"Congratulations, John, on your marriage," he said. "When you make your final report to the European desk back at OSS, send me a copy. It should make for interesting reading."

I squatted down next to him as he mocked my decision to marry Nadia.

"Maybe if you're nice to them, they'll let you in as well," I said.

The Ghurka lifted his eyes from his knife-sharpening task and stared at me. He was not amused by the sarcasm. He lay his kukri on its leather sheath as he continued to lecture me. His limited stature did not detract from his intimidating presence.

"Ridiculous! The whole lot is nothing but a bunch of savages."

"These Lovari helped you pull me out of that labor camp in Nakovo," I said.

"I'm beginning to question that decision."

I decided to ignore that one.

"Any word on orders?" I asked. I stared at the Ghurka's curved blade lying on the leather scabbard, using it as a mirror as I rubbed my eyes in an attempt at getting the redness out from last night's wedding celebration.

"I'm afraid your days as a Gypsy are over before they even start."

"What do you mean?"

"The Germans surrendered. The war's over my friend."

It was May 1945. It felt good hearing the British intelligence officer's word of the Allied victory. "I'm afraid it's time to leave behind the life of a carefree Gypsy and return to your own world."

The man's white teeth contrasted with the dark complexion of his face as he smiled.

"Your orders are to make your way north through the Transylvanian Alps to a Romanian city called Sibiu. Your contact person will rendezvous with you at the train station there."

"How will I recognize him?"

The Ghurka glanced at the scribble written on his piece of paper. He checked for any omissions from the translation of the coded signal received over his radio transceiver.

"Doesn't say. He'll know who you are. I doubt if you'll have any problems. These Romanian communists aren't nearly as interested in rooting out American spies as the Serbs are."

"Aren't you coming along?"

"No."

"Where are you headed?"

"My orders are to head eastward. We have a few other loose ends to clean up now that the war's over. That's all I can tell you."

The Ghurka was far more committed to duty than I was. It made sense that British MI6 would continue using him in communist-controlled territory while the Americans wanted to pull their own man out.

"By the way," the Ghurka said. "I didn't mention in the transmission any of this nonsense with the Gypsy woman."

I waited a moment before responding to his subtle insult.

"I'm bringing her with me. My decision is final on this."

I could see a line become visible on the Ghurka's dark cheek as he reattached the leather scabbard along his belt. The committed British officer wasn't pleased at the decision to mix espionage with personal desire.

"The Allies are not in the business of smuggling Gypsies into the American sector. I used the woman to get you out of Nakovo because it aided in the primary objective. Her role in all of this is now over. "

"I don't care. She's coming with me."

There was controlled anger in the Ghurka soldier's eyes as they turned a shade darker.

"Think about it for a minute, John. This all seems normal right now, but when you return to America to some job as an attorney, do you want some low-class Gypsy woman as a wife?"

I didn't appreciate the negative comment about Nadia, but the man had saved my life and was entitled to some emotional control on my part.

"She's only half Gypsy," I said. "The other half is ethnic German like myself. I don't care what the consequences are back in the states."

I sensed from our previous conversations that the Ghurkha did not view my service record as an undercover operator as exemplary. My decision making since my rescue in Nakovo had only reinforced that impression. Falling in love with a Gypsy, even one as attractive as Nadia, was a breach of his strict code of discipline. Although tied to the woman by a common origin over a thousand years ago, he obviously felt this woman was nothing more than a tool to aid in the mission at hand. Now that my mission was over, keeping the Gypsy woman around seemed a waste of time.

"You have your orders. Do what you want."

The Ghurka walked away in disgust. He knew I had made up my mind, and there was nothing more to say. Within three hours, the Ghurka had abandoned the Gypsy camp and vanished out of the Transylvanian mountain hideout. His mission was completed with his stellar reputation as a Ghurka officer intact. He was gone before I could thank him for saving my life in Nakovo.

"Nadia," I called. I pushed the canvas flap of her tent to the side and entered.

"Yes, John, what is it?"

She stopped running the chipped edge of a decorative plate against the smooth surface of a gray, flat stone and looked up at me.

"It's time to go."

"So soon? Can't we stay a few more days to say goodbye?"

It was going to be a huge step for her to leave this tribe of Lovari Gypsies, giving up the life of a nomad to follow me. I was now Phral, a brother to the Gypsies, but I still felt like an outsider. She knew I could never truly fit into this nomadic lifestyle and that accepting me as her life partner meant leaving her family for good.

"My government has given me a way out of the Russian-controlled area. We have to be in Sibiu in three days if we want to get back to the American sector in Austria."

My mystery contact person didn't know that Nadia was tagging along, which could result in complications in our final escape back to the American sector. I didn't want to mention anything to Nadia about the level of difficulty in smuggling her out of communist-controlled territory, fearing she might change her mind and stay with her vitsa.

For the next several hours, Nadia traded with several woman in her vitsa a few of her personal items in exchange for whatever food could be spared. The trade was practical considering some of her possessions would be too cumbersome to carry on the long walk into Sibiu. Nadia grabbed a few metal pots and several blankets and packed them in a bag sewn together from pieces of burlap. "I have to say goodbye to Bibi," she told me.

I could tell she was terrified at leaving the only family she had known since childhood. There was an uncomfortable silence between us as I followed Nadia to the edge of the camp. She wanted to say a last farewell to the ancient woman who had pulled off the impossible by preserving Nadia's good standing in her adopted tribe of Gypsies.

She ducked under the open flap of the old woman's patched canvas tent as I followed in behind her. Bibi stopped cleaning her pipe and placed her bony arms around Nadia. No words were spoken between the two women, as they held each other one last time in total silence. It was the end of Nadia's nomadic life, and Bibi knew it. The old woman, whose lined face looked like a map of the dusty roads that linked the villages of the Banat together, opened her glossy, dark eyes and stretched her hand out for me to come forward. I could tell by the sincerity of the old woman's embrace that I was no longer perceived as a gadjo. Her cautious air when I was in close proximity to Nadia had vanished like the smoke from her pipe. The three of us sat in a huddle along the floor of her canvas tent.

"You are now a blood brother to the Rom, my friend," Bibi said. "You will be this the rest of your life."

She glanced at the scar on my arm left behind by the blood oath. I sat in silence as the two old friends chatted in the secret language only the Roma understood. "She wants to tell you something," Nadia said to me.

I looked at Nadia as she translated the words coming from Bibi's mouth.

"Always help brothers. Never harm brothers. Always pay when you owe, although not necessarily money, and never be afraid, John. Never be afraid."

I looked at her face and smiled, acknowledging an understanding of the proverb. It was the philosophy of the Roma I had only begun to grasp. These nomadic travelers of the Banat were more than dirty thieves who robbed from the German farmers, as I had learned from my father's stories of his time living in the Hungarian Banat. Their culture and way of life was more complicated than that. The Roma cared little for those who were not of their clan, but to an insider, these dark-skinned nomads showed a level of caring the likes of which I had never felt before. After a last hug, the two of us left Bibi's smoke-filled tent.

"Are you ready to go, Nadia?"

"Yes I am, Jon-neeh," she spoke the American name awkwardly, but I liked the sound of it.

I stuck my fingers through an old rope, which looped around a rolled up blanket filled with supplies, and swung it over my shoulder. Nadia took a last look at the Lovari camp hidden in the Transylvanian Alps and followed me down the incline. The priorities of Nadia's vitsa were now avoiding hunger in the Banat, the former bread-basket to Europe now teetering on the brink of starvation because of the war. The two of us snaked along the edge of the mountain to begin our long journey toward Sibiu to meet my contact person.

Romanian Banat

June 1945

I pushed the blanket off my body, startled awake from my sleep on the dry, valley soil by the reoccurring nightmare that plagued my mind. The image of dead Banat Germans loaded on a wagon for disposal out of Nakovo continued to haunt me, months after my escape from the labor camp.

I looked along the Turnu Rosu Pass, whose dirt road split the Transylvanian Alps down the middle, like a butchered hog ripped open along its belly at a Schlachtfest in Theresiafeld. I could see the naked body of Nadia, kneeling in the distance ahead of me as she gazed into the fading light of the new moon. I moved down the incline and quietly approached her from behind.

"The new moon has come out," Nadia said. "May she be lucky for us. She has found us penniless. May she leave us with good fortune and with good health and with money."

"Do you think the moon is God?" I asked.

She moved off her knees and turned toward me in the darkness.

"God is God, but the moon is for luck."

She returned in silence to her pile of clothing and dressed in the darkness before the light of morning broke over the Transylvanian Alps surrounding us.

"When do you think we'll reach Sibiu?" I asked.

"We'll get there by this afternoon. I want to beg for some food before we head to the train station."

Her travels with the Lovari Gypsies had moved her through this valley many times before. After walking the last ten kilometers through the pass, we knocked on doors of the Romanian, thatch-roofed homes that dotted the road into Sibiu, begging food off the Wallachs who lived there.

Traveling by foot over the last week, I was impressed with Nadia's survival instinct. Her keen eyes caught opportunities at every turn. She acquired an old head scarf at one house and then traded it for a portion of salt at the next one. Her urge to survive never seemed to shut itself off or grow tired as we continued marching northward.

I could see a vandalized sign angled on its side with the name "Hermannstadt" signaling our close proximity to the city of Sibiu. It was the Germanic name of the town during the time when the Transylvanian territory we hiked over was still part of the Austrian empire. We arrived at the train station in the late afternoon, according to our instructions received over the Ghurka's radio receiver.

As I thought about my next move, I took a glance at a leaflet pressed against my hand that braced my exhausted body from collapsing. The flyer was filled with German names of displaced families and the location of refugee camps where they were located in Austria. Returning ethnic German soldiers from the Banat could use the list as a guide in reuniting with their families who had abandoned their villages in Romania for the safety and freedom of the West.

"John?"

"Yes?"

"What's the plan?"

I could tell Nadia wasn't comfortable with the notion of giving up control to a non-Gypsy like myself, even though she had agreed to leave her band of Lovaris to follow me.

"I guess we wait and hope my contact person finds me."

We placed our blankets over a bench in the Sibiu train station and began eating some bread smeared with a thick layer of goose fat given to us by one of the Wallachs. I looked around the station that alternated every hour from frantically busy to abandoned, depending on train arrival times. Occasionally, a Russian in military uniform wandered past us and looked around suspiciously. I always stared at the communist soldier, hoping it would be my contact person in disguise.

Most of the Wallachs moving through the station paid little attention to the two of us, dressed in our filthy, ragged clothing, waiting for my contact to magically appear. My new cover as a poor refugee with his wife of mixed Gypsy origin, trying to find a niche for ourselves in communist Romania couldn't have been orchestrated better if my superiors back on The Farm had planned the whole thing out.

"There he is."

I looked at Nadia's face as she moved her blue eyes in the direction of a man in worker's clothing entering the open waiting area of the Sibiu train station.

"How do you know?" I asked.

"It's him," she said.

Who knows what lead her to believe that was our man. Maybe it was his clothing, not wrinkled enough for a manual laborer or his weight, not malnourished enough, like the typical civilian who had suffered during the war in Romania. Nadia's intuitive ability to spot our contact person must have been honed over years of making a living in the horse trade, noticing subtle nuances in potential buyers as she manipulated them into purchasing one of her broken-down stallions. Call it woman's intuition or a secret power that only the Gypsies possessed. Either way, Nadia seemed to sense the opportunity.

I watched the mystery man take a seat across from us and open a Romanian newspaper, now filled with the latest communist propaganda. The man dressed in wrinkle-free, working clothes sat for several moments until a crackly announcement came over the speakers, starting the crowded station into a massive reshuffling of bodies. The 6 p.m. arrival of a 5 p.m. train triggered the stranger to leave his seat and join the herd of Wallachs passing our bench in a chaotic frenzy. The mystery person moved toward us, and I could feel Nadia reposition her hand closer to the hidden dagger tucked under her long, patched skirt. As the sounds of Wallachs shuffling their luggage echoed through the station, the stranger stopped in front of us for a split second and stared at the two of us. Without a word, the man dropped his propaganda-filled paper on our wooden bench and continued following the crowd of Wallachs toward the late departing train.

I reached for the paper and rolled it up in my hand. Scanning the station, I looked at the faces of roaming Wallachs hustling toward their departing train, worried that one of them might have caught the hand-off of a newspaper and turn us in to the authorities. My contact person made a final glance back at my location, confirming I had the paper in hand before abandoning the Sibiu station for his late-departing train.

"Open it up, and see what's inside," Nadia said.

I began to slowly unroll the crumbled paper with my trembling hands, turning the pages of propaganda with my fingers, now callused from hard work on Reichinger's farm during the last two years. I tossed several pages of empty communist promises to the dirty floor, allowing the rag to mix with a layer of cigarette butts surrounding us. After discarding half the pages, I could see an envelope taped to the center of the black and white print.

I removed the envelope from its position and ripped the fold with my ring finger. I could see the lighter skin tone around my finger leftover from the string used by the Gypsies, supposedly to cure my burning fever. The envelope contained some Romanian currency as well as a passport with my new Austrian identity. The high-quality, fake passport would allow me to cross through the Russian-controlled sector of Austria and into freedom under the Americans.

"I'll go purchase the tickets," Nadia said.

She grabbed the Romanian lei out of my hand and moved toward a wooden booth to get some train passes into Austria. It felt like only yesterday that I had sat on a bench like this one back in Vienna, waiting nervously as I made my debut as a deep undercover operator in Yugoslavia. There was not much left of the young, idealistic lawyer who had enlisted in espionage training several years ago. The son of a German immigrant born in Hungary looking to better himself in life by having an attractive service record tacked on his resume was forever changed. I felt scarred in some way because of my espionage experience in the Banat over the last several years.

"Train bound for Arad, now boarding!"

The crackling sound bellowed out of the speaker, indicating the late arrival of the train that would take us into the American sector of Austria. The shuffling of Wallachs started once again as we scrambled to get a position in the long boarding line.

"How am I going to cross into the American sector?" Nadia asked.

"We'll worry about that later."

Nadia didn't have a valid passport, creating a potential problem when we arrived at the last Russian-controlled train station before crossing into the American sector. I had to figure out a way to smuggle her across, but at this point in time I didn't have a clue.

"Why not give me the money, and I'll go it alone by foot."

"Absolutely not. If you're picked up by the Russians you could be sent to a labor camp."

Back at the Gypsy hideout in the Transylvanian Alps, the Ghurka soldier told me how single women without children were being picked up and loaded onto trains bound for Russia. Communist countries like Romania had a quota requirement of manpower to send to Russia for the reconstruction effort now underway. Stalin was exploiting not only Banat Germans but also other ethnic minorities like Gypsies in the form of slave labor taking place in Russia.

"Ticket please."

An elderly Romanian conductor punched our tickets and wobbled farther down the center aisle of the moving train. I drifted off to sleep, using the upper part of Nadia's muscular arm as a pillow. I considered myself fortunate to have some money in my pocket, allowing me the privilege of riding a train, as opposed to walking out of the Banat.

As the train retraced the path that had brought me into the Banat, I could see out my window the occasional ethnic German village with its rows of whitewashed houses now streaked in brown mud, signaling their abandonment. After a brief stressful stop at the Romanian city of Arad, our train crossed the Tisza river and into the Hungarian Batschka. It was my first time out of the Banat since my arrival three years ago, and it felt good to be free of that mess.

"We've got to plan this out, Hans. Russian guards are going to be crawling all over that last station in Austria."

"I wish I had an answer to give you, but I don't."

As we buzzed through the Hungarian countryside, I moved my eyes away from the window and stared at the sullen face of Nadia. The ease of passing through Russian-controlled territory would end soon, and we'd be forced to confront the difficult task of crossing into the American sector along the Enns river line. I rubbed my arm against her shoulders in a simple gesture to ease the tension.

"I'm sure we're almost at the last Russian controlled station," Nadia said.

"Wait here. Don't move until I get back," I said.

As the train moved ever closer toward our last hurdle with Russian patrol guards, I jumped out of my seat, struggling to balance myself as we continued rolling through the Austrian countryside.

"Watch it!" the Russian said.

"I'm sorry. Excuse me."

As the air breaks jolted the train to a slower speed, I lost my balance as my filthy clothing smothered against a red bandana around the neck of a communist passenger sitting in the aisle seat.

"I'm sorry."

I made a casual gesture to apologize as he pushed me away. As I moved away from the angry passenger, I regretted being polite to him. My hatred for communists now exceeded that of my father. It was now a part of me like the memorized cipher that aided their cause against the German military. I would never forget the brutal killing of all those Banat Germans in Theresiafeld.

The diesel-powered locomotive slowed even further as we approached the border station, separating the American zone from Russian-controlled territory in Austria. I moved toward the front of the train and stopped in the open area, separating the last passenger car and the conductor's private railcar. As I casually glanced through the small, rectangular window dividing the worker's area from the rest of the train, I could see the railroad employees dressed in dark jackets playing cards. They appeared unconcerned about approaching a mythical line marked along the Enns River, which allowed Banat Germans like myself to escape communism for the freedom of the west.

I pulled out a last cigarette and smoked casually as the workers tossed their Hungarian playing cards onto a stack in the center of the pullout wooden table in their cramped quarters.

"Back to your seat!" the conductor said.

"Is this the last stop in the Russian sector?" I asked.

The Romanian looked at me like I was mentally handicapped. It was obvious he heard the question many times before.

"Yes. Next stop, St. Valentin."

I dropped my cigarette onto the metal floor, struggling to keep my balance as the two adjoining railcars slid in opposite directions under my worn out boots.

I walked down the center aisle of the passenger car, catching a last glimpse of the conductor as he began scrutinizing passports. I could feel the humid air amidst the refugee clutter rubbing against the sleeves of my tattered jacket as I pushed down the center aisle back toward my seat. I knew the stakes were high from the Ghurka's intelligence reports. Ethnic German refugees left in Russian-controlled territory faced terrible discrimination or, worse, starvation if sent to a labor camp. The anxiety I felt about the tight controls in place at this border station was now a reality. Only the lucky few with the right paperwork could remain on the train and cross over to the American sector of Austria.

Sweat began dripping down my neck at the realization of Nadia potentially being pulled from the train. I was confident that my passport would let me cross into Austria, but Nadia didn't possess one. I feared the worst, as visions of her dying of hunger in some freezing hole, used for temporary housing of slave labor in Russia, entered my mind.

"Come on!" I said to her. "We have to move!"

"What's the problem?" Nadia asked.

"They're checking. They won't stamp your ticket unless you have a valid pass!"

I grabbed her by the fleshy part of her muscular arm and pulled her out of the seat, moving her toward the rear of the train. We moved through the coaches, avoiding as much eye contact as possible with passengers on both sides of us.

"We've got to jump!" I said.

We moved through the last door of the railcar to an outside balcony fenced in steel. My voice could barely be heard over the rattling of the wheels and the sound of the train engine as I scanned the terrain along the tracks.

"Let me jump, I'm the one without the passport," Nadia said.

"Forget it! We're in this together!"

Even if she managed to sneak across the Austrian border, I knew it would be an impossible task to try and find her again. Nadia would be lost amid thousands of refugees corralled into housing facilities for displaced civilians across the American sector.

"Let's do it!"

Jumping off the train would be more difficult than I had originally thought. Even though the train decreased its speed as we approached the border station of St. Valentin, the tracks were elevated high over the ground, dropping off sharply on both sides like a cliff.

"This isn't the best spot to jump, but we have to do it!"

As the tracks curved in the distance, I could see the train station ahead of me, and I knew that it was now or never.

"Let yourself hit the ground and roll!"

I helped Nadia over the edge of the balcony rail and watched as her ragged skirt lifted like a parachute, dropping off the sharp cliff and rolling out of sight. Seconds later, I followed Nadia and sprang from the train, tumbling along the rough slope trimming the edge of the elevated railroad tracks. As the clicking sound of the train faded,

I stuck my head above the tall grass and looked around the open area, unscarred from the recent war.

"Are you all right?" I asked.

I could see her dark, chiseled features as she adjusted the rear-tie head scarf wrapped around her head.

"I think so," she said. "I haven't done that since my mother and I snuck aboard a cargo train when I was little."

I watched as Nadia focused on the sun above her, trying to get situated in the new surroundings.

"What direction?"

"I'm not sure."

Nadia continued to look along the sharp cliff, following the rail tracks above us as they stretched toward the St. Valentin border station. My confidence in her skill at navigating without a compass increased with each passing day.

"Maybe we should go into town?"

"No," she said. "It won't do us any good. The Enns River is located past the town, and it's too wide to cross from there. We'll have to move south and find a more narrow place to cross."

The entire Enns River in Austria was the boundary line that divided the Russian-controlled communist sector from the American sector we were trying to reach. Nadia's knowledge of the local geography put her in a leadership role as we marched south, putting further distance between the St. Valentin border station and us.

We didn't have anything to eat: the food we had begged off the Wallachs ran dry. As the sun beat down on our exhausted bodies, we followed the river south, trying to find a narrow part to cross. The two of us had been alone together for more than three days now, and I had started to grow more comfortable walking with her in total silence. Our shared hardships over the last several months had propelled us to a level of intimacy that only couples together for a long period of time fully understood.

"Wait a second!" Nadia called.

We rested for a moment along the river's edge, scanning the area around us for any sign of Russian border patrols.

"What do you see?" I asked Nadia.

"That building over there," she pointed to a rundown structure in the distance. "I want to take a closer look at it."

I could barely make out the weathered old barn through the dust along the Austrian pasture. I followed Nadia as we navigated toward the rickety building. It was ripped to shreds, probably from scavengers breaking wooden planks off of it to use for kindling. She stopped and squinted, carefully scanning the exterior of the farm building.

"These people can tell us where to cross," Nadia said.

"How do you know that?" I asked.

"Do you see those markings on the barn?"

"I think so."

I looked at the squiggly lines carved on several planks of wood that dangled from the wooden frame of the building.

"Another vitsa carved them on there to let other Roma tribes know the farmer that lives here is a good person and might help us."

Just then, in the distance past the barn, I caught a glimpse of the border patrol along the edge of the tree line.

"Oh no!" I cried, pulling Nadia down to the dry, dusty ground. As my fingers pressed against the soil, I could feel the difference in its texture relative to the ground I was used to farming in Theresiafeld. It was harder, more clay-like than the fertile fields that stretched across the southern edge of the Banat.

"What's the problem?" Nadia asked.

"Look over there," I said, gesturing to the guards in the distance.

"The communists must be increasing patrols along the border into the American sector," she noted.

The two of us kept our dirt-covered bodies hugging the dry, crusty soil as the two guards approached from opposite sides, toward the field in front of the tree line. I could see a farmer working on the field in front of the approaching guards, unconcerned as they crossed in front of him and headed in opposite directions.

"I say we head down there," Nadia said.

"What if that farmer calls those guards back?"

"The sign on the barn says he can be trusted. The Roma know what to do."

I didn't respond to her. I felt uncomfortable relying on the word of Gypsies marking squiggly lines on the walls of old buildings. Nadia was confident that the engraving etched on the barn indicated the farmer working the field might help us. Even though I was a blood brother to the Lovari Gypsies, I still had a lingering mistrust for the group. Years ago when I was a kid, my father had planted that seed of distrust. Old habits were hard to break.

"Come on," Nadia said.

We moved past the farmhouse down an incline toward the farmer plowing away on his dry soil. As we moved in closer, he pulled back on a set of leather belts and stopped his horse. The belts were frayed and old, cracked like the face of the old farmer from years of hard labor.

The Austrian farmer wiped his wrinkled forehead with a handkerchief, leaning in front of his archaic farming equipment, long abandoned by most of the farmers I had known back in Theresiafeld.

"We want to cross the river into the American sector," Nadia said.

"Doesn't everybody?" he responded.

With his farm in the Russian-controlled territory of Austria, it only made sense that private landowners like this farmer would prefer to be under noncommunist control on the other side of the Enns River. As we spoke, his Austrian dialect was somewhat difficult to understand for a Banater like myself.

"I'll tell you what you need to do," he said. "The border guards will be back shortly. When they move out of sight again, cross over my field past the tree line. The Enns is pretty narrow in that section. It's only about 120 meters across to the American sector."

The farmer seemed rail thin in appearance. Not the gaunt look of starving prisoners back in Nakovo, but a level above that. It was obvious the war had taken a tremendous toll on him physically. I wanted to beg some food off of him, but I backed away, given his malnourished condition.

"Won't those border guards question us when they come back?" I asked.

I could see them approaching in the distance. If I attempted to cross the river right now, they could easily cut me down with their machine guns.

"They won't bug us. Neighbors come down and talk to me all the time. They're used to seeing people in my field."

I dug my leather boot into the hard ground below me, thinking about the risk of trusting this Austrian farmer as the guards moved in closer to his field. He spoke with hardly a hint of anti-German sentiment, and I wondered how he managed to squeeze out a living from such a small piece of ground. I had never run a farm, but I had picked up a little of the business knowledge listening to other farmers gathered around the card table back in Theresiafeld.

"Don't make eye contact with those soldiers," he warned us. "They'll think you're up to something."

As the gun-toting Russian guards approached the farmer's land, we talked of the hardships his family had endured from confiscation of food and equipment. During the war, his location in Austria had given him the privilege of being ripped off by both the Russian and the German militaries. It was similar to the stories I had heard from my late employer, Johann Reichinger, back in Theresiafeld. The patrol guards stopped and stared at the three of us in conversation under the baking hot sun. My body tightened up as the communist guards monitored our activity. Within moments, they returned to their patrol and moved in the opposite direction.

"The window's open, my friends. Go for it!"

As the men with machine guns vanished out of sight, Nadia and I harnessed what little strength remained in our legs and ran across the farmer's field. I caught a last glimpse of the shriveled-up farmer, strapping himself to his old wooden plow to continue with another day of hard labor. I ran toward the last hurdle to reach the American sector, hoping to have the strength of this bony Austrian plowing away in his field. I dropped what few possessions I still carried and removed my shoes in preparation for the swim across.

"Tie them to your belt," Nadia said. "We don't know how far we're going to have to walk before reaching an American once we're on the other side."

I used the shoestrings on my worn boots to lace them securely to my belt loop. The narrow section of the river seemed a good strategic location to cross, but the water flow strengthened as it closed in over the tight area. Nadia removed her dress and head scarf, rolling it into a ball bundled tightly in her traveling bag sewn together from pieces of burlap. I stepped into the cold water, struggling to balance on the smooth rocks like soccer balls greased slick in goose fat. I scooped several handfuls of water into my mouth, hoping to ease the feeling of hunger from an empty stomach.

"Stay with me, Nadia."

She tossed an old, cast iron pan along the river's edge and followed me in.

"I'm ready," she said.

I walked as far as I could before the river's depth forced me to expend energy to stay afloat. The flow of water moved me farther north as my arms drilled into the river like shovels back on Reichinger's farm. My physical condition was more debilitated than when I had made my river escape out of Theresiafeld the night of the Partisan raid. I turned my head partially behind me, catching a glimpse of Nadia pushing along. Our few possessions not abandoned on the other side of the river were tied to her back like a rider to a horse. Our bodies drifted farther apart as the current separated us as we swam. Unlike our journey together on land, we could not support each other as the distance widened between us. The weight of my shoes dangling along my belt pushed against the current, forcing me to work harder to stay afloat. A faint outline of a man carrying a rifle could be seen behind me as I turned my head above the water for air. The river current was stronger than I had anticipated, carrying me ever closer to the Russian soldier downstream. I needed to make the final push across before the soldier's position would be directly behind me within range of his submachine gun. With each rotation of my arm through the flowing water, the pain in my muscles became more unbearable.

"I can't take it any longer," I said to myself.

My arms no longer had the strength to push my malnourished body forward and I let myself sink. It felt good to rest my arms as I drifted down. Shutting my eyes in the darkness, I let my struggle end.

Suddenly, my foot felt the rough surface of the river basin. The depth was far less than I had anticipated. The incremental rest in moving my arms and the awareness of the shallow depth as I approached the shoreline lifted me psychologically. I pushed my legs against the rocky surface of the river basin and forced myself to the surface. Finding the strength to move the last distance, I lay in the shallow on the Enns River's edge like a frog. My head bobbed above the waterline, struggling to maintain my balance in the flowing water as my enemy on the opposite side of the river continued his patrol.

"Where is she?" I asked myself.

I had lost sight of Nadia after letting my body drift below the river's surface before reaching the shoreline. I glanced along the open area, hoping to catch a glimpse of Nadia resting somewhere. I waited for a moment longer and crawled out of the water, struggling to untie the wet knots that secured my shoes to my belt loops. I moved along the river's edge, glancing in all directions to spot my travel companion. She moved out of a section of tall, brown grass some distance from the river.

"We made it," I said.

She nodded her head as she wrung the contents of her bag to dry.

"Didn't you see me hidden in the water along the shoreline?" I asked.

"It would have been bad luck to approach you," she said.

Superstitions learned from her travels with the Lovari clan clung to her like the few possessions not abandoned on the other side of the Enns River.

"Why is it bad luck?" I asked.

"It is *kuntari*, the universal balance of life," she said. "With you in the water, you are like a fish and not in your natural element walking on dry land."

She slipped the last of her damp clothes over her muscular frame.

"You are now the bandolier, John. Lead our new vitsa to good fortune," she said.

She smiled and handed her bag to me. It was her way of acknowledging that I was now in charge in the American sector of Austria. A territory that we would now roam together in search of help.

We walked on an abandoned road in the safety of the American sector for several hours, and I suddenly heard the sound of a rough voice yelling out in front of me. "Get the hell out of the way!" he said. Delirious from lack of food and the intense heat, I had accidentally wandered into the middle of the road, forcing the oncoming jeep to a sliding stop.

"Get out of the way! Move it!"

I stood motionless in the middle of the road as the unshaven soldier stood over the dirt-covered windshield of his jeep, motioning with his hand for me to move to the side. I could tell he was tired of dealing with refugees like myself, flocking into the American sector from Eastern Europe. My ears turned deaf to the sound of the horn blasting from his vehicle as the angry words continued bellowing from his mouth.

"Are you crazy!" the soldier screamed.

I froze as the American soldier jumped from his seat and marched toward me, fuming with anger. I stared at him as Nadia tugged on my arm, fearful of being beaten by the American salivating at the mouth. Over the last year, soldiers had ordered me around in different languages, but my reaction to hearing the English words of anger coming from this particular American was not one of fear, but of relief.

"If you're not off the road in thirty seconds, I'm going to beat the hell out of you!"

The American soldier practically spit in my face as he continued his rant. I could smell his breath as he moved even closer, preparing to slug me across the mouth.

"My name is John Miller," I said. "I'm an undercover officer with OSS. God, am I glad to see you."

I put my arms around the well-fed, angry American and almost began to cry.

✝

"I guess it's time to start looking for a job again."

As the old man spoke, I didn't turn to face him. I watched my spouse press the rosemary bush seedling deep within the pot of soil along the ledge of the kitchen window. My father still felt uncomfortable with a half-Gypsy living in his house, but I could hardly see any outward sign of an untamed nomad remaining in the woman from the Banat that I had married.

"No doubt about it. Things are definitely better in New York," he continued.

"I know! I know!" I responded. "I'll start looking soon."

My father's reminder of the good job prospects for young lawyers with military records in post-war New York was a subtle way of telling me to start getting on with my life. He hadn't showed much outward emotion when I returned home after several weeks of psychological evaluation, but I knew that he had been overwhelmed when he'd heard I was alive.

The dream I had of German colonists moving into the Banat twisting into a nightmare seemed to occur less often with each night's sleep. It felt good to be free of a polarized Banat, a land mass that I had watched repel an extreme ideology of fascism only to absorb another under communism. The war was being put behind me, and it felt good.

"Oh, I almost forgot," he said. "Lisa, hand me that letter."

My father's wife stopped wiping the dish with her white rag and handed my father the stack of mail.

Hans!"

When calling out to get my attention, my father always used the German version of the name John.

"What?" I asked.

I shoveled a last mouthful of chicken soup out of the bowl with my giant, silver spoon. The bad habit of leaving food on my plate after I finished eating seemed to have disappeared after my time in the Yugoslavian Banat.

"The letter."

"Oh."

I stretched my arm over the wooden table, which peeked through a white embroidered tablecloth, grabbing the envelope out of his hand.

"Who's it from?" my father asked.

I waited several seconds as I stared at the name on the return address.

"A priest I knew in Theresiafeld."

Having heard the miraculous story from a Theresiafelder who recently immigrated to New York, I knew Father Peter had survived the machine-gun fire from the Partisan soldiers. I thought I had witnessed his execution from my hidden location in the ravine, so it truly was a miracle that the priest had survived the slaughter. During my debriefing back at OSS, I didn't tell anyone about the illegal killing of Banat German civilians. I was technically on the same side as these Partisan butchers from Yugoslavia, and I was planning to carry the secret with me the rest of my life.

"Was he a friend of yours?" my father asked.

"I'm not sure."

Given the priest's disinterest in cultivating a relationship with me when we were back in the Banat together, I was surprised he had bothered to write me at all. I carefully ripped open the letter from Yugoslavia and began reading the priest's European-style handwriting. The loopy, forward-angled strokes of his lettering style were difficult to make out for an American.

Dear Hans Mueller:

I am writing you from my new assignment in Belgrade. I was pleased to hear that you're still alive and helping some of our more ambitious Theresiafelders find sponsors to emigrate to America. More of them will be coming now that other Theresiafelders are settled in New York and tell about the job opportunities. Other than the occasional complaint of discrimination, most Banat Germans living in Linz, Austria, are starting to return some semblance of order to their uprooted lives.

I'm afraid I cannot say the same thing for the Banat Germans who made the decision to remain in Yugoslavia or the ones who returned from Austria to their original homes when the war ended. Many died of starvation in the work camps or were deported into forced labor in Russia. The last remnants of Banat Germans from Yugoslavia will probably be leaving for good now that their farms have been confiscated by the government and collectivized for the so-called greater good of the people. As a priest in Yugoslavia, I have also felt the hardships under the communist regime. I am often brought before the authorities for questioning about my anti-communist ideas and have spent more than one night in prison, where I am writing you today. It is a struggle to keep my church open in Belgrade, but I know what I am doing is right, and I will never quit.

Recently, a small group of Theresiafelders and I rented several trucks and returned to what's left of our tiny village. I led them to the location where many of our fellow villagers, including myself, were brutally gunned down in a ditch by the Partisan soldiers. Under the cover of darkness, we moved the bodies to a hill on Reichinger's estate overlooking the clear, open pasture that was formed from the drainage of the swamp. The canal project you led is the last great achievement that our people leave behind in communist-controlled Theresiafeld. I conducted a short religious ceremony and marked a stone cross where the bodies were placed in a mass grave. The monument overlooks a newly formed wheat field where the swamp once stood. From the hilltop gravesite, the view of our village and the surrounding area is beautiful.

I think they would like it there.

Sincerely,

Father Peter

www.ingramcontent.com/pod-product-compliance
Lightning Source LLC
Chambersburg PA
CBHW071128200626
46817CB00018B/2483